Still Garden

Grief is not for the faint of heart.

Cisco Mills

Roots OMG

9 798999 042613

www.stillgardenbook.com

ACKNOWLEDGEMENTS

To my beloved wife,

Eileen Colette—whose unwavering encouragement, gentle strength, and radiant creativity sparked the first roots of this journey.

Your work, *Why Plants Die and Other Happy Thoughts*, did more than inspire me, it invited me to listen. To see that healing is not always loud. It is quiet. It is patient. It grows slowly beneath the surface until the time is right to bloom.

Helping bring your book to life opened something tender in me, a reverence for what is unseen, for the holy work of tending sorrow with grace. It taught me that grief is not a wall, but soil. And from it, something beautiful can rise.

Still Garden carries your imprint on every page. Your joy watered it. Your insight pruned it. Your faith in me gave it light.

Thank you for growing this garden with me, for believing in what could be, and for reminding me that even the stillest places can bring forth new life.

CONTENTS

Chapter One

The House That Waited

"Trust in the Lord with all your heart and lean not on your own understanding; in all your ways submit to him, and he will make your paths straight." - Proverbs 3:5-6

THE KEY TURNED IN the lock with the resistance of mechanisms left too long untouched. Metal grinding against metal, sharp enough to make David wince.

He stood on the threshold of his grandfather's house, the brass key warm in his palm, and couldn't make himself step inside.

Late spring sunlight fell through windows that hadn't been opened in months. Dust motes spun in the golden columns stretching from glass to hardwood floor, each particle visible and suspended like the moment itself—caught between before and after, the life he'd known and whatever came next.

David forced himself forward. One step. Another. The floorboards creaked under his weight, announcing his arrival to the empty rooms.

The silence hit him first. Not the comfortable quiet of a house at rest, but a hollowness that pressed against his eardrums until they rang with it. Two months ago, this kitchen had hummed with voices—his mother on the phone coordinating hospice care for her father, the same voice she'd used with countless patients over twenty years of home health nursing. The tap-tap-tap of his grandfather's walker against worn linoleum, the soft beep of medical equipment counting down the hours.

Now there was only the wall clock ticking. An old Westclox his grandmother had bought at a church rummage sale forty years ago. Each tick distinct in the emptiness, measuring time no one was here to witness.

David set his duffel bag by the door. The canvas smelled like his dorm room—stale coffee and the mustiness of textbooks and unwashed laundry. He surveyed the space that was now his, at twenty-three, ancient with grief and impossibly young for what came next.

His lease had ended three weeks ago. The shared apartment near campus felt wrong after graduation—everyone moving forward with jobs and plans while David couldn't figure out which direction to face. Four years studying biology and pre-med courses because they made practical sense, because his father insisted on a stable career path, because he'd been good at science even if medicine had never sparked passion in him.

The key to his grandfather's house had been sitting in his desk drawer since the lawyer sent it in February. Three months of staring at it before he finally used it.

God. He stared into the kitchen where morning light caught on the yellow Formica table. I don't know why I'm here. Everyone else has plans—jobs, grad school, something. And I'm just... here. In this empty house.

It wasn't much of a prayer. But it was honest. David had never been good at talking to God the way his mother managed so effortlessly. Her prayers had sounded like conversations with someone she knew. His were like leaving voicemails for someone who might not check their messages.

His father's voice echoed in his memory, careful and distant the way Robert had been since the cancer took Marie: "Don't get stuck in the past. You need to think practically about your future."

He'd brought charts. Spreadsheets that proved selling was the logical choice.

The words had stung. Partly because they echoed David's own fears. Mostly because they showed how little his father understood what David was looking for.

The house didn't seem abandoned, though. It waited.

White clapboard weathered to the color of old bones, shutters faded from forest green to sage. The wraparound porch sagged on the east side, but the morning glories his grandmother had planted climbed the lattice with stubborn persistence.

Beyond the porch, his grandfather's garden covered just under an acre. Forty years of Marvin's patient work, beds laid out with the precision of someone who understood that good results required time. Six raised beds ran lengthwise down the eastern side, each one eight feet wide and easily thirty feet long, built from reclaimed barn wood weathered silver-gray. The herb spiral his mother had designed stood near the kitchen door, built from stacked stone in a formation that caught both morning and afternoon sun.

Farther back, the fruit trees created their own small orchard—four apple trees in a loose square, the raspberry canes his grandfather had planted when Marie was in elementary school forming a living fence along the western property line. A gravel path wound between the beds, wide enough for a wheelbarrow, dividing the space into sections that appeared both intentional and organic. At the far end, near where the property sloped gently toward the tree line, his grandfather had built a small shed for tools, and beside it, the cleared area where a greenhouse was supposed to go someday.

It was the sort of garden that required devotion, not dabbling. The sort that represented decades of patient investment—soil amendments, careful observation of sun patterns and drainage. The sort that couldn't be maintained by someone passing through.

David stood at the window, watching the raised beds where weeds had begun their patient reclamation. The marigolds his mother had planted along the borders had gone leggy and wild, spent blooms turning brown on stems that reached toward light with desperate optimism.

The marigolds needed deadheading. He remembered Marie showing him how, one summer afternoon when he was ten, her hands moving with practiced certainty. "You cut away what's finished so the plant can focus its energy on new growth. Sometimes ending one process is how you make room for the next."

He hadn't understood then. Now, standing at the window with grief raw inside him, he wondered if she'd known. If every garden lesson had been preparation for this moment.

The whole garden needed attention. David sensed the weight of that need pressing against his uncertainty about whether he was capable of providing it.

The kitchen stretched before him. And there, beside the sink, his mother's coffee mug sat in the dish drainer. Pale yellow ceramic with a chip on the handle.

David's hand reached out before he thought about it.

Stopped halfway.

His fingers hovered in the air above the mug like touching it would make real what he wasn't ready to face.

She'd refused to throw it away, that chip. "Perfect objects don't need grace," she'd said.

He'd been twelve. Mother's Day. Trying to surprise her with breakfast in bed. The French toast had turned out okay—crispy on the outside the way she liked it, though he'd burned the first two pieces and hidden them at the bottom of the trash. He'd arranged everything on the wooden tray his grandfather used for breakfast: the plate, fresh strawberries from the garden, her favorite mug filled with coffee that was probably too strong.

He'd made it as far as the stairs before his sock caught on the carpet runner.

The mug had seemed to fall in slow motion. Yellow ceramic tumbling through morning light, coffee arcing like a dark rainbow, the sick certainty that he was about to ruin everything. It hit the hardwood floor with a crack that sounded like his heart breaking. Coffee spreading in a dark pool. A triangular chip skittering across the floor like an accusation.

David had sunk down on the steps and wept. Not the loud crying of a child, but the silent, shaking tears that came from knowing he'd destroyed what couldn't be replaced.

Marie had appeared in her bathrobe, hair tangled from sleep. She'd taken in the scene—the broken mug, the spilled coffee, her son on the stairs with tears running down his face and French toast going cold.

She'd sat down beside him. Wrapped her arm around his shoulders.

"People matter more than pottery, sweetheart. You're worth a thousand mugs."

She'd kept the chipped mug. Used it every day for the next eleven years. Every morning when David saw it, he remembered what she'd been teaching him: that love doesn't require perfection. That broken objects could be held. That the trying mattered more than the outcome.

Now the mug sat in the dish drainer, chip catching the light, and his throat closed with the understanding that he'd never again watch her wrap her hands around it on a cold morning. Never hear her again hum while she waited for the coffee to cool.

His lungs compressed. Breathing became a conscious choice rather than an automatic function.

He pulled his hand back. Curled it into a fist at his side.

His mother had died three weeks ago. Early May 2024. Marvin had gone first, back in March, his body giving up after ninety-one years the way old trees sometimes decided they were finished. Mom had cared for him through his final weeks while fighting her own cancer, and the effort had accelerated her decline.

Three weeks since Marie. Recent enough that people were still bringing casseroles. Not long enough that David had any idea how to answer when they asked how he was doing.

The dining room table still held the life she'd been living when cancer interrupted it. A stack of library books about native plants, their due dates months past. A half-finished crossword puzzle, her pen resting in the fold. The reading glasses she'd always lost and given up looking for.

Evidence of a person who'd expected to return. Breadcrumbs pointing toward a future that never came.

But David remembered something his mother had said near the end, when the morphine made her honest in ways she hadn't been before. They'd been sitting in the hospice room, late afternoon light coming through venetian blinds in stripes across her blanket.

"You know what I'm most afraid of?" she'd asked. Not waiting for his answer. "That you'll spend the rest of your life trying to be what everyone else needs instead of figuring out who you are."

David had tried to reassure her. Made promises he wasn't sure he could keep.

"Just... don't make me into a shrine, okay?" Her voice had been barely a whisper. "I'd rather you plant something living than preserve something dead."

At the time, he'd thought she was talking about her garden. Now, standing in a house that felt suspended between vigil and abandonment, he wondered if she'd meant something larger.

Through the window, the garden waited. Weeds reclaiming the careful order his grandfather had spent decades establishing. Nature demonstrating its patient indifference to human intention.

The lawyer had outlined David's options in clear, practical terms. Sell the property—the land alone was worth something, three acres on the edge of town. Developers would jump at it.

Or keep it. Live in it. Figure out what came next from inside these walls.

His father wanted him to sell. Robert saw the house as a burden, an anchor tying David to a past that offered no future. "You're twenty-three. You should be starting your career, not playing caretaker to a memory."

But his mother had wanted something different.

David remembered their last real conversation, three weeks before she died. She'd been sitting in the recliner by the sunroom window, wrapped in the afghan his grandmother had crocheted. Outside, March snow had been melting into mud, revealing the dead garden beneath.

"Promise me something," she'd said. Her voice thin but certain. "Come back here. Spend a summer in the house. Give the place a chance to talk to you."

"Mom—"

"I'm not asking you to stay forever. Just... listen. The house knows things. The garden knows things." She'd smiled then. "You might not hear them at first. But if you give it time..."

She'd trailed off. Closed her eyes. Then opened them again, focusing on him with sudden intensity.

"You've spent your whole life trying to be what everyone needs. Maybe this is your chance to figure out what you need."

He'd made the promise. Because she was dying and he would have promised her anything. But also because some part of him wanted to believe she might be right.

The day after graduation, David had packed his duffel bag, loaded his old pickup truck, and driven the forty-seven miles to the house where his mother had grown up. Where his grandfather had spent forty years coaxing abundance from soil. Where the garden waited with patient expectation.

He opened the harvest gold refrigerator. Containers of food that neighbors had brought during his grandfather's final weeks sat forgotten, growing science experiments in the back. He threw away what had spoiled, recognizing some contributors by their distinctive containers—Mrs. Henderson's tuna casserole in the Pyrex dish, Mr. Chen's soup in recycled yogurt containers.

His mother's shopping list clung to the refrigerator, held by a sunflower magnet.

David stared at it. The paper was yellowed at the edges, his mother's handwriting in the blue pen she always used: tomato plants, fertilizer, new gloves for David if he decides to help.

If he decides to help.

Dying, she'd left him room to choose.

David took a steadying breath. Pulled open the cabinet under the sink and found a trash bag. He sifted through what could be saved and what needed to go.

The work was simple. Methodical. The sort of task that required enough attention to quiet his mind without demanding so much that he'd drown in it. By the time he'd finished clearing the refrigerator and wiping down shelves, the morning had stretched toward evening.

He found himself drawn to the sunroom.

The space had been added onto the back of the house sometime in the seventies—walls of mismatched windows salvaged from old buildings, creating a greenhouse effect that kept plants happy year-round. The afternoon sun poured through glass, illuminating dust motes that danced like small miracles.

Plants lined every surface. Jade and spider plants, a Christmas cactus that looked older than David, herbs in terra cotta pots.

And there, in the center of the room on a small table positioned to catch the light, sat a plant unlike any David had seen before.

The pot itself was ancient ceramic, the sort you saw in botanical gardens—glazed in a shade of seafoam green, the kind of vessel chosen by someone who understood that containers mattered. A hairline crack ran down one side that Marvin had glued back together decades ago. The plant growing from it defied easy categorization—part fern, part tropical variety, with broad glossy leaves the color of deep forest that caught and held the light like silk.

David had seen this plant his entire life. At gatherings, holidays, the occasional weekend visit. It had always been here, a fixture as permanent as the house itself.

He'd never paid it much attention before.

Now he found himself staring at it with the uncomfortable awareness that it was staring back.

He reached out. Stopped himself. His hand hovering inches from the nearest leaf.

"Your mother used to talk to me."

David froze.

The voice had come from... no. That was impossible. Clear and present, not quite female but distinctly not male, carrying the kind of patient amusement that comes from watching humans fumble through their lives for decades.

"She'd come here when she was afraid. When the treatments weren't working and she needed to say the words she couldn't say to anyone else."

David's hand jerked back. His heart hammering against his ribs like a trapped bird. He looked around the sunroom, searching for speakers, for some logical explanation.

"I'm not a recording, honey."

The leaves were moving. No breeze stirred the air.

"I'm Samantha. And before you work yourself into a panic, no, you're not losing your mind. I understand why that's your first conclusion, but this is older and simpler than that."

David's rational mind catalogued the situation with clinical detachment. Exhausted. Emotionally overwrought. Processing massive loss. Hearing voices was a known symptom of extreme stress and isolation.

"I'm not a symptom, honey. I know—you're thinking you've finally snapped. Most people do at first. Grief strips away all the padding and leaves you more permeable."

"Plants don't talk."

David said it to the empty room. Or the plant. Or his own fracturing sanity. His voice came out higher than normal, strained with the effort of maintaining composure in the face of impossibility.

"Most don't, no. But I've never been particularly interested in fitting expectations. Think of it this way: some creatures see colors beyond what humans call visible—the ultraviolet paths bees follow, the faint warmth snakes track in the dark. You're standing in one of those unseen frequencies now. Like plants reaching toward light you can't see. Count yourself fortunate or cursed, depending on your temperament."

David sat down hard in the wicker chair. His legs had stopped reliably supporting his weight.

"This isn't real. I'm exhausted. I drove six hours. I'm grieving. My brain is just—"

"Making up a talking plant to cope with loss? Possible. But that would be a remarkably elaborate coping mechanism, even for a clever boy like you."

The voice held gentle humor.

"Your grandfather heard me. So did your mother, especially toward the end when she stopped insisting life had to make sense to be real. And now you can. That isn't madness, honey. That's inheritance."

The casual mention of his family made something tighten in David's chest. He thought about those final months. The way Marie had sometimes talked to herself in empty rooms. He'd assumed she was praying.

"My mother could hear you?"

"Every day for the last six months of her life. She'd come sit where you're sitting, and we'd talk about what she was afraid of. About you. About your father. About running out of time to say everything that mattered."

David sat in stunned silence.

Either he was having a complete psychological break—the sort that required hospitalization and medication and concerned phone calls—or he was talking to a plant named Samantha who claimed to have known his family for decades. Who had witnessed his mother's fear. Who had been here, alive and listening, through everything.

Neither option fit comfortably into his worldview.

"She was terrified you'd spend the rest of your life twisting yourself into what everyone else needed instead of learning who you are, like a plant stretching toward the wrong light, chasing a buzzing fluorescent when you were made for sun. That's why she asked you to come back here. Places like this coax the truth to the surface the way warmth coaxes seedlings through soil."

David's breathing slowed. The voice, whatever its source, carried understanding deeper than anything he'd encountered in months of well-meaning advice.

"You said my grandfather could hear you?"

"Especially after your grandmother died. He spent many mornings right there, letting his grief spill out where someone could hear it. Some of his best conversations were with me. He never told anyone, of course. Humans rarely believe the green things are listening, even though we always are."

A pause.

"Learning to accept impossible truths—that's germination, honey. Seeds cracking open in darkness long before anyone at the surface can see a thing."

David studied the sunroom with new eyes. Imagining Marvin sitting in this chair, carrying on conversations that sustained him. The image didn't seem crazy anymore. It seemed like exactly what his grandfather would do.

"My father thinks I'm wasting my life by coming here."

The words emerged before he could censor them.

"Your father has plenty of opinions. He climbs his ideas the way vines climb a trellis, always reaching upward, away from the messy soil where feelings live. That doesn't make his concerns wrong. It just means they're not the only thing worth growing.

Through the window, David could see the garden stretching toward the back fence. Marvin's careful work now learning to tend itself.

"What am I supposed to do with this?" David asked, gesturing helplessly at the impossibility of his situation.

"Same as with any unexpected gift. You decide whether to receive it or spend your strength trying to explain it away. Like a graft, you can let yourself take to the rootstock you've been given, or keep worrying over why this particular variety was chosen until you never truly join."

"Gift? I'm either talking to a plant or having a nervous breakdown."

"Well, for the first time since your mother died, you're not fixing, planning, or running. You're simply here. That's the beginning of wisdom, honey. And wisdom is what lost young men are most starved for."

David closed his eyes.

The weight of loss and confusion and impossible possibility settled through him like roots seeking purchase in unfamiliar ground. When he opened them, the afternoon light had shifted, filling the sunroom with gold that made everything seem suspended between ordinary and miraculous.

"I miss them."

He said it simply. The words carrying the full weight of months spent pretending that staying busy could postpone learning to live with absence.

"Of course you do. Missing them just means you loved them well. The real question is what you'll do with all that love now that it has nowhere obvious to land."

"I don't know. I just... I don't know."

"Nobody does, at first. It's like learning to garden—you try, you misjudge, some plantings fail and some surprise you and thrive."

A pause.

"You can't rush germination. All you can do is tend the soil, wait, and trust that what's meant to sprout will find its moment."

Outside, a crow called from the maple tree. Somewhere in the garden, bees worked among flowers that had learned to bloom without supervision. The house settled with a sigh that sounded like contentment, as if it had been holding its breath and could exhale now that someone had come home.

David pulled out the small composition book he'd bought at the drugstore. The spiral binding was stiff, the pages pristine. He clicked open his pen—his mother had given it to him at graduation, three weeks before she died—and the sound seemed loud in the quiet room.

He stared at the blank page. All that white space waiting to be filled. Like the summer ahead. Like the house around him. Like his entire life from this moment forward.

His hand moved across the page:

Day 1 - I'm either having a conversation with a houseplant or having a complete breakdown. Either way, she makes more sense than most of the advice I've gotten lately.

Apparently Grandpa and Mom could hear her too. Not sure what to make of that.

God, I asked for direction and got a talking plant. I'm not sure if this is an answer or a sign I need help. But for the first time in months, I don't feel like I'm disappointing someone by being confused.

"What did you write?" came the gentle question.

David glanced up. The plant's leaves caught the last of the afternoon light, and for a moment he could see why his grandfather had spent so many mornings here. Why his mother had come here to speak her fears. This space, this impossible, patient presence, made honesty possible.

"That I don't know if you're real or if I'm losing my mind. But also that... it doesn't matter. As long as it helps."

"Does it matter? If these words help you learn how to live from here? Whether I'm a plant with opinions or your own buried wisdom finally finding a voice, either way, something true is trying to reach the surface."

The question hung in the air like evening mist. Neither demanding an immediate answer nor dismissing the importance of eventually finding one.

David settled into the uncertainty rather than fighting it.

"I'm listening."

He closed the notebook.

"Good. Because they're not gone, you know."

A pause. Leaves catching light.

"They're rooted deeper now. Like bulbs in winter, hidden, not gone. Dormant, not dead. The real question is whether you'll give that love time to push up new shoots, or keep digging the ground apart to prove there's nothing left."

The last light shifted, painting the sunroom in shades of honey and hope. And in the quiet space between grief and healing, between the life he'd shared with his family and the one he would have to learn to live without them, David recognized a new beginning taking root.

Not the absence of sorrow. But the presence of love that had learned to flow in new directions.

The house around him breathed with patient life. And somewhere in the garden, growth was already happening that hadn't been there yesterday.

Chapter Two

CONVERSATIONS WITH THE DEEP

"The purposes of a person's heart are deep waters, but one who has insight draws them out." - Proverbs 20:5

DAVID WOKE TO SILENCE settling like morning dew. Seven days since his arrival, and each awakening was like surfacing from dreams where his old life stood intact.

The disorientation lasted moments now. Replaced by what resembled relief. Not the desperate sort that came from escaping—the deeper relief that arrived when you stopped fighting currents too strong to resist.

God, the prayer rose as he lay in gray light filtering through curtains. I don't know if I'm losing my mind here. But I guess You're working with what You've got, and what You've got is someone who talks to plants.

The couch had memorized his way of carrying exhaustion. He hadn't been able to sleep in either bedroom upstairs yet. His grandparents' room was too sacred to disturb, and his old summer room echoed with too many ghosts of the boy who had believed people you loved would always be there when morning came.

Late May was settling into the rhythm that would become summer. Longer days, warmer afternoons. That green abundance that spoke of earth remembering its work without human supervision.

Through the kitchen window, he could see the garden his grandfather had tended for forty years, now learning to tend itself with varying degrees of success. The six raised beds stretching down the eastern side, each one holding the weight of Marvin's patient investment. Tomato stakes already leaning at odd angles where David had tried installing them yesterday. The herb spiral near the kitchen door where his mother had planted thyme and oregano and rosemary that sent their scents across the morning air.

His phone showed a text from Jeremy from late last night. Short, careful words that said the right things but felt far away. David sent back a thumbs up and set the phone aside.

Morning light was crystalline, painting everything in shades that made ordinary moments feel significant. David carried his coffee toward the sunroom, drawn by the quality of light that gathered there.

"Morning." He settled into the wicker chair that was becoming his. "Day eight of either profound spiritual experience or complete mental breakdown."

"Oh, I'm leaning toward spiritual experience. Breakdowns involve far more wailing and root disturbance—very dramatic, like a plant in full transplant shock. You're far too steady for that."

David snorted into his coffee. "Sorry to bore you."

"Well, 'stable' is a generous term, but you're functional—which is more than I can say for that spider plant in the corner. Poor thing's been having an identity crisis ever since your grandfather forgot to water it three times in a row. Complete loss of turgor. Some species just love theatrics."

"Plants have identity crises?"

"Honey, everything alive has identity crises. We just manage them with more grace because we're rooted, we can't sprint away from discomfort. Being stationary builds character. Forces you to keep reaching for light even when conditions are less than ideal."

They sat in comfortable silence, David watched the morning light shift across the garden. Through the window, he could see Mrs. Rodriguez working in her yard next door, kneeling among what appeared to be a planned garden, her movements slow and deliberate.

"She's building beauty over there. Memorial garden for her husband. Mostly perennials, plants that return year after year without being replanted. Wise choice. Annual grief is exhausting; no one wants to start from bare soil every spring."

David watched as Mrs. Rodriguez stood, brushing dirt from her knees. "That's dark."

"I'm a plant, dear. We have a very practical relationship with death. It's composting in slow motion, nutrients returning to the soil, nothing wasted. Nature keeps efficient books."

The sound of bicycle wheels on gravel interrupted them.

Through the window, David could see a boy coasting down the driveway. Maybe nine or ten, with dark hair that stuck up at odd angles and a serious expression that seemed too old for his face. He was balancing a dish wrapped in aluminum foil on his handlebars.

David met him at the back door. The morning air was cool and sweet, carrying the scent of growing life.

"From my mom." The boy held out what appeared to be a casserole dish, gripping it tight with both hands. "She said you probably weren't eating right."

"That's kind. What's your name?"

"Eli Rodriguez." The boy studied David with frank curiosity. Dark eyes that took everything in but gave nothing back. "We live next door. My mom knew your mom. From around."

David recognized it. The memorial garden. Mrs. Rodriguez. "Well, thank your mom for me. This is thoughtful."

Eli nodded. But didn't immediately leave. Instead, his attention shifted to the window where the sunroom was visible. His expression brightened, the seriousness giving way to recognition. Like seeing an old friend.

"Oh. Samantha's still here." He said it as casually as if he were commenting on the weather.

David's heart kicked against his ribs.

"You know about Samantha?"

"Sure. I come over sometimes and talk to her." Matter-of-fact. Like stating an obvious truth. "Mom thinks I'm making it up, but I'm not."

The world tilted. David set his coffee down before he dropped it.

"You can... hear her?"

"Yeah. Can't you?" Eli looked confused, like maybe David was joking with him.

Before David could respond, Samantha's voice carried through the open window:

"Good morning, Eli. Still stretching upward, I see. You're sprouting faster than bindweed, at least an inch taller than last month."

"Really?" Eli perked up, standing straighter.

"Absolutely. Though I should warn you, the morning glories grew three inches last week. Try not to take it personally. Plants cheat, they have phototropism on their side."

Eli grinned, the first real smile David had seen from him. His whole face changed, became younger somehow.

"I'm gonna be taller than them by summer."

"That's the spirit. Optimistic growth is essential for young mammals—keeps the inner rings from stiffening too early."

The smile faded from Eli's face like someone had flipped a switch. He looked down at his sneakers: scuffed white Nikes with one lace coming untied.

David felt something catch in his throat. Understanding settling over him. The boy's father. Mrs. Rodriguez's husband. The memorial garden.

"I'm sorry about your dad," David said.

Eli nodded. Still not looking up. His shoulders had rounded, making him look smaller.

"It's been over a year now."

Then he looked at David with surprising directness. Eyes that had learned to carry things no nine-year-old should have to carry.

"Does it stop hurting? When you miss them?"

The question landed with unexpected weight. David thought about his mother. About the four weeks since her death. How some days felt lighter and others felt like drowning. How yesterday he'd been fine and then he'd smelled lavender and had to sit down on the kitchen floor and breathe through it.

"I don't know if it stops. Some days it doesn't hurt as much. Then something reminds me and it's like it just happened."

"Yeah." Eli said it like David had confirmed something he'd already suspected.

"Samantha says it comes in waves."

"She's right. Grief has seasons just like gardens. Some days everything is blooming; some days you're breaking down old matter to make room for new growth. Both stages are necessary. Both pass in their own time. Can't rush either—germination follows no human schedule."

Eli smiled. A small thing but real. He waved toward the window—an easy gesture, natural—then climbed back on his bike and pedaled away.

After Eli left, David returned to the sunroom. His hands were shaking.

Relief and confusion churned through him. Relief that he wasn't alone in this impossible thing. Confusion about what it meant that a nine-year-old could share his particular brand of crazy.

"So. Eli can hear you too."

"He can. Has been able to since about three months after his father died. Grief cracked him open—like frost splitting a seed coat. Painful, but it lets new sensitivities in. Necessary for germination, though no one would ever choose the method."

"And his mother?"

"Mara is lovely. Very rooted in practicality. Not much space in her worldview for conversational foliage. She assumes Eli's imagination is doing the heavy lifting—which is partly true. But perception and imagination are intertwined more than humans admit."

David sat down. The wicker creaked under his weight.

"So there are rules to this. Not everyone can hear you."

"'Rules' is such a rigid word. I prefer 'conditions.' Just like photosynthesis needs light, water, and chlorophyll, hearing me requires a certain kind of attentiveness, usually awakened through loss. Your grandfather developed it after your grandmother died. You have it now. Young Eli acquired it early. Premature flowering, you could say."

"But why? Why can some people hear you and others can't?"

"Grief dissolves the insulation most people wrap around themselves. Once it thins, you absorb frequencies you couldn't receive before, like a plant whose cuticle softens in certain seasons, suddenly permeable to what once slid off."

"That's a scientific explanation for an impossibility."

"Honey, I'm a plant. I turn sunlight into food using a process no one fully understands, and I do it while rooted in place. 'Impossible' stopped bothering me decades ago. You'll rest easier once you quit demanding that everything make sense first."

David found both journals: his grandfather's leather-bound one and his mother's spiral notebook. Her handwriting filled pages with observations, sketches, notes about what worked and what didn't. The pages were soft with use, corners turned down, coffee rings marking important passages.

Late May, she'd written. Basil needs first pinching: remove flower buds before they fully open. Counter-intuitive, but cutting back encourages fuller growth. The more you harvest, the more it produces. Like love that way.

He stared at that last line. Like love that way. His mother's habit of finding metaphors in everything. He wondered if she'd written it while sitting in the sunroom, talking to Samantha.

He gathered what he thought might be the right tools. Pruning shears awkward in his grip. Garden gloves too big for his hands, his grandfather's, holding the shape of those larger fingers. Then he headed out to the herb bed with his mother's journal open to the page about basil.

The morning sun was warm on his shoulders as he knelt in the dirt. The basil plants were bushy and fragrant, with small flower buds forming at the tops. According to the journal, he was supposed to pinch these off. But where exactly? How much?

He made himself do it. The stem snapped between his fingers, releasing a sharp, peppery scent. The plant didn't wilt or die. It sat there, identical to before, minus one small flower cluster.

Encouraged, he continued, but his inexperience showed. Some stems he pinched too high. Others he cut too low. One aggressive pinch took off an entire branch.

"This is harder than it looks."

"Most meaningful work is. And just so you know, those tomato plants are watching you massacre that basil and growing increasingly nervous about their future. Plants gossip, mostly through root networks and chemical signals, but trust me, word travels."

David examined his basket. It held an assortment of basil: some properly harvested, most appearing to have been in a fight and lost.

"Well, at least you didn't uproot anything. Plants appreciate enthusiastic mistakes. Shows intention. Attention is the first nutrient, even when technique is questionable."

David was examining his work when he heard a car door slam.

Through the garden, he could see his father's sedan in the driveway. Robert emerging with that expression—jaw set, shoulders squared—that meant he'd come with a purpose.

David's stomach tightened. But he didn't move from where he knelt. Didn't stand up or brush off his hands. He stayed there, waiting, letting his father come to him.

Father, he prayed silently. Help me hear whatever he's trying to say. When I don't like how he says it.

"David?" Robert called, walking around to the back. His dress shoes crunched on the gravel path. "You out here?"

"In the garden."

His father appeared at the garden gate. Wearing work clothes despite it being Saturday: khakis pressed sharp, button-down shirt. He studied David, the basket of mangled herbs, the dirt under his fingernails.

"Trying your hand at gardening?"

"Trying being the key word."

"Learning curve." Robert said it, and David detected what might have been sympathy. "Everything seems simple until you try it yourself."

Brief silence filled with bees working nearby flowers. David could sense his father working up to whatever he'd driven forty minutes to say.

"I wanted to check on you. See how you're managing out here."

"I'm managing. It's quiet. That's mostly what I needed."

Robert nodded, surveying the garden with assessing eyes. David could almost see him calculating. Property value. Maintenance costs. Opportunity cost of a college graduate spending his summer pulling weeds instead of building a career.

"This place meant a lot to your mother. She always said it was where she could think."

Robert's voice had gone softer. The words surprised David.

"Yeah. I'm starting to get that."

Another silence.

"I brought some information." Robert pulled a folder from under his arm. "About property values in the area. What you could expect if you decided to sell, so you have the facts."

There it was.

David's lungs seized. But he kept his voice steady.

"I'm not ready to think about selling yet, Dad."

"I'm not saying you need to decide now. You should have the information to help make an informed decision when you're ready."

David took the folder. The weight was heavier than paper should be. Facts and figures. Market analysis. His father's language of love: providing information, ensuring security, solving problems with data.

"Thanks. I'll look at it."

Robert seemed to relax.

"That's all I'm asking."

"I will. But Dad—" David paused, choosing his words. "The facts aren't the only consideration here. There are other values than what shows up on a market analysis."

His father's jaw tightened. That expression David recognized, frustration being carefully controlled.

"I know that. But a value you can't quantify won't pay your bills."

"Maybe not. But it might teach me what I need to know."

Robert studied him for a long moment.

"Promise me you'll think about it. Really think about it."

"I promise."

His father nodded once. Turned to go. Then stopped, turned back.

"Your mother would want you to be practical about this. She'd want you to have a plan."

The words landed wrong. Sharp. Presumptuous.

Heat flared through David.

"Mom wanted me to come here. She made me promise. So maybe what she wanted was for me to figure this out my own way."

Robert's face closed. That careful mask settled into place.

"I'm trying to help."

"I know." David said it because it was true. Because his father was trying, in the only way he knew how.

After his father left, David stood in the garden for a long time. The folder in his hands was like evidence of a truth he didn't want to admit.

He went inside. Set the folder on the counter without opening it. Then returned to the sunroom.

"Your father loves you, in his own deeply misguided, emotionally constipated way. He's like a plant trying to photosynthesize through a brick wall. Plenty of effort, entirely the wrong direction."

"That's harsh."

"Is it harsh? The man drove forty minutes to hand-deliver reasons you should sell the place where you're finally starting to heal from losing the woman he never figured out how to reach. I'm a plant, and even I can see the irony."

David's throat constricted. Heat and sharpness he wasn't ready to name.

"He's doing the best he knows how."

"Oh, he absolutely is doing the best he knows. Most people are. That doesn't mean the best they know is sufficient for the moment they're in."

Samantha's leaves rustled.

"Your father isn't bad at growing; he's just oriented toward the wrong light. Chasing illumination that can't nourish him. Or you."

"I don't want to be angry at him."

"Want has nothing to do with anger, honey. Anger shows up when there's a gap between what life is and what it should have been—like nitrogen building up in soil. The real question is whether you let it poison the roots or turn it into fertilizer."

David sank into the wicker chair.

That weight he'd been carrying—the one with his father's name on it—was heavier now. More solid. He could sense its edges. Could almost see the words written on it: Where were you? Where were you when she needed you? Where were you when I needed you?

But saying it out loud would make it real.

"I'm not ready. Not yet."

"That's fine. Gardens don't hurry. Neither should you. But eventually that stone you're carrying will get too heavy. You'll either set it down or let it pull you under. Timing is your choice; gravity is not."

David pulled out his journal and clicked open the pen his mother had given him.

It had arrived in his campus mailbox the week after graduation: postage dated three weeks before she died. Inside, wrapped in tissue paper, was this pen. Not expensive, not fancy. Just a good pen. And a card in her shaky handwriting:

David, I wanted you to have this for graduation. I know I won't be there to see you walk across that stage, but I'm so proud of you. Not because you finished, but because of who you're becoming. Use this pen to write your story. Whatever that looks like. Wherever it leads. Love always, Mom

He'd cried then. The first real crying since the funeral. Understanding that she was really gone. That all her careful planning couldn't change the fact that she wouldn't be there to see what came next.

Now he used that pen every day.

Day 8 - Dad came by. Brought market analysis for the house. He's trying to help in the way he knows how: facts and figures and practical solutions.

Samantha says he's growing toward the wrong light. She might be right. But I'm not ready to say that out loud yet.

There's a weight under the surface with Dad. About how he wasn't there during those last months. I can sense it sitting there, like a stone. Getting heavier. But I'm not ready to examine it yet.

God, help me be patient with him. Help me remember he's doing the best he knows how, even when it's not what I need.

Also—Eli can hear Samantha. A nine-year-old kid who lost his father. Grief cracked him open too. I'm not alone in this impossible thing. That matters more than I expected.

He closed the journal.

"I have no idea what I'm doing. Not with the garden. Not with my father. Not with any of this."

"Welcome to being human. None of you know what you're doing. You scatter possibilities and hope something takes root, classic seed dispersal strategy. Quite effective, actually."

"How long did it take my grandfather to know what he was doing?"

"Oh, he never did. After forty years, he still muttered about blights and fickle weather and tomatoes with an attitude. But he learned to enjoy not knowing. Treated the garden like a puzzle instead of a failing. That's the part you're learning now."

David thought about being twelve. Waking early one morning to find his grandfather in the sunroom, having what appeared to be a one-sided conversation with the plants. Young David had frozen in the hallway, embarrassed. His grandfather, talking to plants like they could hear him.

He's lonely, David had thought then. Old age making him eccentric. Grief making him talk to objects that couldn't talk back.

He'd crept back upstairs without getting his water. Had tucked it away as one of those sad realities about getting old.

Now, sitting in that same sunroom, having those same conversations, David understood differently.

His grandfather hadn't been lonely and confused. He'd been grief-wise. Had known that healing required witnesses—even if those witnesses were green and rooted and technically classified as houseplants.

"That's a long way from where I am."

"Honey, you're eight days in. Some processes aren't meant to be solved—they're meant to be lived with. Growth comes from the living, not the solving."

Evening was settling over the garden when David stopped working. His back ached. His hands were blistered where the tools had rubbed wrong. He was fairly certain he'd made several significant mistakes with the tomato stakes.

But the work had been absorbing in a way that surprised him. Physical. Immediate. Requiring attention that left no room for anxious spiraling.

He returned to the sunroom as twilight painted the garden in shades of blue and shadow.

"Thank you," he said to Samantha.

"For what specifically? I need parameters; otherwise I'll assume you're thanking me for the photosynthesis."

"For not trying to fix me. For letting me fumble around and make mistakes without telling me I'm doing it all wrong."

"Well, you *are* doing it wrong. But wrong in the right direction—which is the only wrong worth celebrating. Mistakes made in motion are far better than perfection attempted in stillness."

Her leaves caught the last of the daylight.

"Get some sleep. Tomorrow we'll work on your pruning technique. Which is to say, we'll work on you not committing herbicide through enthusiasm."

"Looking forward to it."

"Liar. But you'll show up anyway, and that's what matters. Half of gardening is simply returning. The other half is learning how not to kill things by accident. You're improving on both fronts."

The garden rested in darkness outside. And somewhere in that breathing space between day and night, David settled into the work that had called him here.

Not the desperate work of trying to fix what was broken. But the patient work of learning to tend what remained—when he had no idea what he was doing.

Like seeds in dark soil. Waiting for conditions they couldn't control. Trusting that growth happened in the hidden places first.

Chapter Three

UNPACKING SHADOWS

"But we have this treasure in jars of clay to show that this all-surpassing power is from God and not from us." - 2 Corinthians 4:7

D AVID HAD BEEN MOVING boxes for three hours, and the living room looked worse than when he'd begun.

Cardboard containers sat open like brown paper flowers across the hardwood floor, their contents spilling in piles that seemed to multiply the longer he studied them. Each box bore labels written in Marie's meticulous script: "Kitchen - Everyday," "Bedroom - Linens," "Living Room - Books & Records"—decisions made during those final weeks when she'd believed there would be time to see everything properly settled.

Lord, David prayed silently as he surveyed the chaos. I thought I was ready for this. Turns out unpacking someone's life is harder than inheriting it.

The spring afternoon had grown warm. Sweat trickled down David's back, making his shirt stick to his skin. Six weeks since his mother's death, and the work of sorting through accumulated possessions was still exhausting, physically and emotionally. Each object carried weight beyond its material substance.

"You're creating quite the archaeological dig over there," Samantha observed from her perch on the windowsill. "Though I should mention most successful excavations involve an actual method. You, darling, seem to be using the 'open everything and panic' approach—like trying to germinate seeds by digging them up every five minutes to check for roots. Ruins the radicle every time."

David sat back on his heels, wiping sweat from his forehead. "I thought I had a system."

"Oh, you do have a system," she continued, leaves rustling with amusement. "It's just a terrible one. You're trying to decide what to keep before you've really seen what you have. That's like pruning a plant you don't understand—clipping blind and hoping you haven't just taken off the main stem."

"So what should I be doing?"

"Well, for starters, you could stop treating your mother's things like they'll explode if you touch them wrong," she said. "Marie packed these boxes knowing someone would open them. She wasn't curating a museum. She was leaving breadcrumbs."

David surveyed the mess, seeing it differently. Not chaos exactly, but the necessary disorder that preceded understanding.

"Breadcrumbs to what?"

"To the fact that the woman you're grieving was far more complex than the saint you've been polishing in your memory," Samantha went on. "People always sand down the edges of the dead. Makes them easier to hold onto—simpler to mourn a statue than a living, flawed human."

The observation stung because it was accurate.

He was examining a box labeled "Marie's Books - Personal" when he heard bicycle wheels on gravel. Through the window, he could see Eli Rodriguez coasting down the driveway with that same serious expression, another covered dish balanced on his handlebars.

David met him at the door.

"From my mom again," Eli said, holding out what appeared to be some sort of pasta bake. The aluminum foil was warm. "She saw you carrying boxes earlier and figured you'd forget to eat lunch."

"Your mom's observant."

"She says it's her superpower." Eli peered past David into the living room, his eyes widening. "Wow. That's a lot of stuff."

"Yeah. I'm starting to think I need an actual plan."

"Mom's good at organizing. She had to pack up all my dad's stuff after..." Eli stopped. His shoulders hunched forward. Then: "Anyway, she's good at it. You want me to ask her?"

Before David could respond, a voice called from the driveway. "Eli? You delivering food or moving in?"

A woman approached: dark hair pulled back in a ponytail, wearing jeans and a t-shirt that had seen many days of hard work. Her face carried the beauty that came from strength rather than symmetry. Her eyes held the awareness of someone who'd learned to read people's needs through their silences.

"You must be Mara," David said.

"And you look like you could use more than casseroles." Mara glanced past him at the chaos. Her voice carried practical warmth. "Eli, go grab the organizing supplies from the garage. The bins and the label maker."

As Eli ran off, Mara turned back to David. "I have some time this morning if you want help. And I might have texted a friend who's good with this kind of thing. She's a nurse, so she's got crazy hours, but if she can make it..." She read his face. "Is that okay?"

David hesitated. The instinct to say he was fine battled against the obvious evidence that he was drowning.

"You didn't have to—"

"I know I didn't have to. But I wanted to." Her voice was matter-of-fact. "Besides, this is what people do. We show up. We help."

David was pulling out another box when he heard tires on gravel again.

Through the window, he saw a small sedan. Not Mara's van.

His pulse jumped before his mind caught up with why.

Eileen's car. That silver Honda she'd had since junior year.

The warmth that spread through his chest was immediate. Relief that she'd actually come. Nervousness about what her presence here meant. Gratitude that someone from his former life had chosen to show up in this house full of ghosts and half-unpacked boxes.

He watched her emerge, gathering something from the passenger seat with that same careful precision he remembered from their shared classes. She was wearing weekend clothes: jeans and a soft green sweater, hair pulled back.

She was here. In his grandfather's driveway.

He wasn't sure if he was ready for this. But he was certain he didn't want her to leave.

Eileen emerged carrying a bag from the local coffee shop. When she saw him standing in the doorway, her expression shifted. Uncertainty breaking into something that might have been cautious relief.

"Hi," she said. Simply. Then, after a breath: "Mara texted. Said you might have company but could use more hands." Her voice got quieter. "I had the day off and thought... I wasn't sure if you'd want me here. But I wanted to try."

The honesty of it—her admission that she wasn't sure, that she'd taken a risk by coming—loosened something inside him.

"I'm glad you came," he said. The words came out rougher than he intended.

"Yeah?" Her shoulders relaxed.

"Yeah. I—" He gestured helplessly at the chaos behind him. "I'm pretty bad at this. At all of it."

"I brought coffee," she said, holding up the bag with a small smile. "Figured we could at least caffeinate our way through the bad-at-it part."

"That sounds perfect."

The four of them, counting Eli, who returned with an impressive array of organizing supplies, settled into a rhythm that felt surprisingly natural.

Mara had a gift for cutting through paralysis, asking simple questions that helped David make decisions without making him feel judged. Eileen worked beside him, sorting photographs and letters into chronological piles with methodical attention.

"Before we get too deep into this," Mara said, settling onto the couch, "what are you actually trying to accomplish here? Are you preserving everything as your grandfather left it, or figuring out how to make this space yours while honoring what came before?"

David opened his mouth to answer, then realized he didn't know. "I guess... both? Neither?"

"That's honest. So maybe the first step is deciding which boxes to open today and which ones can wait until you have more clarity."

"How do I know which is which?"

Eileen glanced up. "Maybe start with the ones that feel the most necessary? The ones you keep thinking about?"

"That box labeled 'Marie's Books - Personal' keeps catching my eye."

"Then maybe that's your answer."

David pulled the box closer.

Inside, he found books on plants and gardening, field guides to local birds, a well-worn copy of Pilgrim at Tinker Creek. And beneath those, wrapped in tissue paper, a collection of ceramic birds. Small sculptures in various colors: blue jays, cardinals, wrens. Each one detailed. Each one with a tiny imperfection. A chipped wing here. A cracked beak there.

"She loved these," Mara said. "Said they reminded her that imperfection didn't mean worthless. That broken could be beautiful if you stopped demanding perfection."

David held a blue jay with a chipped wing, remembering how his mother had kept it on her desk during the final months.

"Because perfect things don't need grace," she'd said once. "But these—these I can appreciate as they are."

"Your mother had a gift for making spaces feel alive," Mara continued. "She understood that honoring the past meant building on it, not freezing it in time."

Eileen had been listening while she worked. Now she glanced up, her voice careful.

"She taught me that. During... when I was helping."

David's hands stilled on the ceramic bird.

"When you were helping?"

Mara and Eileen exchanged a brief glance. It was Mara who answered.

"The women from church. We rotated through during your mom's final weeks. Helped with meals, garden work, just... being present when she needed it."

David looked at Eileen. A new understanding settled over him.

"You were part of that?"

Eileen nodded, not quite meeting his eyes. "I should have mentioned it earlier. I didn't know if—" She stopped. "I wasn't sure how to bring it up."

"How long?"

"The last eight weeks or so. After my brother's accident in January, I was struggling. Your mom heard about it through the church network and reached out. We'd meet for coffee, talk about how to be present for someone who was suffering without trying to fix it." Eileen's hands had stilled on the letters. "When she got sick in March, it seemed like the least I could do was show up."

David sat back against the couch.

"I didn't realize. During those final weeks, I was so focused on Mom that I didn't see anyone else."

"You were surviving," Mara said. "Nobody expected you to notice everything. You were watching your mother die. That takes all the attention you have."

Eileen was quiet, then: "I wanted to say something at graduation. Or at the funeral. But I didn't know how to bring it up without it seeming like I was claiming something. A relationship with your mom that you didn't know about." Her voice got quieter. "That felt private."

David studied her, this person who'd been more present in his mother's final weeks than he'd realized.

"Thank you," he said finally. "For being there. For her."

"She was easy to show up for. Even when it was hard."

"Your mother collected broken birds and broken people," Samantha's voice drifted from the sunroom, audible to David and Eli. "She always recognized the grace in what everyone else called damaged. Cracks made it easier for the light to get in, she said."

Eli, who'd been organizing the ceramic birds on the coffee table, glanced toward the sunroom. The corner of his mouth twitched but he said nothing. He arranged the blue jay with the chipped wing apart from the others, as if it were standing guard.

It was Eileen who found the Bible.

She pulled it from the box of personal books, handling it with reverence. Not the small bedside Bible David had found upstairs. This one was larger, heavier, the leather cover worn smooth at the edges. Pages marked with a dozen different colors of ink visible through the closed book, edges of yellow and green and blue bleeding through like stained glass.

David's breath caught.

This was the one. Her real Bible. The one where she'd done the actual work.

"This looks important," Eileen said, holding it out. "Different from the one upstairs."

"Yeah." David's voice came out rough. "That one was for quick comfort. This is where she wrestled."

He took it from Eileen's hands. The weight settled in his palms, dense with years of reading and rereading and arguing and questioning.

His hands trembled as he opened to a random page. His mother's careful annotations bloomed across the margins in three different colors. Questions, prayers, arguments with God, evidence of an inner life far more complicated than he'd understood.

"She marked it up like a scholar," Mara said, peering over his shoulder. "Different colors for different themes. Yellow for comfort passages, green for hope, blue for prayers and questions."

David opened to the Psalms and found a passage marked heavily in blue ink. Next to it, she'd written:

David doesn't know it yet, but he has a gift for tending. Not just plants—people, relationships, broken places that need attention. God, help him see what I see in him.

The date beside it: April 15, 2024. Three weeks before she died.

He had to sit down.

His legs gave out, and suddenly he was on the floor, back against the couch, the Bible open on his lap. His mother had seen something in him that he'd never been able to name for himself. Had written it down as a prayer in those final weeks when every word cost her energy she didn't have.

"You okay?" Eileen's voice was concerned. She'd moved closer, crouching beside him. Her hand touched his shoulder lightly, anchoring.

"Yeah. Just..." He couldn't take his eyes off the words. "She wrote about me. About seeing something in me that I don't see."

"She saw it because it's there," Mara said, sitting down beside him on the floor. "Your mother had a gift for seeing people—not for who they pretended to be, but who they were capable of becoming."

"She wrote that three weeks before she died," Mara added. "We were having coffee here, and she was worried about what would happen to you. Not worried you couldn't handle it. Worried you didn't see your own gifts."

David sat with that. The knowledge that his mother had spent her final weeks writing prayers about his calling, seeing in him what he couldn't yet see in himself.

"Thank you," he said. To Mara. To Eileen. To the room and the house. "For being here. For helping with this."

"You don't have to do it alone," Eileen said. Simply. Certainly.

And for the first time since he'd arrived at this house, David believed her.

They worked through the afternoon, making slow progress. The room transformed—not into a new space exactly, but into a space that held both past and present without choosing between them.

David kept reading. Found more passages where his mother had wrestled. In Job, she'd written: I don't know where You were, but I know where I am. Afraid. Angry. Here. In Romans 8: Doesn't mean everything that happens is good. Means God can make good out of the worst circumstances. In Ecclesiastes: Planting and plucking might be the same work. Trusting the gardener to know the difference.

"She wasn't peaceful about dying," David said. "She was angry. Scared."

"She was human," Mara said. "Marie wrestled with her faith more than most people knew. She told me once that easy faith wasn't real faith. That real belief required you to stay engaged when you wanted to walk away."

A faith that was alive because it was honest enough to include doubt.

After Mara and Eli left, and Eileen's sedan followed a few minutes later, David stood in the living room surrounded by the evidence of the day's work.

"That was productive," Samantha said from the kitchen after the door closed behind the last car. "Though I did notice Eileen couldn't hear me."

"No," David confirmed. That strange mixture of isolation and specialness settled over him again.

"She seems well-rooted," Samantha added. "Practical. Good with her hands. The sort of person who arrives when she says she will—steady as an established root system holding soil in place during a storm."

"She is."

"And you like her," she said, not bothering to shape it as a question.

It wasn't a question. David's face heated.

"We're friends. She's been supportive—"

"Oh, stop," Samantha chided gently. "The question isn't whether you're interested, honey. The question is whether you're in season. A plant can form buds in winter, but forcing blooms before the frost has passed only damages the tissue."

David sat in his grandfather's reading chair, too tired to argue with a plant about his romantic life.

"I don't know if I'm ready for anything beyond surviving right now."

"Fair enough," she said. "Just remember—surviving and living aren't the same. One keeps you breathing; the other lets you grow. Eventually you'll have to decide which one you came here to do."

He should have stopped there. Should have gone to bed.

Instead, exhausted from the day's emotional work, he found himself climbing the stairs. Retrieving a box from the closet. The one he'd opened once, two weeks ago, then closed immediately with shaking hands.

Medical records. Documents from the hospital. Items his father had gathered and packed away like evidence.

The photograph was near the top.

Marie in a hospital room during one of her chemotherapy sessions, based on the IV stand visible at the edge of the frame. Someone, a nurse, had captured her when she thought no one was watching.

This wasn't the composed woman who'd smiled bravely for visitors.

This was his mother stripped of all performance. Her face drawn tight with pain, every line telegraphing agony. Her hands folded in prayer, but there was nothing peaceful about the gesture. It looked like wrestling. Demand. Someone holding onto faith with white-knuckled desperation because letting go would mean drowning.

The memory slammed into him:

That day. He'd been in the hallway getting coffee. Escaping, really. The smell of antiseptic and fear. Fluorescent lights too bright. Medical equipment beeping, tracking, counting down.

When he'd returned to the room, the IV pump was beeping, that urgent sound that meant a problem. Marie's face had been twisted, trying not to scream. The nurse adjusting settings with practiced urgency.

"I need five more minutes," Marie had gasped. Not to the nurse. To God, maybe. To herself. To death. "Five more minutes before I start crying."

David had frozen in the doorway.

Unable to go in. Unable to turn away. Watching his mother fight to maintain control while her body betrayed her and the poison meant to save her destroyed her from the inside.

He hadn't stayed.

Had turned around. Gone back to the hallway. Sat on a bench near the elevators where he couldn't hear the beeping or see her face or feel the weight of his own uselessness.

She'd never mentioned it. Had never said "Where were you?" or "I needed you."

David stared at the photograph now. Understanding with devastating clarity what it showed: his mother's honest faith. The version that looked like suffering. That included rage and demand and Why are You doing this to me?

His hands were shaking.

"She was praying," he said to Samantha. His voice was rough. "In that photograph. She's praying and she looks like she's dying."

"She was doing both," Samantha said quietly. "Dying and praying. Not with serene smiles and soft lighting—she died angry, questioning, demanding answers from a God who stayed maddeningly silent. But she kept talking. For her, real faith was less about calm acceptance and more about refusing to hang up the line."

"I wasn't there," David said. The admission tore out of him. "That day. When this was taken. I left."

"Of course you left," Samantha replied, her tone free of judgment. "You were twenty-two, watching poison tear through your mother's body in the name of saving her. Your nervous system did what it had to do. Stepping out of the room was not betrayal; it was survival."

Samantha's voice carried no judgment.

"The question was never whether you stood beside her every single moment," she continued. "The question is whether you'll let yourself be human in a memory you keep trying to rewrite. Can you forgive the boy you were for reaching his limits inside an impossible storm?"

David sat with that.

The photograph showed him what he hadn't been able to see then: his mother's tremendous courage. Her refusal to pretend suffering was anything less than devastating. Her insistence on staying in conversation with God when that conversation was mostly screaming.

He picked up her Bible. Opened it to the page she'd marked heavily. Found the words that suddenly made sense:

I don't know where You were, but I know where I am. Afraid. Angry. Here.

Here. When "here" was unbearable. When "here" required more courage than David had been able to witness without breaking.

He set the photograph down on the coffee table. Next to the ceramic birds with their broken wings. Next to his mother's Bible with its color-coded arguments with God.

Evidence of a woman who had been more complicated than a saint. More honest than peaceful. More faithful because she'd included the doubt.

He pulled out his journal, too exhausted to write much:

Day 22 - Found Mom's real Bible. The one where she wrestled. She doubted more than I knew. Wrestled with God more than I understood. That makes her faith more real, not less.

Found a photograph from the hospital. Her praying while the chemo was destroying her. I wasn't there that day. I left because I couldn't watch.

She never said "Where were you?" Never made me feel guilty. But I feel it anyway.

Mom wrote that I have a gift for tending broken places. Three weeks before she died. Not sure I believe that yet. But maybe that's what I'm doing here: learning to tend what's broken. Including myself.

God, help me understand what it means to inherit faith without trying to copy it. Help me make it my own.

He closed the journal.

Tomorrow he would work in the vegetable beds. Tonight, he would sleep in a house that was becoming his own.

The work of inheritance, he was beginning to understand, wasn't about preserving the past unchanged. It was about letting the past transform into wisdom that could feed the future.

Like bulbs pushing through spring soil. Breaking through what was dead to reach what was possible.

Chapter Four

READING THE MARGINS

"But I cry to you for help, Lord; in the morning my prayer comes before you. Why, Lord, do you reject me and hide your face from me?" - Psalm 88:13-14

T HE MORNING AFTER UNPACKING his mother's possessions, David woke before dawn with the Bible already on his mind.

The worn leather cover. Pages soft as tissue from constant handling. Colors of ink marking different seasons of her spiritual journey—all waiting downstairs on the kitchen counter.

God, he prayed while pulling on yesterday's clothes, *I'm not sure I'm ready to see her like this. But maybe that's the point.*

He made coffee in his grandfather's ancient Mr. Coffee, then carried both a mug and Bible to the sunroom, where morning light gathered like honey poured slow. The wicker chair creaked its familiar welcome as he settled.

The leather was warm under his palms. Smooth where his mother's hands had held it, rougher at the edges. He could almost sense her presence in the weight of it.

"You're up early," Samantha observed. "Ready to meet her properly, then. Most people spend years tending comfortable myths about their dead parents. Takes courage to look at who they were beneath all the titles. It's like examining the root system instead of just admiring the leaves—unsettling to see all the tangled, vulnerable parts, but it's the only way to understand how anything ever grew."

The pages fell open naturally to passages his mother had returned to again and again. The margins were dense with annotations in different colors. Yellow for comfort, green for hope, blue for prayers. But the system was more complex than that—some passages had all three colors layered, showing her returning to the same verses in different seasons, finding different meanings as circumstances changed. The ink had bled where tears had fallen, faint halos around certain words that had mattered intensely.

The early notes in black pen were confident, practical. *Trust in the Lord with all your heart* was underlined firmly, with her notation: *Easy to say before you know what you're trusting Him with.* The handwriting was strong, certain—the script of someone who believed in clear answers.

"She wrote most of those early notes in that first year after diagnosis," Samantha said. "When she still believed that bright thoughts and tidy theology could bargain with cancer. As if faith were a coupon you could hand over at the register in exchange for more time. Like trying to negotiate with photosynthesis—polite, but entirely beside the point."

David's coffee cooled as he read, watching his mother's handwriting grow shakier, her observations more honest as treatments progressed. Confident black pen gave way to pencil during weeks when her hands shook too much for precision, then back to pen in colors that marked different emotional territories.

In Job, the margins were cramped with wrestling. The handwriting was smaller, tighter, like she was trying to contain what was too big for the space provided. *Where were you when I laid the foundation of the earth?* highlighted in yellow, with her response in blue ink: *I don't know where You were, but I know where I am. Afraid. Angry. Here.*

David's vision blurred. He blinked hard.

"She was angry," he said, barely above a whisper. "At God. Really angry."

"Of course she was angry," Samantha replied, her voice gentler than usual. "Illness like that burns away polite answers and leaves whatever's true underneath. And for what it's worth, anger makes excellent fertilizer when you let it break down. All that emotional nitrogen returning to the soil, ready to feed something new."

A loose paper fell from between the pages of Psalms.

A printed handout with "Riverside Cancer Support Group" at the top.

David's heart beat faster. Discussion questions about dealing with doubt during serious illness. His mother had answered them in pencil, cramped to fit the small spaces.

Do you ever feel angry with God?

Every day. Some days all day. Anger is love with nowhere to go.

The words hit him like a physical blow. David had to set the paper down. His hands were shaking too much to hold it steady.

"I never knew she went to a support group," he said, his voice rough. "She never mentioned it."

But that wasn't quite true. Thursday evenings. Every Thursday at 7 PM, for almost two years. Marie would say she was "going out for a bit" or "meeting with a friend." David had been in college for most of it, too absorbed in his own life to question where his mother went every Thursday evening.

Now he understood. A room full of people wrestling with mortality and rage and the impossibility of dying when you weren't finished living yet. A space where his mother could be honest about her anger at God, her fear of leaving David unprepared, her rage at the unfairness of having time measured in months instead of decades.

She'd never told him. Had protected him from knowing how scared she was. How angry. How human.

But he had known, once.

He'd buried the memory because it was too uncomfortable. Too different from the composed mother he preferred to remember.

He was twenty-one. Spring break, senior year. Marie had been in treatment for almost eighteen months. The cancer had metastasized. The doctors were talking about "managing symptoms" rather than "fighting for cure."

He'd woken at 2 AM. Thirsty. Padded downstairs in bare feet, trying to be quiet.

The light in the sunroom had been on—a golden rectangle spilling into the dark hallway.

Marie was there. Kneeling on the floor in front of the wicker chair, Bible open on the seat cushion. Her body folded forward, forehead pressed against the chair's arm, shoulders shaking with silent sobs.

David froze in the doorway, watching his mother break in ways she never allowed anyone to see.

"I can't do this," she whispered. Not to David. To God, maybe. To herself. "I can't leave him. He's not ready. I haven't prepared him enough. Please—a little more time. Let me finish teaching him how to be okay without me."

Her voice was raw, desperate. Nothing like the calm, accepting tone she used during the day when visitors came with casseroles and platitudes about God's plan.

"I'm so angry with You," she continued, the intensity making the whispered words feel loud in the quiet house. "Is this how You answer prayers? By taking people before they're done? Before their children are ready? What Father does that?"

David backed away. Retreated to the kitchen. Got his water. Crept back upstairs without letting her know, without offering comfort or presence or acknowledgment.

He'd been too young. Too scared. Too overwhelmed by the depth of her pain to know how to respond.

The next morning, she'd been composed again. Making breakfast. Asking about his plans. Performing strength so convincingly that David had wondered if he'd dreamed it.

But he hadn't dreamed it. He'd witnessed his mother's honest faith. The version that included rage and demand and *Why are You doing this to me?* The version that was nothing like the peaceful acceptance everyone pretended grief required.

"I need some air," David said now, his lungs constricting. "This is too much."

"Of course it's too much," Samantha said. "You're meeting your mother as a whole human instead of just Mom. That always rearranges the roots—like discovering a plant you thought was annual is actually perennial. Suddenly the growth rings make sense, but you have to revise the story you've been telling yourself." Her leaves shifted. "Walking helps move heavy things through the system. Your mother used to take laps around the block when her Bible margins got too loud for sitting still."

He grabbed his grandfather's old denim jacket—holding the faint scent of pipe tobacco Marvin had given up decades ago—and stepped outside into the late May morning that smelled of cut grass and warming earth.

The neighborhood was quiet with the peace of suburban morning routine. A distant lawnmower provided gentle percussion. Birds called from various territories—cardinals, blue jays, the persistent chattering of house sparrows. David walked without destination, letting his feet choose the path while his mind tried to absorb what he'd discovered.

The sound of weeping made him glance up from his thoughts.

Not quiet weeping. Raw. Unguarded. The kind of crying that didn't care who heard.

Across the street, tucked behind a black iron fence that looked older than the town itself, the small cemetery served the older part of the neighborhood. David had walked past it countless times during childhood visits but had never paid it much attention.

Now, in the clear morning light, he could see someone kneeling beside a granite headstone about thirty yards from the gate.

A young woman, maybe his age or younger. Her blue hair caught the morning sun—not subtle, but vivid, electric, the color so intense it seemed to glow against the subdued greens and grays of the cemetery. She'd arranged yellow roses at the base of the stone, their petals tight with morning dew.

But it was the way she grieved that stopped David in his tracks.

Her whole body curved around the sorrow she was holding—shoulders rounded, head bowed, one hand resting on top of the headstone like she was maintaining physical connection with whoever lay beneath. She wasn't trying to hide her tears. Wasn't apologizing for them. Wasn't performing the careful, private grief that society expected.

She was just there. Raw and honest. Letting the loss move through her without trying to manage how it looked.

There was something in her posture—the way she held her sorrow without self-consciousness, without the careful containment that usually accompanied public displays of emotion—that reminded David powerfully of his mother's honesty in the Bible margins.

Here was someone else living the questions. Someone else who understood that love required presence, required the patient work of coming back to what mattered even when it brought pain.

The blue hair triggered a memory from years ago.

He and his mother, visiting Grandpa Marvin one summer. He'd come downstairs to find Marie in the kitchen with purple streaks in her hair. Not subtle highlights—actual purple. Bright and defiant and completely unlike the practical woman who wore nursing scrubs and kept her nails short.

"Mom. What did you do to your hair?"

She'd touched the purple self-consciously. "Do you hate it?"

"I... no. I just. It's really purple."

"I know." A smile, uncertain. "I saw a girl at the grocery store with blue hair and I thought—why not? Life's too short to only have brown hair."

His dad had hated it. David remembered now—the way Robert's face had closed when he'd seen it. The careful neutrality: *That's quite a statement.*

The purple had lasted three weeks. Then Marie dyed it back to brown. David had never asked why.

Now he wondered if she'd been trying to claim something for herself. Some small rebellion against the practical, put-together, strong-for-everyone-else version she maintained. Some visible marker that she was more than Mom, more than Nurse Marie, more than just Robert's wife who kept the household running.

The purple had been her equivalent of this woman's blue hair. A way of saying: *I'm here. The person I am is visible underneath all these roles I perform.*

The young woman glanced up, perhaps sensing his presence, perhaps simply taking a break from the intensity of her grief. Her face was streaked with tears she hadn't bothered to wipe away. Her eyes were red-rimmed but not apologetic—brown eyes, dark and direct, carrying the awareness of someone who had learned that grief was to be witnessed rather than hidden.

Their eyes met across the cemetery's careful landscaping—the manicured grass, the walking paths of crushed stone, the old oak tree providing shade over the oldest graves.

She didn't look away or apologize for her emotion. Instead, she nodded. Not invitation, not dismissal—acknowledgment. The nod said: *I see you seeing me. I'm not ashamed.*

David nodded back, holding her gaze for a moment before continuing his walk.

As he passed the cemetery gate, something caught his eye. A small rectangle of white near the base of the iron fence, half-hidden in the grass where the wind must have carried it.

A business card. Simple design. "Maya's Canvas" printed above a local address. A small paintbrush icon in the corner. On the back, handwritten: *Art heals what words can't reach.*

David picked it up. The card was slightly damp from morning dew. He looked back toward the cemetery, toward the blue hair and yellow roses and honest grief.

He pocketed the card without quite knowing why.

He carried with him the image of blue hair and unashamed tears and yellow roses arranged with the care of someone who understood that caring for the dead was its own form of faith. Its own way of insisting that love persisted beyond the boundaries of physical presence.

When he returned twenty minutes later, he found a text from Eileen: "Staying at the B&B on Main Street instead of driving back. Yesterday was a lot. Want company for breakfast?"

He typed back: "Just saw this. That would be good."

She arrived ten minutes later, carrying coffee and scones from the local bakery. They settled on the wide porch steps, the morning warm but not yet hot. A breeze carried the scent of roses and fresh-cut grass from Mr. Chen's yard next door.

"So," Eileen said after a comfortable silence. "Yesterday was intense."

"Yeah. Finding Mom's Bible..." David trailed off.

"Did you read more this morning?"

He nodded. "She was angry at God. Really angry. And I remembered something I'd buried."

He told her about the 2 AM scene. His mother kneeling, weeping, demanding answers from God. How he'd retreated instead of going to her.

Eileen listened without interrupting.

"Makes sense though," she said finally. "Being angry when you're dying and leaving people you love behind."

"I always thought her faith was stronger than mine. Like she had something I didn't."

"Maybe she did. Years of practice wrestling with doubt and staying with it anyway." Eileen took a sip of coffee. "That's not weakness. That's strength."

David studied her. The way she sat comfortably on the worn steps, not worried about dirt or grass stains. The way she spoke about faith without making it sound simple or easy.

"Thank you," he said. "For coming. For being here."

"I wanted to be here." She met his eyes, and David sensed a shift between them—what had been potential becoming more defined. "You're not the only one figuring out life, you know. I'm trying to learn how to be present with people who are grieving without trying to fix them."

"You're good at it. The being present part."

"I'm learning. Mostly by being there and hoping I don't mess it up too badly."

From inside the house, Samantha's voice drifted through the open window: "She's well companion-planted. Deep roots, steady presence, good exchange of what matters underneath. Excellent nutrient-sharing potential."

David pressed his lips together, fighting a smile.

They talked for another hour. About Eileen's work at the hospital. About families she was learning to support. About how hard it was to sit with other people's pain without trying to solve it. About David's slow discovery that grief wasn't something to overcome but something to hold.

When Eileen gathered her things to leave, she paused by her car.

"I'm coming back next weekend. If you want company for whatever project you're working on."

"I'd like that," David said. And meant it.

After she left, David returned to the sunroom. He pulled the business card from his pocket, studied the simple design. Maya's Canvas. The woman with blue hair who wasn't ashamed to grieve in public.

"That went well," Samantha observed when the house settled quiet again. "Eileen, I mean. Not that I have any opinions about whatever you've been turning over in your pocket like a seed you're not ready to plant."

"There was a woman at the cemetery," David said. "Blue hair. Crying at a grave. She wasn't hiding it at all."

"Ah," Samantha's leaves rustled with what might have been recognition. "Blue hair. Yellow roses. Yes. She came once, years ago, when your grandfather was still alive—brought coffee and stayed for an hour. That grief frequency I mentioned? She's tuned to it too. Lost her brother. Twin, if memory serves. Some losses split the trunk right down the middle."

David looked up sharply. "You know her?"

"She came by once, years ago. When your grandfather was still alive. Brought coffee and stayed to talk for an hour." Samantha paused. "Interesting that you noticed her. That frequency I mentioned—the one grief opens up? She's tuned to it too. Lost her brother. Twin brother, if I remember correctly."

David stared at the card in his hand. *Art heals what words can't reach.*

"Should I—"

"Should you what? March over there and introduce yourself because you both know how to weep in public?" Samantha's voice held gentle amusement. "Give it time, honey. These things have their own seasons. Connections are like seeds—you don't force them open. They know when conditions are right."

David pocketed the card again. He'd hold onto it. See if the right moment arrived.

He pulled out his journal:

Day 23 - Read more of Mom's Bible. Found the support group handout. Every Thursday for two years, she went to a cancer support group and was honest about her doubt and fear and rage.

I never knew. She protected me from seeing how scared she was while she was teaching me to be brave.

Remembered something I'd buried. Finding her at 2 AM, kneeling in the sunroom, begging God for more time. "I can't leave him. He's not ready." I retreated instead of going to her. I was too scared to witness her breaking.

Saw a woman at the cemetery. Blue hair, yellow roses, raw tears. She wasn't hiding her grief—she was honoring it. Like Mom honored her faith in those margins. Giving it room to be messy and real.

Found her business card. Maya's Canvas. Samantha says she knew her—says she can hear Samantha too. Another person tuned to the grief frequency.

Eileen came by. She's coming back next weekend.

God, help me learn to honor my faith the way Mom honored hers—with honesty and anger and persistence. Help me understand that doubt isn't the opposite of faith. Maybe it's faith that's honest enough to ask hard questions.

Evening settled over the garden. Through the window, fireflies began their work—small points of light rising from the grass like stars trying to find their way home.

"She would be proud of you," Samantha said as evening settled, her tone soft. "Not for tidying boxes or saying the right things—but for having the courage to read what she wrote in the margins. For letting her be complicated instead of polishing her into something flawless and untouchable."

"How do you know?"

"How do I know?" she echoed. "Because she told me. Near the end, she said she'd scattered breadcrumbs through that Bible—not to make you copy her faith, but to show you that real belief could hold doubt without cracking. She didn't want you rehearsing her answers. She wanted you to see that staying in the conversation mattered more than sounding certain. Be present. Care for what needs tending. The rest grows in its own time."

The garden rested in growing darkness. And somewhere in that breathing space between day and night, David learned a new way to honor his mother's memory—not by trying to replicate her faith, but by having the courage to develop his own.

Complete with doubt and anger and the patient work of holding questions that might never have easy answers.

Chapter Five

STORM AND TRUTH

"Yet you desired faithfulness even in the womb; you taught me wisdom in that secret place." - Psalm 51:6

THE PHONE CALL CAME early June, on a gray morning when the weight of approaching summer felt more like burden than blessing.

David had been at the house for nearly a month. The careful distance his father had maintained since the funeral was beginning to read less like respect and more like avoidance wearing patience's mask.

He stood at the kitchen window, watching clouds stack themselves on the western horizon. Not the soft white cumulus of fair weather—these were darker, denser, the bruised purple-gray that meant real storms. The air had that heavy quality, thick with moisture and the electric anticipation of pressure about to break.

God, David prayed as he watched morning light struggle through the gathering clouds, *I sense what's coming and I'm not ready for it. Help me.*

His coffee had gone lukewarm in his hands. The kitchen smelled of the grounds he'd measured out an hour ago, mixed with the particular mustiness of old houses before rain: dust and wood and the ghost of decades of cooking. Through the open window, he could smell the garden too: wet soil from last night's brief shower, the green sharpness of tomato leaves, the faint sweetness of the roses his grandmother had planted along the fence thirty years ago.

The week since reading his mother's Bible had shifted something fundamental. Her willingness to be angry with God, to question everything, to keep returning when faith felt impossible—all of it had been giving him courage he hadn't known he was building toward. If she could be that real with the divine, maybe he could be that real with his father.

His phone rang at eight-thirty.

Robert's number glowed on the screen.

David's stomach tightened. His free hand gripped the edge of the counter, knuckles whitening against the old Formica.

He let it ring twice before answering.

"David." Robert's voice carried the controlled efficiency of someone conducting business, but underneath David could hear uncertainty wearing authority's mask. "How are you settling in?"

"I'm settling. The house is peaceful. The garden needs work, but it's manageable."

"Good. That's good." A pause that stretched too long. "And your plans? For the fall semester?"

There it was.

Outside, the first gust of wind moved through the maple tree, setting its leaves to restless whispering. David watched them shiver, green going silver as the undersides caught what remained of the light.

"I'm taking some time. To figure out life." David heard his own voice sound younger than he'd intended. "The house gives me space to think."

"Space to think." Robert repeated the words like evidence being entered into a case he was building. "David, I've been patient about this, but summer's here. Registration deadlines are passing. You can't put your life on hold indefinitely."

"I'm not putting my life on hold. I'm trying to figure out what my life is."

Through the window, the storm clouds had swallowed more of the sky. The light in the kitchen shifted, dimming as if someone were slowly turning down a lamp. David could feel the barometric pressure dropping—that subtle heaviness in his sinuses, the way sound seemed to carry differently when the weather was about to change.

"Son, I know losing your mother has been difficult—"

"Do you?"

The words came out sharper than he'd intended.

A crack opened in him. Sudden. Bright. Painful.

"Do you know how difficult it's been? Because from where I'm sitting, you handled her dying by working longer hours. And her death by trying to manage everyone else's grief instead of experiencing your own."

"That's not fair—"

"Isn't it?"

David's face heated. His breath came faster, shallow in his chest. The phone was slick in his palm—he was sweating despite the cool morning. His heart hammered against his ribs with the insistence of something trying to escape.

"Where were you when she was scared about the diagnosis? Working late. Where were you when the chemo made her too sick to drive herself to appointments? Business trip. Where were you when she needed someone to sit with her while she cried?"

"I was providing for the family—"

"You were hiding, Dad."

The words hung in the air like the charged stillness before lightning.

"You were so afraid of watching her die that you chose to be absent for how she lived. While she was dying. You just... you weren't there."

Thunder rumbled in the distance—still far off, but approaching. David could feel it in his chest, that low vibration that resonated with something primal. The storm was coming whether anyone was ready for it or not.

The memories flooded back, unbidden and unstoppable.

Second round of chemo. Marie was having a bad reaction: fever spiking to 103, nausea so severe she couldn't keep water down. David had been home for Thanksgiving break. He'd found her in the bathroom at 3 AM, curled on the cold tile floor, too weak to stand.

The fluorescent light had been harsh, unforgiving. It showed every line of exhaustion on her face, every shadow under her eyes. She'd been wearing her old bathrobe—the blue one with the fraying hem that she refused to replace because it was comfortable.

"Where's Dad?"

"Houston. Client meeting." Her voice barely a whisper against the tile. "He'll be back Friday."

It was Tuesday.

David had lifted her—shocked at how light she'd become, how the cancer and treatment had whittled her down to angles and determination. He'd driven her to the ER himself, 3 AM roads empty and surreal. Sat with her for eight hours while they rehydrated her through IV, the fluorescent lights buzzing overhead, the smell of antiseptic and fear thick in his throat. Held the basin when the nausea medication didn't work fast enough. Called Robert's cell three times. Left messages that grew increasingly desperate.

Got a text back six hours later: *In meetings all day. Keep me posted. Love you both.*

Or October. The afternoon light had been golden, almost mocking in its beauty. Marie's hair was falling out in clumps—she'd find them on her pillow, in the shower drain, tangled in her brush. She'd asked Robert to come to her oncology appointment—the one where they'd discuss whether the current protocol was working.

"I really need you there." Her voice had carried that particular vulnerability she rarely allowed anyone to hear. "I don't want to hear this news alone."

"I'll try, honey. But the merger is happening this week. You know how these things are."

She'd gone alone.

Driven herself to the cancer center. Sat in the waiting room with its careful neutrality, its magazines about hope and survival. Walked into the consultation room by herself.

The appointment was devastating.

The cancer wasn't responding.

They'd need harsher treatment. More aggressive. More destructive.

She'd driven home with that news rattling around inside her like broken glass. Made meatloaf because it was Tuesday and Tuesdays were meatloaf nights. Asked David about his classes, his friends, whether he'd decided on a major yet.

Robert got home around 9 PM. Loosened his tie. Asked how the appointment went.

Marie said "Fine."

Robert accepted that answer and turned on the news.

"When did you move out?" David asked now, his voice flat as hammered metal. "Before she died or after?"

Outside, the wind had picked up. The maple's branches swayed and creaked, leaves showing their pale undersides in continuous silver waves. Rain began to spatter against the windows—fat drops that hit the glass with audible impact, each one a small percussion.

He'd found out from Mara. An envelope addressed to Robert at a different street, discovered while sorting mail that had accumulated. A small apartment across town. Six months of separate addresses that no one had thought to mention.

They'd been living separately for about six months before she died, Mara had said carefully. *She didn't want to tell you while you were finishing school. Didn't want you to worry.*

Six months. His mother had been dying and dealing with a separation she'd hidden to protect him.

"Six months before," Robert said finally. The controlled efficiency had cracked; underneath was something rawer. "We thought we'd wait until things were more stable. Until you'd graduated. Until—"

"Things never got more stable. She died."

"I know."

"Did you come back? After things got worse? After the cancer spread?"

Terrible pause. The rain was falling harder now, drumming against the windows in sheets. Lightning flickered somewhere to the west, still distant but closing.

"I stayed at the apartment. But I was there every evening—"

"You visited."

David's voice cracked on the word.

"You visited your dying wife instead of being with her. You maintained separate residences while she was trying to survive cancer and a failing marriage simultaneously. While she was scared and in pain and needed someone to hold her hand at 3 AM when the fear got too big."

There had been a day. Late February. Three weeks before she died.

Marie woke up clearheaded for the first time in days. The morphine levels had been adjusted. Enough to manage pain without drowning her in fog. She'd had a window of lucidity, precious and brief as the last warm day before winter.

She wanted to sit in the sunroom. The morning light was soft, golden, forgiving. She asked David to make chicken salad because she could actually taste food again—the morphine dulled everything, made eating a chore rather than pleasure, but today she was hungry. Actually hungry.

David had watched her eat half a sandwich. Watched her smile—really smile, not the brave performance she'd been managing for months. She'd looked almost like herself. Like his mother before the diagnosis, before the treatments, before the careful march toward ending.

"Call your father," she said. Wiping her fingers on a napkin, that familiar gesture he'd seen ten thousand times. "I want him to come for lunch. While I can still have a real conversation."

David called. Left a voicemail, trying to convey urgency without panic. "Mom's having a good day. A really good day. She'd like to see you. Can you come by for lunch?"

Robert texted back three hours later: *Stuck in meetings all day. Tomorrow maybe? Tell her I love her.*

Tomorrow Marie was back in bed. Pain spiking through the medication. Too exhausted to sit up, to eat, to do anything but drift in and out of consciousness.

That window of clarity had closed.

Robert came by the next evening. Stood in the doorway of her bedroom while she slept, her breathing shallow and labored. Stayed for ten minutes. Said he didn't want to wake her.

Left.

"She waited for you," David said now.

His voice breaking like something that had held too long.

"That last good day. She made chicken salad with her own hands though holding the spoon exhausted her. She wanted to have lunch with you. Wanted to talk while she could still talk. While she was still her. And you were in meetings."

He heard his father make a sound.

Like something breaking.

"You didn't come the next day either. Or the day after that. By the time you came, she couldn't talk anymore. Couldn't really connect. That window closed, Dad."

David pressed his palm flat against the window glass. Cool and wet with condensation, the storm's breath seeping through. Outside, rain poured down in silver curtains, transforming the garden into an impressionist blur.

"And you missed it because meetings were more important than your dying wife's last good day."

Silence. Thick with years of unspoken pain.

The storm had arrived in full now—rain hammering the roof, wind driving sheets of water against the windows, thunder rolling across the sky like furniture being moved in heaven's attic. The kitchen had grown dark enough that David could see his own reflection in the glass, ghostly and uncertain.

"I don't know how to fix this," Robert said finally. His voice carried defeat more honestly than any authority he'd tried to claim. "I don't know how to make any of it right."

"You can't fix it." David's anger softened a fraction—not forgiveness, but recognition that destruction wasn't the goal. "That's what I'm learning here. Some circumstances can't be fixed. They can only be grieved. Learned from. Carried."

"And you think hiding in your grandfather's house is the answer?"

"From everything I said, that is what you come back to?"

David shook his head, though his father couldn't see it.

"I think this house is teaching me to be quiet enough to hear my own voice again. I think being alone with my grief long enough to understand what it's teaching me—maybe that's necessary. Maybe that's the work I need to do before I can figure out anything else."

Another long silence. Less charged with conflict now. More heavy with the weight of recognition: two people standing in the wreckage of things that couldn't be unsaid.

"What do you want from me?" Robert asked. Genuine uncertainty rather than defensive challenge. "What would help?"

"I want you to stop trying to manage my grief. Stop trying to fix me according to your timeline." David's voice cracked again—he was so tired of cracking. "And I want you to do your own work of grieving her instead of avoiding it by focusing on everyone else. Including me."

"I don't know how."

Three words. Honest in a way Robert rarely allowed himself to be.

"Neither do I. That's why I'm here. Trying to learn."

When they hung up, Robert's last words were careful: "I need some time to think about what you said."

"Take all the time you need."

David meant it.

The phone went silent in his hand.

David stood in the kitchen, rain hammering the windows, coffee long cold on the counter. He felt emptied and full simultaneously: hollowed out by what he'd finally said, filled with the strange lightness of burdens set down.

He sank into a kitchen chair. Put his head in his hands.

His whole body trembling with the aftermath of adrenaline and emotion. His throat ached from words he'd held for weeks. His eyes burned but wouldn't produce tears—too wrung out for crying, too exhausted for anything but sitting in the wreckage.

The storm raged outside, indifferent and necessary.

"That sounded necessary," Samantha observed from the sunroom, her voice carrying through the doorway. "Like lancing an infection that's been building pressure for months. The body hates that kind of pain in the moment, but you can't leave the rot sealed in and expect health. You can't plant anything good in poisoned soil. Sometimes you have to let the pus and toxins drain out before the ground can hold new roots."

David walked to the sunroom on unsteady legs. The room was dark with storm-light, rain streaking the windows in patterns that looked like tears. Samantha's leaves glistened with the humidity, droplets of condensation catching what little light filtered through.

"I don't know if it helped anything or made everything worse. I may have destroyed whatever relationship we had left."

"You're asking the right question," Samantha continued when he reached the doorway. "What's the difference between damage that ruins something and damage that makes room for new growth? I've watched trees come through storms that looked catastrophic—branches ripped away, bark stripped, whole limbs gone. But here's the secret: wind doesn't usually take the healthiest branches. It finds what's already weak, what the tree hasn't shed on its own, and tears it free." Her leaves stirred as if remembering old weather. "Your father's carrying a lot of deadwood—avoidance, absence, carefully measured distance. You didn't shatter the trunk today. You let the storm take what was already weighing the living parts down."

She paused, letting the metaphor settle.

"Your father needed pruning, David. Those dead branches—the avoidance, the absence, the careful distance he's maintained—they were weighing down whatever's still alive between you. You didn't destroy the foundation. You cleared deadwood. That's different."

"I wasn't trying to hurt him."

"No. But you were tired of pretending his absence didn't hurt you. Those aren't the same thing. One is cruelty; the other is honesty. "You weren't trying to wound him," she said. "You were finally telling the truth about the wounds you've been carrying. Those are different things. Plants don't pretend they're fine when they're starving. They wilt when they're thirsty, yellow when they're depleted. Humans hide your symptoms and then wonder why nothing grows right."

"I need to move," David said finally, his body restless with unspent energy. "I can't sit here and think anymore."

"Garden work helps when words can't reach what's knotted up inside," Samantha added, her tone softening. "Your mother knew that. She'd go out in the rain sometimes, soil turning to mud around her feet, and say it felt like the sky was crying with her. Like she didn't have to hold all the sorrow alone because the weather was shouldering some of the weight."

David pulled on his grandfather's old work jacket—canvas worn soft at the elbows, smelling of soil and pipe tobacco and decades of patient labor. The rubber boots by the back door were cracked but still waterproof. He stepped out into the rain.

The storm had gentled to steady downpour—not the violent hammering of earlier but something more sustainable. Persistent. The kind of rain that soaked through everything without violence, that turned soil to workable mud and washed dust from leaves.

The air smelled of wet earth and green growth and ozone, that particular sharpness that followed lightning. David breathed it in, letting it fill spaces the phone conversation had hollowed out.

He made his way to the herb bed, rain immediately plastering his hair to his forehead. Cold water ran down his face, into his collar, along his spine. His jeans soaked through at the knees the moment he knelt in the soft earth.

The weeding was easier after the rain. Dandelions that had resisted his efforts for weeks came up now with their entire taproots intact—long pale tendrils sliding free of the loosened soil with a satisfaction that felt like completion. Each weed he pulled left a small hole that immediately began filling with rain, tiny pools that would drain and settle and leave space for what should grow there instead.

David worked without thinking. Let his hands find the rhythm of grip and pull and release. The rain ran down his arms, soaked through his gloves until his fingers pruned inside the wet fabric. His back began to ache from bending—that deep muscle fatigue that came from sustained effort. His knees grew numb against the cold ground.

But the work was settling something that words couldn't reach.

He moved from the herb bed to the tomato rows, staking plants that had listed in the wind. The wet twine was difficult to work with, slippery and uncooperative, but he managed serviceable knots that would hold until he could do better in dry weather. He cleared debris from between the rows—sticks blown in by the storm, leaves torn loose, a bird's nest that must have fallen from the maple.

The cucumber vines needed redirecting. He guided them gently toward their trellis, careful not to break the delicate tendrils that were reaching for something to hold onto. The leaves were broad and rough against his wet palms. Water pooled in their creases like small offerings.

At some point, the rain mixed with tears on his face. He wasn't sure when the crying started; just became aware that his chest was heaving with something more than exertion, that the salt on his lips wasn't only rain. He let it happen. Let the sky cry with him the way his mother had described. Let the grief move through his body and into the soil he was working.

The garden received it all without judgment. Absorbed the water and the work and the wordless sorrow. Converted it, the way gardens did, into something that could feed growth.

By the time David came back inside, he was soaked through completely—water squelching in his boots, jacket heavy enough to drag at his shoulders, jeans plastered to his legs like a second skin. He was muddy to the elbows, dirt ground into his knuckles, soil dark under his fingernails.

He was exhausted in a way that felt earned.

The rain had gentled to a drizzle. Watery sunlight was breaking through the clouds in the west, turning the wet garden into something that glittered.

Three days after the confrontation, Jeremy called.

David was in the sunroom, watching the garden steam gently in the afternoon sun, when his phone buzzed.

"Hey." Jeremy's voice was careful. "So, your dad called me. Mentioned you two had a... difficult conversation."

David's stomach dropped.

"He called you?"

"Asked if I thought you were having a breakdown." Jeremy's voice held wry amusement. "I told him you were having a breakthrough. That maybe he should consider the difference."

"What did he say?"

"Got quiet. Which honestly might be the most productive response your dad's ever had to anything." Jeremy paused. "I told him that running away to Portland taught me that healing doesn't happen according to anyone else's timeline. That sometimes the bravest choice is staying in the difficult place until you've learned what it has to teach."

Gratitude washed through David—warm and unexpected.

"I should have been there more," Jeremy said. His voice going quieter, more honest. "During her treatment. Those last months. I ran, David. I ran and you stayed. That wasn't fair to you."

"You were dealing with your own challenges—"

"I was avoiding. There's a difference." Jeremy's honesty was startling in its directness. "Seeing her in pain, seeing her get weaker, watching someone I loved disappear by inches... I couldn't handle it. So I found reasons to stay in Portland. Told myself I was giving you family space when really I just couldn't watch her die."

David sat with that admission. The parallel to Robert was obvious—two people who loved Marie, both unable to be present for her suffering.

"You're thinking about coming back?"

"Yeah. Maybe." Jeremy paused. "Been working on paintings about grief. About loss and presence and what it means to witness someone's ending. But I realized I can't finish them in Portland. Need to be in the place where it happened. Need to face what I ran from."

When they hung up, Jeremy's last words stayed with David: "You did the right thing with your dad. It doesn't feel like it yet. But you did."

A week after the confrontation. Late evening. The house had settled into its nighttime quiet—that particular silence of old houses resting, floorboards cooling, walls releasing the day's heat.

David was reading his mother's Bible in the sunroom, trying to understand her faith through the archaeology of her annotations, when his phone buzzed.

His father's name on the screen.

David's heart kicked. He had to set the Bible down. Had to sit with his hands pressed flat against his thighs until they stopped trembling.

He opened the message.

Need time to think about what you said. It wasn't wrong.

That was all.

No elaboration. No promises. No defensive explanations or counterarguments. Just acknowledgement that David's truth had landed and was being considered.

David stared at the message for a long time.

The words blurred and sharpened and blurred again. Such a small thing—two sentences, fourteen words. But they represented something Robert Mills almost never offered: admission that someone else might have a valid perspective.

It wasn't an apology. It wasn't an agreement to change. It wasn't resolution or reconciliation or any of the things David had imagined this conversation might eventually produce.

It was recognition.

It was enough. For now.

He carried the phone to the sunroom, held it up so Samantha could see.

"Ah," Samantha said when he held the phone up, her leaves rustling with something like satisfaction. "Soil needs rest after it's been turned over. You don't rip through a field with a plow and then toss in seeds five minutes later—you let the clods settle, give the organisms time to adjust to the light and air. Your father's inner landscape just got tilled, David. Every story he's told himself about those years, every carefully buried justification—you dragged them to the surface and exposed them. Now the small unseen workers have to get busy."

She paused, letting the teaching develop.

"That's what decomposition is," she went on. "Breaking down what was into something that can feed what might be. It's not pretty, and it never moves as quickly as impatient hearts would like. But you can't rush it any more than you can hurry a seed to sprout. Tear open the shell too soon, you don't get growth—you get ruin."

"How much time?"

"However long it takes," Samantha replied when he asked how much time. "And I know that frustrates you. Humans adore timelines—charts and forecasts and estimated arrival dates. But growth doesn't follow your schedules. You keep digging up what you've planted to see if it's working, you'll kill it. Some things you speak once and then leave buried, trusting the dark to do its work."

Her leaves caught the lamplight, shadows moving across the wall like slow breath. "You did your work, David. You said what needed saying. That was your part. Now you tend the ground you're responsible for—your grief, your garden, your calling. Let his soil settle without your hands in it for a while. In time—soon or far off—you'll see what takes root. But today? Today you rest from the turning and trust that truth, once spoken, knows how to grow without your supervision."

"You did your work, David. You spoke the truth that needed speaking. Now you wait. You care for your own garden. You let the soil settle. And eventually—maybe soon, maybe not—you'll see what grows."

David typed back: *Take all the time you need.*

He meant it.

That night, he sat with his journal for a long time before writing.

The house was quiet around him. The garden rested in darkness outside the window—recently cleared of weeds, recently tested by storm, recently worked with more competence than he'd brought to it a month ago. Somewhere out there, seeds were doing their invisible work. Roots were reaching deeper. Bulbs were storing energy for seasons he couldn't yet imagine.

Day 37 - Dad texted. Said what I said wasn't wrong. Didn't say more than that. Don't know if this is the beginning of resolution or acknowledgment before more silence. Don't know if I should hope.

But something has shifted. I can feel it. Like the garden after rain—same plants, same beds, same soil. But everything washed clean. Everything settling into new positions.

Jeremy called. Said he's thinking of coming back. Said he ran from watching Mom die and he needs to face that. Two people I love, both struggling with the same limitations. Not villains. Just humans who couldn't sit with suffering.

Mom knew that about them. I found a note in her Bible—she'd written it about Robert specifically: "He loves through planning and providing. Not through presence. I have to stop asking him to be someone he isn't." She RELEASED him. Let him love in the only way he could manage.

I'm not there yet. Don't know if I'll ever be. But I understand something I didn't before: some people can't be present for pain. Doesn't mean they don't love. Means they have limits. We all do.

Samantha says I can't rush growth. Have to let soil settle after being disturbed. Have to trust that telling the truth matters even if I don't see what grows immediately.

God, help me be patient. Help me trust that truth serves purpose when the aftermath is uncertain. Help me care for my own garden while I wait for what I planted in my father to take root.

He closed the journal.

Outside, the garden rested in darkness. Stars had emerged now that the storm clouds had moved east. The air smelled clean and new—that particular freshness that followed rain, as if the world had been rinsed of dust and sorrow and was ready to try again.

Faith, David was beginning to understand, might be exactly like this. Trusting processes that happened underground. In darkness. In ways that couldn't be rushed or monitored or controlled.

His mother had known that. Had lived it through her illness and her doubt and her persistent returning. Had kept the conversation going with a God she was furious with because maintaining connection mattered more than maintaining composure.

Maybe he could learn it too.

One uncertain day at a time. One truth spoken without guarantee. One seed planted without certainty of harvest.

The work continued when the outcome remained uncertain.

Perhaps especially then.

Chapter Six

LEARNING TO LISTEN

"The wise listen and add to their learning, and the discerning get guidance."
- Proverbs 1:5

T HE MORNING SUN CLIMBED higher as David stood in the garden with his mother's journal open to a page titled "Early Summer Care."

Five days had passed since his confrontation with his father. Five days of Robert's silence punctuated by that single text: *Need time to think about what you said. It wasn't wrong.* The waiting was its own kind of work, not the active labor of weeding or watering, but the harder discipline of sitting with uncertainty while something stirred in darkness.

David had thrown himself into the garden with desperate focus, as if dirt and sweat could fill the space where resolution should be. The alternative was to pace the house and check his phone every ten minutes, which he'd done the first two days until Samantha pointed out he was wearing a path in the hardwood.

His mother's handwriting stared up at him from the journal page, each letter formed with the precision she brought to everything important. *Third week of June: Side-dress tomatoes with compost tea. Check for hornworms daily—they can strip a plant overnight. Harvest basil regularly to prevent flowering.*

The instructions looked straightforward enough on paper. But as David surveyed the garden with its complex network of plants and relationships, paralysis settled over him. A robin called from the oak tree, its song sharp and insistent in the morning stillness. The scent of warming earth mixed with the green sharpness of basil and something sweeter: the roses along the fence, still struggling but producing a few determined blooms.

God, he prayed, the words forming without conscious decision, *I don't know what I'm doing. With the garden. With Dad. With any of it. But I'm here. Help me learn to read what I'm supposed to be seeing.*

"You're overthinking again," Samantha observed from her spot near the kitchen window, her leaves stirring as the breeze slipped through the open door. "Marie used to wear a groove in that garden path when she tried to solve everything in her head instead of with her hands. Plants don't respond to mental gymnastics, honey. They respond to water, nutrients, and the slow repetition of care. Your worry isn't reaching their roots—only your attention is. And right now your attention is scattered across forty different storms instead of resting on the one living thing in front of you."

"What if I kill everything?" David asked, his voice coming out smaller than he'd intended. He knelt beside the first tomato plant, the soil dark and crumbly against his knees, cool where morning shadow still lingered. "What if I can't read whatever signals these plants are supposedly sending?"

"Then you'll learn what dead plants look like and try not to repeat whatever killed them," Samantha said, her voice patient rather than scolding. "That's how your mother learned. That's how your grandfather learned before her. Marvin killed more seedlings in his first decade than you'll probably ever own. Plants are far more forgiving than humans—they don't sulk or hold grudges when you overwater or miss a feeding. They wilt, yellow, drop leaves. All of it is communication, not punishment. They're sending honest status updates and hoping you'll adjust conditions before the damage goes past recovery. No passive-aggressive silence. No cryptic hints. Just a clear physical response to reality. Humans could take notes."

David consulted the journal again. His mother's recipe for compost tea filled the margins beside a careful sketch of a bucket, the drawing showing exactly how far from the stem to pour, how much liquid to use per plant.

He filled a five-gallon bucket with aged compost from the bin behind the greenhouse. The material was dark and crumbly, smelling like earth after rain, rich and loamy with a faint sweetness that spoke of decomposition completed, death transformed into fertility. He added water from the hose, watching it darken to the color of weak coffee. The smell intensified, organic and alive, not unpleasant but unmistakably the scent of things returning to soil.

The bucket was heavier than he'd expected. Much heavier. Water sloshed over the rim as he carried it toward the tomato row, splashing across his shoes and creating dark spots on the gravel pathway. His arms burned with the strain, biceps trembling by the time he reached the first plant. His pour landed too fast, too much: a deluge that created an instant puddle around the plant's base. Nothing like his mother's careful diagram.

"Less like a flash flood, more like a steady front moving through," Samantha suggested. "Think about how real rain behaves when it's trying to be useful—it seeps, it lingers, it gives the soil time to drink. Roots don't form a neat little column straight down; they spread, they wander, they explore sideways as much as deep. You're feeding the whole root zone, not baptizing the stem. Slow it down. Let the water work its way in instead of skating off the surface."

David moved to the second plant, attempting to correct his technique. But the compost tea had other ideas about where it wanted to go. It splashed onto leaves, creating brown stains that looked like evidence of plant abuse. It pooled in low spots, attracting flies that appeared with supernatural speed. By the time he'd worked through half the tomato row, his arms were shaking from the weight of the bucket, sweat running down his back despite the early hour. His jaw ached from clenching. The garden resembled the scene of a minor disaster. Muddy archipelagos spreading between plants, his shoes thoroughly soaked, his technique improving only marginally.

"Am I killing them?" David asked, surveying the mess.

"Plants have survived worse than enthusiastic incompetence," Samantha said, tone dry but kind. "They've outlasted ice ages, volcanic winters, and your grandfather's first five years with pruning shears—which, I assure you, were apocalyptic from a horticultural standpoint. Right now your method is less precision irrigation and more 'throwing water in the general direction of the problem and hoping for the best.' Messy, but not fatal. Marie flooded half this garden her first season, misread a fertilizer label and scorched an entire row of beans, and executed three perfectly innocent rose bushes before she understood how hard to cut. You're not failing. You're just right on schedule."

The sound of bicycle wheels on gravel announced Eli's arrival.

David glanced up, wiping sweat from his forehead with the back of his hand. The gesture left a streak of dirt across his skin, but he didn't notice. The boy coasted down the driveway with his usual careful attention to steering, his dark hair sticking up at its perpetual odd angles. Behind him came Mara on foot, carrying her familiar toolbox with the ease of long practice. And Eileen's silver Honda pulling in with its quiet engine, the car David had come to recognize by sound.

"Morning, David. Morning, Samantha," Eli called as he dismounted, leaning his bike against the garden gate with practiced ease. His voice carried across the garden, natural as breathing.

David caught the flicker of confusion that crossed Eileen's face—the question forming in her expression before she smoothed it away. She couldn't hear Samantha. The reminder was like a splinter working its way deeper each time it happened, small but persistent, marking a boundary between them that David didn't know how to address. She was here, learning the garden, becoming part of this strange new life—but there was a frequency she couldn't access, a conversation she would never hear. He didn't know what that meant for whatever was growing between them.

"You're doing it too much," Eli said, kneeling beside one of the muddy spots. His small hands touched the sodden soil with the unselfconscious authority of someone who'd learned to read earth the way other children read picture books. "Mom says people do that a lot. They try really hard but don't pay attention to what the plant actually wants. Like talking at someone instead of listening to them."

"The community here has a way of sharing knowledge," Mara added, approaching with her characteristic blend of practical wisdom and gentle teaching. Her hands were already dusted with soil—she'd been working in her own memorial garden this morning, the one she'd built for her husband. "Eileen mentioned she'd learned some sustainable techniques from nursing students who volunteer at community gardens. Thought she might share some insights."

Eileen nodded, her presence radiating the thoughtful attention David was beginning to recognize as essential to who she was. She smelled faintly of hospital soap and good coffee, the combination somehow becoming familiar, even welcome. "In nursing, we learn to read subtle signs—changes in posture, color, how patients hold themselves, what they're not saying as much as what they are. Plants show stress and health in similar ways. The language is different, but the skill is the same. Paying attention to what's actually happening instead of what you expect to see."

She moved toward the rose bushes along the garden's edge, drawn by something David hadn't noticed. Her steps slowed as she got closer, and her expression shifted—concern replacing the gentle confidence she'd carried a moment before.

"Oh," she said, almost to herself. "Marie's roses."

David followed her gaze. Several of the rose bushes his mother had cared for were struggling—brown spots spreading across leaves, canes that were brittle and dry, buds that had never opened. He'd been so focused on the vegetables, so consumed with the tomatoes and the compost tea and the mechanics of not killing things, that he hadn't registered the roses' distress.

Eileen knelt beside one of the worst specimens, her fingers gentle on a withered cane. Sadness lived in her face—the recognition of something beloved that was failing despite everyone's best efforts. Her lips moved, almost imperceptibly. No sound. The barest whisper of motion.

She was praying.

The realization struck David with unexpected force. Not a long prayer, not a formal petition—just her lips moving in what was clearly a conversation with someone he couldn't see. Her eyes were open, focused on the damaged plant, but her attention was divided between what was visible and what was invisible.

David had seen this before. The memory surfaced sharp and clear, summoned by the echo of posture and presence.

Late summer, two years ago. He'd been home for a long weekend between sophomore and junior year. Marie had been in treatment for about six months—past the initial shock, into the grinding middle section where hope and fear traded places daily. The roses had been struggling then too, some fungal infection the garden center couldn't quite diagnose despite three different treatments.

He'd found her in the garden at dawn. She was kneeling in the dirt in her worn jeans and one of Marvin's old flannel shirts—the red one that was too big for her, that smelled like pipe tobacco even though Marvin had quit smoking fifteen years earlier. Her hands were pressed flat against the soil around the struggling bushes, fingers spread wide as if she could feel the roots through the earth. Her lips were moving in quiet conversation.

David had stopped in the kitchen doorway, coffee forgotten in his hand, concerned that his mother talking to roses indicated something was slipping, that the treatments were affecting her mind in ways no one had warned them about.

But then he heard her voice—barely above a whisper, but carrying in the morning stillness:

"I know You don't fix problems just because I ask. That's not how this works, and I've lived long enough to stop expecting it. But I'm asking anyway. For these roses that survived my mother-in-law, survived the drought of 2012, survived everything I've done wrong in this garden. For these blooms that make me remember what beauty is when everything else is dying by degrees."

Her voice had broken. Tears running down her face, falling into the soil like an offering. But she hadn't moved, hadn't wiped her eyes, hadn't done anything to interrupt the conversation she was having.

"I'm scared," she continued, and the rawness in her voice was nothing like the composed woman who smiled for visitors and told everyone she was handling circumstances fine. "I'm so scared. And I don't know how to do this. Don't know how to die well or leave him prepared or make peace with any of it. But I'm here. I'm showing up when showing up is all I can manage. I figure that has to count for something."

She'd stayed there for twenty minutes, talking to God like He was sitting beside her in the dirt. Not asking for miracles. Not demanding explanations. Just being honest about her fear and her exhaustion and her desperate need to matter beyond her own death. Just staying in conversation when the conversation was mostly questions without answers.

David had backed away. Returned to the kitchen. Poured his cold coffee down the sink and made a fresh pot. Pretended he'd just woken up when she came inside forty minutes later with soil on her knees and something like peace on her face.

He'd never mentioned witnessing her prayer. Had filed it away as a private moment he wasn't meant to see, a glimpse behind the curtain of his mother's careful composure.

Now, watching Eileen kneel in almost the exact same spot, lips moving in that same quiet conversation, he understood what his mother had been doing. Not talking to herself. Not losing her mind. Praying the way gardeners worked—with hands in the soil and attention on what needed care, with honesty about what she couldn't fix and presence despite her limitations.

Eileen stood after a minute, brushing soil from her knees. Her eyes met David's, and there was no embarrassment there. Just acknowledgement. Just the quiet recognition of someone who'd been caught doing something true.

"I pray over patients I can't fix," she said simply. "Your mom taught me that. Said it was better than pretending I had control I didn't have. Seemed right to do the same for her roses."

David's throat tightened. The memory of his mother kneeling in this same spot pressed against his chest like a physical weight.

"She did that," he managed. "Prayed over things she couldn't fix. I saw her once. Didn't know what she was doing then."

"Now you do."

It wasn't a question. Just acknowledgment that understanding sometimes arrived late, after the person who could have explained it was gone.

By mid-morning, David's hands were stained with compost tea and his knees ached from kneeling on the garden path. But the paralysis that had gripped him earlier had eased into something more like focus. The garden no longer read like a test he was failing. It was a conversation he was learning to participate in—fumbling, imperfect, but present.

"You're getting it," Eli said, that rare smile brightening his serious face. "You're beginning to listen instead of just following the recipe."

"Is that what listening means? Paying attention to how plants respond?"

"That's part of it." Mara pointed to small holes in a tomato leaf that David had missed entirely—tiny crescent shapes along the edge, evidence of something feeding in the night. "But it's also noticing problems before they become disasters. That means something's been eating. Hornworms, most likely. Your mom's journal talks about them."

They searched through the tomato plants together, parting leaves, checking stems. Two fat green hornworms were nearly invisible against the foliage—their camouflage so perfect that David would have walked past them a dozen times without noticing. Eli showed him how to remove them, plucking them off with surprising confidence and dropping them in a bucket of soapy water.

The process was vaguely murderous, but Mara explained that it was necessary.

"Everything's eating or being eaten in a garden," she said. "Your job is to help the plants you care about survive what wants to consume them. It's not cruel—it's how ecosystems work. Your mother understood that. She wasn't sentimental about it. She was practical about protecting what she'd chosen to nurture."

David thought about that as they continued through the morning. How caring meant choosing. Deciding which lives to protect and which to sacrifice.

How his mother must have made these decisions constantly—pulling weeds that were simply plants in the wrong place, removing pests that were only trying to survive, cutting back growth that competed with what she valued more.

The work was sacred. Not in a religious sense exactly, but in the way it required presence and attention and constant small acts of care that added up to larger significance. Like prayer, maybe. Being present, paying attention, making choices about what to nurture and what to let go.

When Mara and Eli left around noon, Eileen lingered. They worked together in comfortable silence, organizing tools, emptying the remaining compost tea around the rose bushes in a last attempt to give them whatever strength they might need.

"Thank you," David said as they worked. "For coming. For the prayer earlier. For... all of it."

Eileen paused, a watering can in her hands, the afternoon light catching the silver streaks in her dark hair that he hadn't noticed before. "Your mom taught me that. Praying over what you can't fix. I was with her once when she got bad news from the doctor."

The words landed like a stone in still water, sending ripples outward.

The memory came flooding back—not Eileen's memory, but his own, triggered by her words.

He'd been there that day. Spring semester, junior year. He'd come home for spring break, planning to sleep late and eat home cooking and avoid thinking about finals. Marie had an appointment—routine scan, routine bloodwork. Supposed to be in and out, nothing to worry about, she'd be home by lunch.

He'd gone with her. Sat in the waiting room playing games on his phone while she disappeared into the warren of examination rooms and imaging suites. The waiting room had smelled like antiseptic and anxiety, like coffee from a machine and magazines no one actually read.

When Marie emerged forty-five minutes later, her face had been composed. Perfectly controlled. The mask she wore when she was managing something too big to show.

She'd smiled at David. Said everything was fine. Said they'd needed to adjust her medication schedule, nothing to worry about. Said they could go home now and she'd make lunch.

In the car, she'd been quiet. David had put on music—filled the silence with bass and guitars so he didn't have to notice his mother's white-knuckled grip on the steering wheel, the way her jaw was clenched tight enough to crack teeth.

At home, she'd gone straight to the garden. Hadn't taken off her good shoes—the low heels she wore to appointments, now sinking into soft soil. Hadn't changed out of her nice blouse. Had walked directly to the roses and knelt in the dirt like she was falling more than kneeling.

David had watched from the kitchen window. Her shoulders were shaking. Her forehead pressed against the earth. Her lips moving in that same silent conversation.

He hadn't gone to her.

Hadn't asked what the doctor had really said. Hadn't offered presence or comfort or even acknowledgment that he'd seen her breaking.

Had accepted her lie about medication adjustment because the truth was too big to hold, because he was twenty years old and still believed that if he didn't look at the monster directly, it might not be real.

Later, much later, after she'd died, he'd learned what that appointment had revealed: the cancer had spread. The current treatment wasn't working. They'd need to try something more aggressive, with worse side effects and lower success rates.

She'd gotten that news alone. Robert had been in meetings—always in meetings, always somewhere else when presence was required. She'd worked through it alone. Then came home and knelt in the garden to pray over roses while her son pretended not to notice she was falling apart.

"She went straight to the garden afterward," Eileen said, unaware of the memory she'd summoned. "Knelt beside her roses. Talked to God like He was right there listening. Not asking for miracles—just staying present with the hard thing instead of running from it."

David swallowed hard. His eyes burned with tears he didn't want to explain.

"I don't know how to do that," he admitted. "The praying. I mean, I try. But it feels awkward. Like I'm talking to myself and hoping someone's eavesdropping."

"Maybe that's okay." Eileen set down the watering can and met his eyes directly—no judgment there, just understanding. "Maybe it's supposed to be awkward at first. Like learning any new language, you stumble over words until eventually they become natural." She paused. "Your mom said faith wasn't about certainty. It was about being present when you weren't sure anyone was listening. That's what I saw her do. Every day. Especially when everything was falling apart."

The words settled into David like seeds finding prepared soil. Maybe prayer was like gardening—something you learned by doing. Season after season. Until your hands knew the work even when your mind couldn't explain the mystery.

"I should go," Eileen said, glancing at her watch. "I'm on shift at seven."

"Thanks for coming."

"Anytime." She smiled, and warmth spread through David's chest—unexpected, welcome, slightly terrifying. "Text me if you find more hornworms. I want to know if my patient observation skills translate to pest identification."

After she left, David stood in the garden surveying the morning's work. The tomato plants looked more settled, their leaves turning toward the afternoon sun with what might have been gratitude. The roses still struggled, but he'd done what he could for them—compost tea and quiet prayer and presence. Maybe that was enough. Maybe being there, paying attention, caring for what was in front of him when outcomes were uncertain was the whole job.

Around three o'clock, restlessness drove him out of the house.

The afternoon heat pressed down like a physical weight, thick and humid, the kind of June warmth that made shirts stick to skin within minutes. David walked without destination, feet choosing the route while his mind wandered. He passed the church where his mother had attended, its white steeple rising against clouds that were building in the west. Passed the small downtown with its handful of shops—the hardware store, the bakery, the place that sold antiques and local crafts.

The cemetery drew him without conscious decision.

His feet simply turned toward the gates, following some internal compass that pointed toward grief. He found his mother's grave easily now, no longer needing to count rows or reference the small map they'd given him at the funeral. The headstone was simple, the grass around it still not quite established, the earth still settling from the disturbance of burial.

Someone was sitting on the bench nearby.

Blue hair, faded now from sun and time, but unmistakable. The same woman from weeks ago, from the day he'd found her business card at the cemetery and carried it home like a talisman. She was crying, shoulders shaking with grief that couldn't be contained or controlled.

David hesitated. He'd seen her once before, observed her from a distance, taken her card without introducing himself. Should he approach now? Pretend he didn't recognize her? His mother would have known what to do—would have sat down beside a grieving stranger and said exactly the right words.

He walked over and sat on the far end of the bench. Not close enough to intrude, but close enough to signal presence. Solidarity, maybe. The acknowledgment that grief was less lonely when witnessed.

She glanced over at him, eyes red-rimmed, mascara smudged in dark streaks down her cheeks. But she didn't seem angry at the interruption.

"Sorry," she said, her voice rough. "I'm a mess."

"Me too," David replied. "Different day, same mess."

She laughed—a short, wet sound that was half sob. "Is your mess also about someone who died too young and left you wondering what you're supposed to do with all their unfinished business?"

"Yeah. My mom. Cancer. Few weeks ago."

"My brother. Car accident. Three years now." She gestured to a nearby grave—a headstone David hadn't noticed before, though it must have been there every time he visited. "I come here every year on his birthday and dye my hair his favorite color. It's silly, but—"

"It's not silly." David studied her blue hair, the way the faded color caught the afternoon light. "Rituals don't have to make sense to other people. They have to mean something to you."

The woman examined him for a moment—really looked, the way people did when they were deciding whether to trust a stranger.

"You're Marie's son. David."

"How did you—"

"Small town. Plus, your mom talked about you all the time at the coffee shop. I'm Maya. I run The Grind." She wiped her eyes with the back of her hand, smearing the mascara further. "Your mom was one of my best customers. Always ordered the same thing—large black coffee and whatever pastry I was trying to get rid of. Said it was her job to help me work through my experimental baking failures."

David's heart kicked against his ribs. The business card in his pocket. *Maya's Canvas. Art heals what words can't reach.* He'd been carrying it for weeks, waiting for the right moment to introduce himself, and here she was—not in her coffee shop but in the cemetery, raw and real in a way that felt more honest than any planned meeting could have been.

"I have your card," he said. "Found it here, actually. A few weeks ago. I've been meaning to come by the shop, but—"

"But it's easier to carry the intention than to follow through." Maya's smile was knowing, tear-streaked but genuine. "Story of my life. I've been meaning to do a lot of things for three years now."

Junior year, fall semester.

The memory surfaced unbidden—David had been home for a long weekend. Marie had suggested they go out for coffee instead of making it at home. "I want to support a local business," she'd said, that particular brightness in her voice that meant she had an agenda beyond the stated reason. "And there's someone I want you to meet."

The Grind had been small and welcoming, smelling of fresh bread and espresso and something baking in the back that might have been muffins or might have been a beautiful disaster. The walls were covered with local art—paintings and photographs and mixed media pieces that rotated monthly. Behind the counter, a woman with purple streaks in her hair was wrestling with a pastry that appeared to be experiencing structural failure.

"Marie!" she'd called out when they entered, her face lighting up with genuine warmth. "And you must be David. Your mom talks about you constantly. I know way too much about your academic achievements for someone who's never met you."

David had been embarrassed—his mother bragging to strangers, making him seem more impressive than he felt.

"Maya's an artist," Marie had explained while they waited for their order. "She inherited this building from her brother. Turned the back into a studio space where she teaches free art classes to kids who can't afford lessons. She's doing important work here."

"It's just coffee," Maya had said, bringing over their drinks and what looked like a deconstructed croissant that had experienced architectural collapse. "And experimental pastries that mostly fail. But your mom insists on eating my mistakes. Says failure is part of the creative process."

They'd sat for an hour. Marie fully present, asking Maya about her art, about her brother's memory, about the studio space and the community she was building. David had been restless, impatient, wanting to get back to the house where he could check his phone without being rude.

"You're creating legacy," Marie had said. "Turning grief into something that serves others. That's sacred work."

Maya's eyes had filled with tears. "Some days I don't know if I'm honoring him or just avoiding dealing with losing him."

"Maybe it's both. Maybe that's okay. Maybe the best way to deal with loss is to let it transform into something useful." Marie had smiled. "Like composting. Everything returns to feed new growth."

David remembered being impatient with the conversation, with his mother's way of finding meaning in everything, with her insistence on connecting with people he saw as strangers. He'd been twenty years old and certain that deep conversations with random coffee shop owners were a waste of time.

Now, sitting on a cemetery bench with that same woman, he understood what he'd been too young to see: his mother had been building something. Creating connections. Modeling what it looked like to be present for people whose grief made them isolated.

She'd been teaching him when he was too impatient to learn.

"Your mom used to say grief doesn't have an expiration date," Maya said. "That the people who love us don't get to decide when we're done working through loss."

"When did she say that?"

"About a month before she died. I was having a bad day—it was my brother's birthday—and she sat with me while I cried into her coffee. Didn't try to fix it or tell me it would get better. Just sat there and let me fall apart." Maya met David's eyes. "You look like her. Same eyes. Same way of holding your shoulders like you're carrying weight but trying not to show it."

The observation landed with unexpected force. David had been trying so hard to manage his grief properly, to work through it efficiently, to move toward some imagined endpoint where he'd be whole again. But maybe that wasn't how it worked. Maybe grief was more like the blue hair ritual—something you did honestly even when you couldn't prove it was working.

"How do you know when you're doing it right?" he asked.

"You don't." Maya stood, brushing off her jeans. "You keep doing it and see what happens. Some days you cry on cemetery benches. Some days you dye your hair colors that make people stare. Some days you wake up and realize you went an hour without thinking about them, and then you feel guilty for forgetting." She paused. "The point isn't to do it right. The point is to do it honestly."

She turned to walk away, then stopped.

"Your mother believed in you. Talked about how you were going to do important work in the world."

"I don't even know what I'm doing next week."

"Maybe that's the point. Maybe inheriting someone's faith in you means you get to figure out what that looks like on your own terms." Her smile was warm despite the tear tracks. "She'd be proud of you for staying here and trying to figure things out instead of running."

"How do you know I'm staying?"

"Because you're walking around town at three in the afternoon looking like someone who's deciding if he belongs here. Because you stopped to check on a crying stranger instead of crossing the street." Her expression softened. "Plus, I've got that card you mentioned. Means you've been thinking about connection even when you weren't ready to pursue it. That's how it starts."

David walked back as the afternoon light turned golden, slanting low across the gardens and rooftops he passed. Someone was grilling somewhere nearby. The smell of charcoal and meat mixing with the ever-present scent of cut grass and summer heat. Maya's words echoed in his mind: *The point isn't to do it right. The point is to do it honestly.*

The garden was settling into evening when he arrived, shadows lengthening across the beds, the air cooling slightly as the sun dropped toward the tree line. He found himself drawn outside anyway—not to work, but simply to be present.

The tomato plants he'd fed that morning already looked different. Not dramatically so, but more upright, more purposeful, as if they'd received something they needed and were responding with quiet gratitude. Maybe it was his imagination. Maybe plants really did respond that quickly to proper care. Maybe the difference was in him—in how he was seeing rather than what he was looking at.

The roses still struggled. But he'd done what he could for them—compost tea and quiet prayer and the patient work of presence when results were uncertain.

God, David prayed, standing among the beds his mother had worked, *I don't know how to do this. The praying. The caring. Any of it. But I'm here. I'm trying. Help me learn what Mom knew—how to stay with what I can't control. How to keep the conversation going when the other side is silent.*

The prayer was clumsy, unpolished. But it was honest. And maybe, as Eileen had suggested, that was enough to begin with.

"You met Maya properly," Samantha observed when he came back in, evening light pooling around her pot. "I noticed you've been carrying that card like a seed packet you weren't sure when to open. And instead of some tidy introduction over a carefully brewed latte, you collided in the wild—two people doing grief honestly instead of trying to arrange it into something presentable."

"I had her card for weeks. Kept meaning to introduce myself."

"And instead you met in a cemetery where you were both doing grief honestly instead of managing it properly. More authentic that way," she continued. "Volunteer seedlings often grow tougher than anything started in trays and transplanted on schedule—they find their own way to the light without human supervision. She's been expressing her brother's death out loud since it happened, like a plant that thrives on full sun. Your mother worked through hers mostly in the shade—private prayers, quiet margins, wrestling no one saw until she let a little light in at the end. Neither way is wrong. They're just different adaptations. Some plants close their stomata in heat to conserve water; others open wide and let the excess burn off. Different mechanisms. Same goal: survive."

David settled into the kitchen chair with a glass of water, watching the last light fade from the garden. "She said rituals don't have to work perfectly to be worth doing."

"Maya's developed grief wisdom that fits her soil conditions," Samantha said. "She needs witnesses the way some plants need a trellis—her sorrow climbs better when it has something to lean on. Your mother needed solitude to be honest. She did her best wrestling where no one could see the leaves shaking." Samantha's leaves shifted, catching the last light. "The question isn't which of them you should copy. The question is what actually leaves you more rooted instead of more depleted. You won't know until you've tried different ways of grieving and noticed which ones help you stand instead of collapse."

The day's accumulation of lessons circled through his mind: Eli teaching him to read plants, Eileen connecting nursing observation to garden care and showing him what prayer as presence looked like, Maya demonstrating that honest expression mattered more than proper management. All of it orbiting the same central truth: paying attention was more important than getting everything right on the first try.

His phone buzzed.

David's heart kicked. He picked it up with hands that weren't quite steady.

A text from his father. The first since that brief acknowledgement five days ago.

Still thinking. Saw something about a scholarship that reminded me of you. Want to talk about it when I'm ready. Soon.

Not an apology. Not resolution. But not silence either. A door left open rather than slammed. Acknowledgment that the conversation was continuing even when words weren't flowing—that seeds planted might take time to sprout.

"Progress isn't fond of announcements," Samantha said when his phone buzzed and he read the message. "You almost never see the most important changes when they're happening. You don't watch a radicle emerge in real time—the first root breaks through in the dark where no one's looking. Dig up the seed every day to check on it and you'll snap the very thing that's trying to hold the plant in place." Her leaves rustled like a quiet shrug. "You turned your father's soil over. Now something underneath is testing the idea of growing differently. Your job isn't to supervise. It's to resist the urge to keep clawing at the same spot and instead keep tending the ground you've actually been given."

David typed back: *I'll be here when you're ready.*

He meant it.

Outside, the garden rested in gathering darkness. Roots working invisibly beneath the soil. Plants converting stored sugars, preparing for tomorrow's photosynthesis. The roses struggling but not yet surrendered. The tomatoes standing a little straighter than they had that morning.

Faith, David thought, might be exactly like this. Learning by doing. Season after season. Until your hands knew the work even when your mind couldn't explain the mystery.

And grief might be like Maya's blue hair: a ritual worth performing even when its effectiveness was uncertain. An act of love that mattered more for its honesty than its perfection.

Tomorrow there would be more listening, more learning, more opportunities to practice the attention that turned work into relationship. Tonight, he would sleep with soil under his fingernails and the quiet satisfaction of someone who'd spent the day learning new languages.

One conversation at a time. One plant at a time. One uncertain prayer at a time.

Like roots finding their way in darkness, doing the hidden work that would eventually break through into light.

Chapter Seven

WHAT WAS HIDDEN

"My God, my God, why have you forsaken me? Why are you so far from saving me, so far from my cries of anguish? My God, I cry out by day, but you do not answer, by night, but I find no rest." - Psalm 22:1-2

T HE BOX HAD BEEN sitting in the corner of his mother's old room for six weeks.

Sealed with packing tape that had yellowed in storage, the cardboard softening at the edges from humidity. David had moved it twice—once to vacuum underneath, once to reach the window when a late-season wasp had gotten trapped against the glass. But he'd never opened it.

Medical paperwork, the label read in his father's efficient block letters. *Insurance. Bills.*

Nothing he wanted to see.

But it was Tuesday afternoon, and the garden didn't need him the way it had been needing him. The tomatoes were staked properly now. The weeds were under control. He'd achieved something approaching equilibrium in the beds his mother had tended, and the work that had consumed him for weeks had gentled into maintenance rather than rescue.

Which left him with time. And attention. And the box that had been radiating avoidance from the corner like a dark star pulling at the edges of his awareness.

The air pressed thick and humid against the windows, the kind of atmospheric pressure that came before summer storms. Thunder rumbled somewhere distant—not yet threatening, but promising. The light through the windows had taken on that peculiar yellow cast that meant weather was building.

God, David prayed as he stood looking at the box, *I don't know what's in there. But I think I need to see it. Help me be brave enough to look at what I've been avoiding.*

He fetched scissors from the kitchen drawer.

"Finally tackling that box?" Samantha observed from the sunroom, her leaves rustling in the cross-breeze from the open windows. "It's been sitting there like a seed in suspended animation—nothing wrong with it, just locked up. Some seeds need winter, some need fire, some just need their shell cracked so water can get in. This box is the same. Your avoidance has been the seed coat. Whatever's in there has been waiting on one thing: you deciding to open it."

"I don't know if I'm ready," David admitted.

"Nobody ever is," Samantha replied. "Readiness isn't a feeling, it's a discovery. Seeds don't sit around wondering if today's the day—they notice moisture and warmth and start. The first root breaks out whether the seed feels prepared or not."

David knelt beside the box. The tape split under the scissors with a sound like tearing fabric—sharp, final, the kind of noise that couldn't be undone.

Inside, manila folders organized with his father's usual precision: *Hospital Bills - Paid, Insurance Claims - Processed, Treatment Summary, Final Expenses*. Each one a small monument to suffering reduced to paperwork, to pain made manageable through documentation and systematic filing.

David pulled folders out mechanically, not really examining the contents. Numbers that represented his mother's body failing in increments small enough to bill by procedure code. Dates that marked the eighteen months between diagnosis and death like waypoints on a map to somewhere he'd never wanted to go.

He was nearly through the box when his hand touched something that wasn't a folder.

Cloth. Soft fabric wrapped around something rectangular.

David's hands stilled. His heart began beating faster, that animal awareness that something significant was about to surface.

He pulled it out carefully.

A composition book wrapped in one of his mother's silk scarves—the emerald green one she'd worn to church, the one that smelled faintly of her perfume even now, mixed with the mustiness of storage. The scarf fell away in his hands, revealing a notebook with a cover that had been handled until the edges were soft.

No label. No title. Just Marie's handwriting on the first page in careful script:

Private. For after.

David's throat closed.

He opened to the first entry.

October 12th. Two weeks after diagnosis.

I bought this notebook today. The oncologist says I should document my treatment—symptoms, side effects, questions for next appointment. But I think I need to document something else. The thoughts I can't say out loud. The fears I can't tell David or Robert or anyone who needs me to be brave.

So this will be my honest place. Where I can fall apart without witnesses. Where I can question everything without making anyone else afraid.

The kitchen tilted sideways.

David's vision blurred at the edges. His hands began shaking so badly that the notebook trembled, pages rustling like leaves in the wind.

She'd kept a journal. His mother had kept a journal through her entire treatment, and no one had known. She'd written down what she wouldn't say. She'd documented the suffering she'd worked so hard to hide.

He turned the page.

October 15th.

First chemo tomorrow. I'm terrified. The nurse was cheerful, explaining side effects like she was describing possible rain in the forecast. "You might feel nauseous. You might lose your hair. You might experience fatigue." Might. As if these things were optional. As if I had any choice in how my body would betray me.

Robert keeps saying everything will be fine. David keeps asking if I'm okay. Everyone wants me to be optimistic. Positive. Fighting.

But I don't feel like fighting. I feel like I'm standing on train tracks watching the light get closer and I can't move. Can't run. Can only wait for impact.

God, I know You're supposed to be here with me. But I've never felt more alone.

David's breath came shallow now, his chest constricting. He should stop reading. Should put the notebook away and come back to it when he was stronger. But his eyes kept moving across the pages, pulled forward by terrible momentum.

November 3rd.

Hair is falling out. Found clumps in the shower drain this morning. Spent twenty minutes crying in the bathroom where no one could hear. Then I came out and smiled and told David everything was fine.

I'm becoming an expert liar.

Why does faith have to hurt like this? I pray and pray and nothing changes. The cancer doesn't respond. The treatments destroy me. And God is silent. Completely, devastatingly silent.

Maybe I don't have enough faith. Maybe if I believed harder, trusted more, questioned less, things would be different. But I can't stop the questions. They pile up like unread mail, demanding attention I can't give.

The words blurred. David realized he was crying—not the quiet tears he'd grown accustomed to, but raw, gasping sobs that came from somewhere deeper than conscious control.

She'd been lying. All those times she'd smiled and said she was fine, all those assurances that treatment was going okay, all that careful composure—underneath was this. Terror. Loneliness. The sense that God had abandoned her when she needed Him most.

David turned more pages, his hands shaking so badly he could barely hold the notebook.

January 8th.

David came home this weekend. He looks at me with such fear in his eyes. Like I'm already gone. Like he's trying to memorize me before I disappear.

I wanted to tell him I'm scared too. That I don't know how to die well. That I'm angry at everything—at my body, at God, at the unfairness of leaving him before he's ready.

But I can't make him carry that. He's twenty years old. He should be worrying about finals and girls and what to do with his life. Not watching his mother turn into a skeleton who can't keep food down.

So I lie. I smile. I pretend.

And inside I scream.

David's legs gave out.

He sat down hard on the floor, his back against the bed, the notebook in his lap. His whole body shaking with something between grief and rage and guilt so intense it felt like drowning on dry land.

She'd been screaming inside while he'd been too young and too scared to hear it. She'd been carrying agony she wouldn't share because she was trying to protect him. And he'd let her. He'd accepted her lies because the truth was too big to hold.

"I didn't see it," David said, his voice coming out raw, scraped thin. "She was falling apart and I didn't see it because I didn't want to see it."

Thunder rolled closer now, the storm tightening its approach. The light through the windows had gone greenish-yellow, that peculiar color that meant serious weather building. But David couldn't move, couldn't do anything but sit there reading his mother's documentation of suffering he'd been too afraid to witness.

March 2nd.

Robert moved out today. We both pretended it was temporary. "Just until you're feeling better," he said. As if I'm going to feel better. As if we're not both facing the truth that he can't watch me die and I can't pretend I don't need him to be present.

I released him. Told him it was okay. That I understood.

And I do understand. Some people can't sit with suffering. It's not weakness exactly. It's just... limitation. We all have them.

But God, it hurts. To be dying and separated. To know that he loves me but can't be in the room with me. To understand that love isn't always enough to overcome fear.

David's hands clenched on the notebook. He'd known about the separation—Mara had told him. But reading his mother's words about it, seeing her try to understand Robert's absence while she was dying—it cracked something in his chest that hadn't yet broken.

April 15th.

David was here today. I had a bad reaction to the new protocol. He sat with me for two hours while I was too sick to speak. His face—I'll never forget his face. Pure terror. Like he was watching me drown and couldn't reach me.

Then he left. Made excuses about finals. About needing to study.

I wanted to tell him it was okay. That I understood. That watching someone suffer is its own kind of torture.

But he left before I could say anything.

And I realized: I've taught him to run from pain. By hiding mine. By pretending I was okay when I wasn't. I've taught him that suffering should be private. That grief should be managed alone.

What kind of legacy is that? What kind of faith am I modeling? The kind that hides? That pretends? That maintains appearances while screaming inside?

God, forgive me. I'm failing him even while trying to protect him.

The memory slammed into David with physical force.

He'd been there. That day. The day she was writing about.

Late spring, end of sophomore year. He'd driven home because Marie had a difficult treatment scheduled: the procedure where they'd warned her the side effects would be worse than usual. More aggressive protocol. Higher toxicity. Last chance to get the cancer under control.

The infusion room had smelled like antiseptic layered over something organic and wrong, that particular hospital smell no amount of cleaning could quite eliminate. The fluorescent lights were too bright, making everything look washed out, unreal, like they were all actors in a badly lit play. Four other patients sat in their recliners getting their own poisons dripped into their veins, all of them trying to maintain privacy in a space that offered none.

Marie's chair was by the window. She'd insisted on that spot—said she liked being able to see trees, needed something alive and growing to look at while chemicals destroyed her from the inside.

David had sat beside her in the uncomfortable visitor's chair, his backpack at his feet, a textbook open on his lap that he wasn't reading. The words swam across the page meaninglessly while he watched his mother's face for signs of what was coming.

The infusion had begun okay. Marie talking about the garden, about what needed planting in the next few weeks, about whether the roses would bloom this year. Normal conversation. Surface conversation. The kind that kept fear at bay by refusing to acknowledge its presence.

Then the shift.

David saw it in her face first—the way her jaw tightened, her breathing changed, going shallow and deliberate. Her hand on the armrest went white-knuckled, the tendons standing out sharp beneath skin that had gone thin and fragile.

"Mom?" His voice had sounded young even to himself. Scared.

"It's fine." She'd forced the words out between controlled breaths. "Just... nausea. It'll pass."

But it hadn't passed. It had gotten worse. David watched his mother's face transform from composed to barely controlled to someone drowning while still breathing air. She'd pressed her hands together in her lap—not casual, not comfortable, but with desperate intensity. Her knuckles went white. Her whole body tensed against something he couldn't see, couldn't fight, couldn't make stop.

"Should I get the nurse?" David had asked, his own hands shaking, not knowing what to do, feeling useless and young and completely inadequate to this moment.

"No. No, they can't... there's nothing they can..." Her words came out fragmented, gasping, each one costing her something to produce. "Just... stay. Please stay."

So he'd stayed. For two hours. Watching his mother suffer. Utterly helpless. His stomach churning with sympathetic nausea. His breath coming too fast. The room feeling too small, too hot, the walls pressing in until he couldn't get enough air.

A nurse had come eventually. Adjusted the IV, given Marie medication for the nausea that didn't help, offered professional sympathy that was kind but didn't change anything. The nurse's face had been carefully neutral, but David saw pity there—the kind healthcare workers learned to mask but never quite eliminated.

His mother had gripped the armrest until David thought the plastic might crack. Breath catching in sharp involuntary gasps she tried to muffle. The chemical smell of the IV sharp in his nose. The mechanical beeping of monitors marking time in systematic increments. The fluorescent lights making everything too bright, too exposed, too real.

When the worst seemed to pass, not gone but diminished to something bearable, Marie had reached for his hand with fingers that trembled from more than medication. Cold fingers. Shaking so hard he could feel it in his bones.

"I need you to understand something important," she'd said, her voice rough, scraped raw from holding back screams. "We don't always get to know the why. But we can choose to trust anyway. Promise me you'll remember that."

He'd promised. Of course he'd promised. He would have promised her anything to make the pain in her eyes diminish even slightly.

Then he'd left. Made excuses about finals, about needing to study, about having to get back to campus before it got too late. He'd kissed her forehead and run.

She'd let him go. Of course she had. Had smiled—actually smiled—and told him to drive safely. Had protected him from seeing how much his leaving cost her.

He'd sat in his car in the hospital parking lot for twenty minutes, shaking, crying, feeling like the worst kind of coward. But he hadn't gone back in. Had started the engine and driven away while his mother sat in that infusion chair alone with her suffering and her unanswered prayers.

Now, sitting on the floor of her old room with her journal in his hands, David understood what he'd been too young and too terrified to see: he'd abandoned her in her worst moment. Not because he didn't love her. Because he loved her too much and couldn't bear to watch her die by inches.

But she'd needed him to stay. Needed someone to witness what she was enduring. And he'd run because his own fear was louder than her need.

"I was so selfish," David said into the quiet room, his voice breaking. "She was suffering and all I could think about was how much it hurt me to watch. I made her death about my loss instead of her pain."

He turned back to the journal, pages blurring through tears he couldn't stop.

April 20th.

Five weeks left. Maybe less. The doctor couldn't look me in the eye when he said it.

I'm not ready. I'm not finished. David isn't prepared. I haven't taught him enough. Haven't shown him how to be okay without me. Haven't given him permission to grieve honestly instead of managing it quietly.

The prayers don't work anymore. Or maybe they never worked. Maybe I've been talking to myself this whole time, creating the illusion of conversation to make the silence feel less empty.

But I keep praying anyway. Keep returning to it. Keep folding my hands and forming words even when no answer comes.

Because what else is there? What else can I do when my body is failing and my faith feels like holding water with cupped hands?

I pray because giving up would mean admitting that all of this—the suffering, the fear, the desperate hope that kept getting crushed—was meaningless. And I can't accept that. Won't accept it.

Even if God never answers. Even if I die still asking why.

I'll keep showing up. Because showing up is the only faith I have left.

David stood up, the journal falling from his hands.

He needed to move. Needed to do something with the rage and grief tearing through him like storm winds. His hands were shaking. His whole body vibrating with something too big to contain.

He walked outside.

The storm was close now, clouds stacked dark and heavy overhead, the air electric with approaching violence. The light had gone strange—greenish, heavy, making everything look too vivid, too real, edges too sharp. Thunder rolled continuously, no longer distant but immediate, surrounding.

The garden stretched before him. His mother's garden. The beds she'd worked while dying. The plants she'd watered while her body destroyed itself from the inside. The weeds she'd pulled while praying prayers that went unanswered.

David grabbed the first weed he saw and yanked.

It came up with satisfying violence, roots tearing free from soil with the kind of force that felt appropriate, that felt right. He moved to the next one, and the next, pulling with increasing aggression. Not being careful about what else he might be disturbing. Soil flying. His fingers digging into earth like he could claw his way down to some deeper truth.

"Easy there," Samantha called from her window. "Those weeds aren't offended by your emotional state, but your tomatoes will be. Their roots sit shallow, right in the top layer with all the tender feeder roots. Yank hard enough close to the stem and you don't just pull weeds—you tear at the whole system. Grief works like that too: if you rip at it in a fury, you end up damaging the parts you were trying to protect."

David ignored her, moving to the tomato plants themselves. Several had grown crooked despite his attempts at staking, leaning in directions that made the whole row look drunk. He grabbed a stake that was listing badly and jerked it upright, jamming it deeper into the soil with more force than necessary. The wood protested, groaning as he drove it down.

His hands were already bleeding—small cuts from rough stems and his own violence. He didn't care.

The tomato plant shuddered. A few leaves tearing where the ties held too tight, the sound of green tissue ripping. David's breath came ragged now, his chest heaving.

"That's crossed the line from maintenance into destruction," Samantha observed, her voice edged with warning. "I get the urge—sometimes you have to admit something's already broken. But those plants didn't fail your mother. They're just doing what she planted them to do: keep growing. You're angry at the disease and the silence, not the tomatoes."

The first drops of rain hit—fat, warm, heavy. David stood there while the sky opened. Water poured down, soaking through his shirt in seconds, running into his eyes, mixing with tears he couldn't stop and didn't want to stop.

He was drowning in air.

Drowning in rain and grief and the crushing weight of understanding that came too late. His mother had suffered alone. Had prayed alone. Had died asking questions that never got answered. And he'd been too young and too scared and too selfish to truly see her.

Lightning split the sky close enough that he felt the electricity crackle through the air. Thunder followed immediately—the crack of it so loud it felt physical, vibrating through his chest like a second heartbeat. Samantha was yelling something from the window, but he couldn't hear her over the storm, over the roaring in his own ears.

The rain came harder, turning the garden paths to mud, water pooling around his feet, the tomato plants bending under the deluge. Everything becoming indistinct through the downpour, shapes blurring, boundaries dissolving.

David fell to his knees in the mud.

His hands pressed flat against the soil the way he'd seen his mother do, the way he'd watched her pray over roses when faith was all she had left. The rain poured down on his bent back. The earth was soft and yielding beneath his palms.

"I'm sorry," he said into the rain, his voice breaking. "Mom, I'm so sorry. I didn't see you. Didn't stay with you. Didn't understand what you were carrying."

No answer came. Just rain and thunder and the terrible emptiness of speaking into a void.

"God," he continued, not knowing if he was praying or screaming or both, "I don't understand. I don't understand why she had to suffer like that. Why her prayers went unanswered. Why faith had to cost her everything. I'm so angry. At myself. At You. At the whole brutal universe."

Lightning again. Closer. The smell of ozone sharp in the air.

"But she kept praying," David said, his voice raw. "Even when You stayed silent. Even when nothing changed. She kept returning to it. Kept folding her hands. Kept forming words into the emptiness."

He stayed there, kneeling in the mud while rain pounded down, his mother's journal back in the house documenting suffering he'd been too young to witness fully, too afraid to sit with completely. The garden she'd worked for received him the way it had received her—without judgment, without answers, just presence and soil and the patient work of roots growing in darkness.

Eventually, the rain calmed down. Not stopping, but shifting from violent downpour to steady persistence. David's breathing slowed. His hands were covered in mud, bleeding from small cuts he didn't remember getting. His clothes were soaked through, heavy with water. But the storm inside had moved through the worst of its violence.

He stood slowly, unsteadily, and went back inside.

He was standing in the kitchen, dripping rainwater onto the floor, when his father's car pulled into the driveway.

Robert hadn't called ahead. Hadn't texted. He just appeared, climbing out of his sedan with something tucked under his jacket to protect it from the rain.

David opened the door before his father could knock. They stood regarding each other across the threshold: David shirtless and muddy, still breathing hard; Robert in his usual business casual, looking older than David remembered, more worn.

"Bad time?" Robert asked.

"Seems to be the theme today," David said, stepping back to let him in.

Robert's eyes went to the journal on the floor where David had dropped it. His face shifted—recognition, maybe, or old pain finding new expression. "You found it."

"You knew about this?"

"I found it when I was packing up her things." Robert set down a plastic grocery bag, pulled out a clear hospital bracelet. "This was with it. Thought maybe you should have both."

David took the bracelet. The plastic was smooth, yellowed, his mother's name printed in small black letters: MARIE MILLS. The date of admission. Her birthdate. The clinical documentation of a person reduced to identifying information.

He remembered when this bracelet had been cut off.

Final admission. Marie had been moved to hospice care, the transition from "treating" to "managing comfort," a semantic shift that meant everything and nothing.

David had driven up from school. Finals were beginning but he'd told his professors there was a family emergency, which was true though calling imminent death an "emergency" felt absurd. This was the slowest emergency of his life.

The hospice nurse had been kind, efficient. She'd explained what to expect—the stages of dying, the physical changes, the timeline that was both predictable and impossible to predict. "Could be days. Could be a week. Everyone's different."

Marie had been semi-conscious, pain medication keeping her comfortable but making communication difficult. She'd squeezed David's hand when he arrived, a weak pressure that said *I know you're here* without words.

The nurse had removed Marie's hospital bracelet with special scissors designed not to cut skin. The plastic falling away to reveal the red mark it had left on her too-thin wrist.

"Do you want to keep this?" the nurse had asked, addressing Robert.

Robert had taken it wordlessly, his face doing that thing where he was experiencing too much and showing too little. He'd slipped it into his pocket without looking at it.

David had been annoyed—why did his father get the bracelet? David was the one who'd been there for treatments, for the hard days, for suffering his father had been too afraid to witness.

But he hadn't said anything. Had swallowed the resentment. Had focused on his mother's labored breathing instead of his own petty grievances.

Now, holding that same bracelet years later, David understood differently. His father had carried this in his pocket through the funeral, through the weeks and months after. Had kept this small plastic artifact of his wife's suffering close when he couldn't keep his wife.

"I couldn't watch her suffer," Robert said abruptly, the words coming with the force of something held back too long. "That's why I wasn't there. I couldn't walk into that hospital and see her in pain and know there was nothing I could do."

"At least you had a choice," David said, his voice harder than intended, sharp-edged. "I had to watch. I was there for treatments, for bad days, for every time she tried to pretend she was okay."

His hands shook, the bracelet rattling between his fingers.

"I know you were." Robert's voice was tight, his jaw working. "I know. And I should have been stronger. Should have been able to be there."

"She needed you," David said, years of unspoken resentment surfacing. "And you hid. We all did, in different ways. But she didn't get to hide. She had to endure it. And I just found her journal—" his voice cracked, "—and it shows how much she was enduring while we were all too scared to truly see her."

Robert picked up the journal from where it lay on the floor. His hands trembled as he opened it, read a few lines. David watched his father's face crumble—actually crumble, like a structure giving way under weight it couldn't hold.

"I loved her," Robert said, his voice breaking. "I didn't know how to love her through that."

"She needed you to be there," David said, fresh tears hot on his face. "She needed us both to witness what she was going through. To stay with her in it instead of running."

"I know." Robert's voice was barely above a whisper. "I know that now. But knowing it doesn't change that I failed her. That we both did. And it's too late."

They stood in the kitchen while rain pattered against the windows, the journal and hospital bracelet between them like evidence. Two men who'd loved the same woman and failed her in different ways, standing in the wreckage of their inadequacy.

"I should go," Robert said finally, setting the journal down carefully. "I just... I wanted you to have the bracelet. To know I kept it. That I've been carrying her with me even when I couldn't be present with her."

He turned toward the door. David felt something shift between them—not forgiveness, not resolution, but acknowledgment that they'd both been drowning in the same sea of inadequacy.

"Dad."

Robert turned back.

"Thank you for coming. For bringing this." David gestured at the bracelet, his hand still shaking. "For admitting you didn't know how."

Robert nodded once, his throat working, then left. His car backing down the driveway and disappearing into the rain-soft evening.

David stood alone in the kitchen, holding the hospital bracelet, the journal open on the table beside him. His mother's words staring up from the page, documenting suffering he'd been too afraid to witness, faith that had persisted despite silence, love that had endured despite pain that should have destroyed it.

His phone rang. Eileen's name on the screen.

For a moment, he considered not answering. He was too raw, too exposed, too stripped bare. But his hand moved before his mind could override it.

"Hey." His voice came out rough, scraped thin.

"David." Eileen's voice carried immediate concern. "Are you okay? The storm was bad—"

"I found something today," David interrupted. "In my mom's things. A journal she kept. During treatment."

Silence on the other end. Then, quietly: "What did it say?"

"Everything she couldn't tell us." David's throat tightened. "How scared she was. How alone she felt. How her prayers went unanswered. How she kept praying anyway."

Another pause. "That must have been hard to read."

"She wrote about me. About the day I left the infusion room because I couldn't watch her suffer anymore." His voice cracked. "She understood why I left. But she needed me to stay. And I ran because I was drowning in my own fear."

"You were twenty years old," Eileen said gently. "You did the best you could."

"It wasn't enough."

"David." Eileen's voice was firm now, cutting through his spiral. "Your mom didn't write that journal to make you feel guilty. She wrote it to be honest. To document that faith doesn't mean pretending suffering isn't real."

David looked at the journal, pages filled with his mother's careful handwriting, her questions and fears and persistent prayers. "How do you know?"

"Because she told me once that honesty was the only faith worth having. That pretending to be okay when you're not—that's not faith. That's performance." Eileen paused. "She loved you enough to hide her suffering from you. But she also loved you enough to document it. So someday, when you were ready, you could see that faith doesn't require perfection. It requires presence."

The words settled into David like seeds finding soil.

"She kept praying," he said, more to himself than to Eileen. "Even when nothing changed. Even when God stayed silent. She kept folding her hands and forming words into emptiness."

"Yes," Eileen said simply. "That's what faith looked like for her. Not peace. Not answers. Just the refusal to give up on the conversation even when the other side stayed silent."

After they hung up, David sat with the journal and the bracelet and the rain-washed evening. His mother's words teaching him what he'd been too young to learn while she was alive: that faith could look like suffering, that prayer could look like wrestling, that honest presence was the whole job even when you had no guarantee anyone was listening.

"Some growth only happens in darkness," Samantha said into the quiet. "Bulbs sit through whole winters underground. Seeds wait out droughts and frosts until conditions finally match what they need. Your mother's suffering went that deep—down into places you couldn't see. It didn't make sense, but it built something in her. A kind of faith that could hold agony and hope in the same set of roots. She's still teaching you that now, through what she left buried in these pages."

David placed the journal on the table next to his mother's Bible, the two documents forming a conversation—her public wrestling in the margins, her private wrestling in the pages. Evidence of a woman who'd maintained faith not because it made circumstances better, but because giving up on conversation would mean admitting that suffering was meaningless.

He prayed differently now. Not trying to sound composed or grateful or faithful in the way he thought he should be. Just honest.

God, he prayed into the gathering darkness, *I don't understand. I don't understand why she had to suffer like that. Why her prayers went unanswered. Why faith had to cost her everything. I'm angry—at myself, at You, at the brutal mechanics of disease and death. But she kept at it. Kept praying when You stayed silent. Maybe that's the faith she's teaching me. Not the kind that gets answers. The kind that keeps asking questions anyway.*

No answer came. But David hadn't expected one. Prayer wasn't about getting answers anymore. It was about being honest enough to admit the questions, faithful enough to keep returning despite the silence.

Like his mother had done. In hospital rooms and gardens and the pages of a journal she knew he'd find someday.

Over the next few days, David returned to the journal often—sometimes late at night when sleep wouldn't come, sometimes in the morning before working in the garden. Each time, he saw new layers. Not in the words themselves, but in what they represented. His mother's refusal to hide her struggle. Her insistence that suffering be witnessed honestly, even if only by herself in the privacy of pages no one else would read while she was alive.

"You're learning the language," Samantha observed one evening as David sat with the journal and Bible spread on the table. "Prayer as wrestling instead of performance. Like roots pushing through rock and clay hunting for water—harder than growing in loose soil, but the root system that survives that kind of pressure is stronger, wider, better suited for hard seasons. Your mother grew roots in unforgiving ground. Now she's showing you how to send yours down the same way."

The journal stayed on the kitchen table beside his mother's Bible and the hospital bracelet. Not hidden away like his father had hidden them, but present, visible. A reminder that faith could look like suffering and prayer could look like fighting and both could be truer than peaceful acceptance ever was.

It wasn't resolution. But it was truth. And truth was what his mother had asked him to honor—even when truth hurt more than comfortable lies.

Like prayers prayed in hospital rooms, hands folded not in serenity but in desperation, words torn from the deepest places, conversations continued when no answer came. Faith that looked like wrestling because sometimes wrestling was the honest response to suffering.

David was beginning to understand that his mother's gift wasn't peaceful faith. It was fierce faith—the kind that refused to pretend, the kind that persisted even when the other side stayed silent, the kind that could hold agony and hope without dropping either one.

He was learning. Not perfectly. Not peacefully. But honestly.

And maybe honesty was the only faith that ever mattered.

INTERLUDE: THE SOIL OF LOSS

The silence of the house gives way to the sound of storms.
What once felt frozen in memory begins to move again,
unsettled. Roots stretch under the weight of rain, pressing
deeper where eyes cannot follow. Grief asks us not to stay still,
but to grow where the ground has cracked.

"To everything there is a season, and a time to every purpose
under heaven." – Ecclesiastes 3:1
Storms remind us that seasons change. The season of silence
shifts to the season of testing. Here, grief is no longer a
shadow but a teacher, demanding that we learn to endure, to
bend, and yet to stand.

In Marie's handwriting, tucked into her Bible margin:
"Don't be afraid of the storms. They water what you cannot
see."

Chapter Eight

THE SCHOLARSHIP

"In their hearts humans plan their course, but the LORD establishes their steps." - Proverbs 16:9

TWO WEEKS HAD PASSED since Robert left the hospital bracelet on the kitchen table. Two weeks of silence that felt less like punishment and more like the careful quiet that followed difficult honesty—the space needed after soil had been turned, before new seeds could be planted.

David had learned to read his father's rhythms over the years. The retreat into work after emotional exposure. The processing time required before any conversation could continue. So when Robert's truck pulled into the driveway on a Saturday morning—earlier than his usual visits, the sun still low enough to paint long shadows across the garden—David's stomach tightened with familiar anticipation.

The smell of coffee reached the porch before Robert did. Two cups from the diner downtown, the good kind in real ceramic mugs that required returning. A peace offering. Or at least an opening gesture.

"Morning," Robert said, climbing the porch steps with careful attention to the fourth one that creaked. He'd been meaning to fix that step for years, had brought tools on at least three occasions, never quite gotten around to it. "Thought you might want decent coffee."

"Thanks." David accepted the mug, the ceramic warm against his palms, the heat seeping into his fingers. His father's hands weren't quite steady—whatever conversation was coming had cost Robert effort to prepare for.

The coffee was black, no sugar, no cream, the way Marie had always taken it, the way David had begun taking it since moving here. Bitter and strong and somehow comforting in its refusal to be anything other than what it was.

They stood on the porch for a moment, both regarding the garden where morning light was reaching the tomato plants. The storm damage from two weeks ago had been cleaned up, but evidence remained: the way certain plants leaned despite new stakes, the disturbed soil along pathways, the fresh growth emerging from places that had been torn.

"Garden's coming along well," Robert observed, genuine surprise in his voice. "Better than I expected, honestly."

"It's teaching me things." David sipped the coffee, letting the heat and bitterness ground him. "Lessons I didn't know I needed."

"How are you doing?" Robert asked, the directness catching David off guard. "Really doing. Not just surviving."

The lines around his father's eyes had deepened since David had last looked closely. The careful way Robert held his coffee mug, like it was the only thing keeping his hands occupied and steady.

"Some days better than others." David paused. "I found Mom's journal. The one she kept during treatment."

Robert's face did something complicated: recognition, old pain, a careful closing. "I know. I saw it when I was packing her things. Left it there thinking... I don't know what I was thinking. That you'd find it when you were ready, maybe."

"It had things she never told me. About the separation. About how much she was suffering while pretending to be okay." David's voice tightened. "About me leaving that infusion room because I couldn't handle watching."

"She understood why you left," Robert said quietly. "She told me that later. Said you were drowning in your own fear and she couldn't ask you to stay."

The admission hung between them, another layer of honesty adding to the foundation they were slowly, awkwardly building.

"I've been thinking about what you said," Robert continued, his voice steadier now, like he'd rehearsed this part. "About me hiding. About not being there."

David waited, his pulse picking up.

"You weren't wrong." Robert met his eyes, held them. "I was hiding. But I was also... I thought I was providing. Keeping things stable. Making sure that when you came out of this—however you came out of it—you'd have options."

He reached into his jacket pocket and pulled out a thick envelope. Official university letterhead visible through the window.

"Which is why I need to show you this."

David's hands trembled as he took it. The paper was heavier than it should be, the weight of significance.

"It came three weeks ago," Robert said. "I've been carrying it around. Trying to figure out the right time. Trying to figure out if there was a right time."

David opened the envelope, his fingers fumbling with the flap. Inside, nested between official documents and formal language, was an acceptance letter. Scholarship information that made his breath catch.

Dear Mr. Mills,

We are pleased to inform you that you have been selected to receive the Marie Patterson Memorial Scholarship...

The words blurred. David had to blink hard to keep reading. Full tuition. Four years. Stipend for books and living expenses. All wrapped in a name that made his throat close.

"Marie Patterson?" His voice came out rough.

"Different Marie." Robert's voice was rough too. "We lost her to cancer five years ago. She was nineteen. Environmental science major. Her parents established the scholarship to honor her memory."

The coincidence felt too sharp, too pointed. Another Marie. Another family transformed by cancer. Another attempt to make meaning from loss.

"How long have you been working on this?" David asked.

"Since March." Robert's voice broke slightly. "Since it became clear that your mother... since it became clear I was going to be responsible for making sure you had options after she was gone."

David's mind flashed back to March, spring semester senior year. He'd been focused on finals, on graduation preparations, on the slow dissolution of his mother's health that he experienced through phone calls and weekend visits.

But Robert had been doing something else entirely.

Early March. A specific weekend surfaced in David's memory with sudden clarity.

He'd driven home because Marie had asked him to come—said she wanted to see him, wanted to talk. When he'd arrived, she'd been more tired than usual, sleeping most of the afternoon. But Robert had been there, unusually present for a Saturday, sitting at her bedside with paperwork spread across his lap.

"Where's Dad going?" David had asked when Robert left later that afternoon, briefcase in hand despite it being the weekend.

"Meeting about paperwork," Marie had said, her voice tired, barely above a whisper. "Financial planning things."

David had assumed it was estate planning—wills and trusts and the grim administrative work of preparing for death. He'd been relieved not to be included in those conversations.

"You were meeting with the scholarship committee," David said now, understanding shifting like tectonic plates. "That Saturday I came home in March."

Robert nodded. "With university financial aid officers. The application required extensive documentation. Letters of recommendation. Your academic transcripts. Evidence of community engagement and commitment to place-based learning."

"Mom wrote a letter?"

"About your character. Your dedication. Your capacity for caring about things beyond yourself." Robert's voice grew rougher. "She wrote it while she could still hold a pen without shaking. Took her three days because she could only write for twenty minutes at a time before the exhaustion overwhelmed her."

The image of his mother—hands trembling from treatment, fighting exhaustion and pain—spending precious energy writing a scholarship recommendation landed in David's chest like a stone. She'd been planning for his future when she had none. Investing strength she didn't have in opportunities he hadn't known to pursue.

Something shifted. Not forgiveness exactly, but recognition. While he'd been drowning in grief, his father had been planning. While he'd been angry about Robert's absence, Robert had been building a different kind of presence.

The work of love looked different depending on who was doing it.

"The deadline passed while I was deciding whether to stay here," David said, reading the dates more carefully.

"I submitted everything in early April. Figured if you decided to leave, you'd have somewhere to go that mattered. And if you decided to stay..." Robert gestured at the letter. "The scholarship has provisions for delayed enrollment. Gap years. Community-based learning projects. Your situation qualifies for all of it."

"You thought of everything."

"I tried to." Robert's smile was tired, sad. "That's what I do. Your mother used to say I loved through planning. That I showed up with spreadsheets when what people needed was just... me being there. She wasn't wrong."

The words hung in the air, heavy with admission.

"She wrote that in her journal," David said quietly. "About you loving through planning and providing. About releasing you from the obligation of presence because she knew it would destroy you both."

Robert's face crumbled slightly, that careful control fracturing. "You read that part."

"I read all of it. About the separation. About her asking you to leave. About her refusing to let you come back when she got sick because she knew you'd just shut down." David's hands tightened on the mug. "She understood your limitations. I'm still learning to."

"I didn't know she was documenting all of that," Robert said, his voice barely above a whisper. "I didn't know she was writing it down for you to find."

"Maybe she knew I'd need to understand someday. That knowing you tried—even if trying looked different than I wanted—maybe that matters."

They stood in silence, the morning sounds of the garden filling the space between them. A robin calling from the oak tree. Bees already working among the squash blossoms. The world continuing its patient work regardless of human complications.

"I couldn't watch her suffer," Robert said finally, the words coming with visible effort. "Every time I saw her diminished by treatment, I shut down. Became useless. She said I helped more by handling logistics (bills, insurance, practical things) than by trying to be emotionally present when I clearly wasn't capable of it."

"At least she gave you permission to step back," David said, not unkindly. "I didn't get that choice. I had to watch."

"I know you did. And I know that cost you." Robert's jaw worked. "The scholarship was my way of... I don't know. Making sure that when you were ready to build something new, you'd have resources to do it. Marie died believing I was capable of doing that much right. I don't want to prove her wrong."

The sound of bicycle wheels on gravel interrupted them. Eli coasting down the driveway with his usual careful attention, though this morning he was pedaling faster, excitement visible in his posture.

"David! The beans are ready!" Eli called before he'd even come to a complete stop. "We should harvest today before they get too big!"

"Yeah," David said, his voice sounding distant even to himself. "Yeah, okay."

But he didn't move, couldn't quite make his body cooperate. He stood there holding the letter, staring at nothing.

Eli approached with careful attention—the same quality he brought to plants, noticing what wasn't being said.

"You okay?"

"I don't know," David admitted. "My dad just... there's a lot happening."

"That's okay," Eli said with nine-year-old matter-of-factness. "Sometimes not knowing is the honest answer."

The simple wisdom of it made David's throat tight. He managed a nod.

"I'll start on the beans," Eli said. "Come when you're ready."

David watched him head toward the garden, a child who already understood that some things couldn't be rushed, that people needed time to process what hurt.

"That was a substantial information delivery," Samantha observed from her window, her voice gentler than usual. "Like getting yanked out of your pot, told about a storm front, and handed a new fertilizer schedule all at once. Your father just dropped past failures and future possibilities in the same hole. That's a lot of root disturbance in one morning."

"He was working on this while she was dying," David said. "While I was furious he wasn't present, he was planning for after."

"Both can be true," Samantha replied. "He failed at emotional presence and excelled at logistics. Humans act like that's a contradiction; it isn't. Roots don't all do the same job—some anchor, some hunt for water. Your father's taproot is planning. His emotional roots are... stunted. Marie knew that. She worked with what he could offer instead of demanding what he couldn't grow."

David sank into the porch chair, the acceptance letter still in his hands. "I'm angry at her," David said. "For not telling me about the separation. For making decisions without me. For dying with secrets."

"Of course you're angry," Samantha said. "She pruned information without your consent. Protected you in ways that also excluded you. That's real impact; you're allowed to name it. Being buried doesn't make her beyond critique—it just means she can't explain herself anymore. You're standing here with the consequences and no chance for clarification. Frustration is reasonable. Anger is honest."

The permission landed with unexpected weight.

"Marie wasn't perfect," Samantha continued. "She made pruning decisions about what information to share and what to withhold. Some of those decisions were wise. Some were debatable. But being dead doesn't make her infallible; it just means she can't explain herself anymore. You're left trying to understand her reasoning through what she left behind. That's frustrating. Anger is a reasonable response to frustration."

"What would she want me to do about the scholarship?" David asked.

"I can't speak for Marie," Samantha said. "But I know what she believed about inheritance: deep roots and new branches. Stability and stretch. If you only cling to the past, you fossilize. If you only chase new growth, you uproot. Healthy plants do both—anchor and explore."

David looked toward the beds. "I don't know how to be rooted and growing at the same time."

"Nobody does until they practice," Samantha said. "Most big choices aren't between good and bad—they're between different kinds of good that lead to different kinds of growth. You could spend your life paralyzed by 'what if,' or you can choose honestly and let God, time, and consequences do their quiet work."

From the garden, Eli shouted about the beans. David stood.

"You should help him," Samantha added. "Work settles what words churn up. Hands in the soil will understand this long before your head does. Roots are already adjusting down there, even when you can't see a single thing move."

David walked toward the garden, the acceptance letter folded in his pocket, his breath still not quite reaching the bottom of his lungs.

The garden stretched before him in late morning light—nearly an acre of his grandfather's patient work, each bed a testament to decades of attention. The six raised beds ran lengthwise down the eastern side, their weathered barn wood silvered by years of sun and rain. Tomato plants climbed their stakes with determined vertical reach, leaves catching light like green hands open to possibility.

The herb spiral his mother had designed rose in its careful stone formation near the kitchen door, positioned to catch both morning and afternoon sun. The smell of thyme reached him even from here—clean, almost medicinal, that scent that intensified in heat. Oregano and rosemary sent their fragrances across the warming air, mixing with the earthier smell of turned soil and the green abundance of things actively growing.

Bees moved through the beds with single-minded purpose, their humming a constant backdrop beneath bird calls and the rustle of leaves in the breeze. A monarch butterfly drifted past, orange wings catching sunlight as it investigated the zinnias along the garden's edge—bright pinks and yellows and reds that drew pollinators like prayer flags marking sacred space.

The garden didn't care about scholarship deadlines or family secrets or the weight of decisions that needed making. It kept growing, kept reaching toward sun, kept doing the patient work of being alive whether anyone was watching or not.

Eli had filled one basket already, the beans glossy and perfect. He looked up when David approached, his serious face brightening with satisfaction.

"Look how good these are. Your mom would be proud."

The casual invocation of Marie landed in David's chest with surprising force. Would she be proud? Of the garden, maybe. Of his indecision about the scholarship, probably not.

"Can I ask you something?" David said, kneeling beside Eli in the soft soil.

"Sure."

"How do you know when you're making the right choice? About anything?"

Eli considered this with the gravity he brought to all questions. "Mom says you don't. You just choose honestly and then deal with what happens. She says being scared of choosing wrong is worse than choosing something and learning from it."

Mara's wisdom, delivered through her nine-year-old son with perfect clarity.

"That's good advice," David said.

"Mom's good at advice. Less good at following it." Eli grinned. "But she's trying."

They worked together in comfortable silence, harvesting beans with the careful attention the task required—pulling gently so as not to damage the plant, checking each bean for size and ripeness, leaving the smaller ones for future harvest. The repetitive motion was soothing, grounding, allowing David's mind to settle while his hands did familiar work.

That afternoon, after Eli had left with a basket of beans for his mother, Eileen's silver Honda pulled into the driveway.

David was on the porch, the scholarship letter spread on the small table, when she climbed out carrying a covered dish and a thermos. Exhaustion showed in everything—dark circles under her eyes, her shoulders hunched slightly forward, her movements more deliberate than usual, like each action required conscious thought.

"Morning," she called, though it was well past noon. "Brought banana bread. And coffee, though you look like you've had plenty."

"Dad brought some earlier. First real visit since..." David gestured vaguely at the space where Robert had stood.

"How did it go?" Eileen climbed the porch steps, the covered dish balanced carefully, her movements precise in a way that suggested she was running on fumes and pure determination.

"Complicated." David showed her the acceptance letter. "He brought this. Along with some history I'd only partially known from Mom's journal."

Recognition crossed Eileen's face as she read the scholarship details. "The Patterson scholarship. David, that's... that's significant. Do you know what this represents?"

"Dad said she was nineteen. Environmental science. Cancer."

"I knew her," Eileen said quietly, settling into one of the porch chairs. "Marie Patterson. We were in the same support group for a few months before she died."

David's breathing shallowed. "What was she like?"

Eileen poured coffee from the thermos with hands that trembled slightly. "She was determined to make her time matter. Even when treatment was destroying her, she was researching, planning, thinking about how to bridge traditional farming wisdom with modern environmental science. She talked about wanting education that served place rather than extracted from it."

"That's what the scholarship funds?"

"Her parents established it to honor that vision. They specifically wanted to support students committed to place-based learning—people like you who understand that real education happens through engagement with communities and land, not just in classrooms." Eileen looked toward the garden. "Students trying to learn how to tend what matters."

The weight of it settled over David. The scholarship wasn't just financial aid. It was inherited possibility—the dreams of a dead girl transformed into opportunity for the living.

"Are you okay?" David asked, really looking at Eileen for the first time since she'd arrived. "You look exhausted."

The question seemed to surprise her. "Why do you ask?"

"Because you look like you've been working five twelve-hour shifts without sleeping between them. And because you're doing that thing where you're holding yourself very carefully, like if you relax you'll fall apart."

Eileen's laugh was short, without humor. "Observant."

"Learned from someone who knew how to see people."

For a moment Eileen didn't respond. Complex emotions worked across her face. When she spoke, her voice was controlled—too controlled.

"I'm doing a pediatric oncology rotation. Children's ward." She took a long drink of coffee, her throat working as she swallowed. "It's harder than I expected."

David waited, giving her space.

"There's a little girl. Six years old. Leukemia." Eileen's hands tightened on the mug, knuckles going white. "Her name is Sophie. She asks me every morning if today's the day she gets to go home."

She stopped. The rest of the sentence hung unspoken in the air between them—the knowledge that Sophie wouldn't be going home, that the question would soon stop being asked because Sophie wouldn't be there to ask it.

"I'm sorry," David said, meaning it deeply. "That's terrible."

"Part of the job. I knew what I was signing up for." But her voice betrayed the cost, the way knowing and experiencing were entirely different things.

"Knowing and living aren't the same."

"Your mother used to say that. About faith. That it wasn't about understanding suffering, it was about surviving it without becoming bitter." Eileen met his eyes, her own too bright. "I'm trying. Some days are easier than others."

They sat in silence, the afternoon sounds of the garden providing backdrop to grief that needed acknowledgment but not solutions.

"The scholarship deadline is in two weeks," David said finally. "Dad wants an answer by then."

"And what do you want?"

"I want to honor Mom's vision without being trapped by it. I want to stay here without closing myself off. I want..." He gestured helplessly. "I want contradictory things."

"Most important decisions aren't between good and bad options," Eileen said. "They're between different goods. That's what makes it hard—not that one choice is wrong, but that multiple choices could be right in different ways."

The permission it offered—to stop searching for the one perfect answer—settled into David like rain into thirsty soil.

"Can I tell you what your mom told me once?" Eileen asked.

David nodded.

"She said she'd stopped praying for specific outcomes. That she used to pray for healing, for more time, for answers about why she got sick. But eventually she started praying for something different: for discernment. For the ability to trust that God could work with whatever choice she made, that she didn't have to control outcomes through perfect decision-making."

David's breath caught. "That sounds harder than just getting an answer."

"It is." Eileen's smile was sad but warm. "But maybe that's the point. Maybe faith isn't about having certainty about the future. It's about trusting that you can make honest choices and God will meet you in whatever comes next. Your mom said it was the only way she could keep praying—by releasing the need to control how things turned out."

The photograph David had found in the box of medical records. His mother's face twisted in prayer that was wrestling. Her refusal to pretend suffering was less than it was. Her insistence on staying in conversation when no answers came.

"So I just... choose? Without knowing if it's right?"

"You choose honestly. Based on what you value, what you're being called toward. Not based on fear of disappointing someone or making the wrong move." Eileen stood, gathering her things—she had a shift starting in two hours. "Your mom would want you to choose growth over preservation. She'd want you to honor what she began by building on it, not by freezing it like a museum exhibit."

After Eileen left, David sat with the scholarship materials as afternoon wore into evening. The choice before him was more complex than simple acceptance or rejection—it was about how to honor multiple visions simultaneously, how to stay rooted while growing, how to tend inheritance without being trapped by it.

God, he prayed into the gathering darkness, *I don't know which choice honors You. I don't know which choice honors Mom. I don't even know if those are the same question anymore. But Mom taught me to pray for discernment instead of certainty. So help me see clearly. Help me choose honestly. And then... just be there with me, whatever happens next.*

No answer came. But David was learning that prayer wasn't about getting immediate responses. It was about trusting that God could work with whatever choice he made—that faith was less about controlling outcomes and more about showing up honestly to decisions and then living with what came next.

The garden rested in darkness, plants breathing into the night air, roots working invisibly underground, the patient work of growth continuing whether anyone was watching or not.

And somewhere in the city, Eileen was beginning her shift in the pediatric oncology ward, sitting with Sophie who wouldn't be going home, learning her own lessons about tending what mattered when what mattered most was learning when to hold on and when to let go.

Prayers offered without certainty of outcome. Conversations continued when the other side stayed silent. Faith that was less knowing and more choosing to show up honestly, trusting that God could work with whatever came next.

David was learning his mother's language—prayer as wrestling, faith as discernment, love as releasing control while staying present. It wasn't the faith he'd expected to inherit.

But maybe it was the faith he needed.

Chapter Nine

STILL GROWING

"I am reminded of your sincere faith, which first lived in your grandmother Lois and in your mother Eunice and, I am persuaded, now lives in you also." - 2 Timothy 1:5

THE MORNING AFTER HIS father's visit, David woke with the scholarship letter still sitting on the kitchen table.

He'd read it four times the night before. Each reading revealed new details—the program's focus on sustainable agriculture and community health, the emphasis on place-based learning, the requirement for a capstone project that served the local community. Marie Patterson had been nineteen when she died. Her parents had channeled their grief into something that would keep growing, keep helping, keep creating possibility from loss.

God. The prayer rose without conscious thought. *I don't know what to do with this. Mom spent her last strength writing a letter so I'd have options, and I'm terrified of choosing wrong. Help me figure out what she was pointing me toward.*

The prayer felt clumsy. Unfinished. But he was learning that prayers didn't need polish to matter.

Coffee helped. The garden helped more: an hour of early morning work before the heat set in, checking tomatoes, pulling weeds, the simple physical labor that let his mind work without forcing it. Samantha was quiet this morning, which David appreciated. Sometimes her wisdom was exactly what he needed. Other times, the silence was its own teaching.

By mid-afternoon, the humidity had turned oppressive. The kind of heavy air that made every movement feel like swimming. David worked in the tomato rows, checking for hornworms and blossom-end rot, when Eli appeared at the garden gate with his bike and the expression of someone who needed somewhere to be that wasn't home.

"Hey," David called. "Come to help or supervise?"

"Help," Eli said, dropping his bike in the grass with the unselfconscious abandon of nine-year-olds. "Mom's working a late shift. She said I could come here if you didn't mind."

"Never mind. Grab gloves from the shed?"

Eli disappeared and returned with gloves three sizes too big, making his hands look like cartoon mitts. He held them up and wiggled his fingers, grinning, and David was struck by how young he was—still a kid despite the grief that had found him early.

They worked together in a comfortable quiet, Eli more focused than most nine-year-olds David had known. He'd learned to tell ripe tomatoes from almost-ripe, learned to check undersides of leaves for pest damage, learned that squash bugs deserved no mercy. Samantha had been teaching him, David knew, the same way she'd been teaching David. Botanical wisdom translated for whatever age needed hearing it.

After twenty minutes, Eli set down a tomato and turned to David with the sudden focus that meant a real question was coming.

"Does it get easier?" he asked. "Missing someone?"

David's hands stilled on the vine.

This was the question everyone wanted answered and no one knew how to ask directly. Leave it to a nine-year-old to just say it.

"Yes and no," David said, choosing honesty over comfort. "It doesn't hurt as much. Or it hurts differently. Like..." He searched for the right words. "Like the sharpness goes away but the ache stays. You get used to them not being there, which feels like betrayal but isn't."

Eli pulled off his gloves and sat down between the rows, and David joined him, both of them cross-legged in the dirt like they were having a campfire conversation instead of talking about dead fathers.

"I can't remember what my dad's voice sounded like anymore," Eli said, his voice small. "Mom showed me videos and I can hear it then, but when I try to remember without the videos, it's gone. That makes me feel bad. Like I'm forgetting him."

David's chest tightened.

"I have that too. With my mom. Her voice is getting fuzzy in my memory. I have to listen to the voicemails she left to remember exactly how she sounded."

"Does that mean I didn't love him enough? If I'm forgetting?"

The question landed like a stone in David's chest.

"No," David said firmly. "It means our brains can't hold everything perfectly. But the important stuff stays: how they made you feel, what they taught you, the ways they were present for you. Those don't fade."

Eli picked at the dirt, not looking up. "I dream about him sometimes. And in the dreams he's not dead yet, and I know he's going to die but I can't tell him because it's a dream. Then I wake up and remembered it had already happened and I couldn't stop it."

"That sounds really hard."

"It is." Eli's voice wavered. "Do you get those dreams?"

"Sometimes. With my mom. I dream she's still sick and I'm trying to help but nothing works. Then I wake up and she's already gone and I never got to save her."

They sat together in the heavy afternoon air, two people at different life stages working through the same impossible reality—that people you love die and you can't stop it and you have to figure out how to keep living anyway.

"Samantha says death is like winter," Eli offered. "Plants go dormant but they're not really gone. The roots are still there underground, just resting. And in spring they come back."

"What do you think about that?" David asked, curious how Eli was sitting with Samantha's teaching.

Eli's face scrunched up in concentration. "I think... people aren't plants. My dad isn't coming back in spring. But maybe the stuff he taught me is still there? Like roots underground?"

"That's wise," David said, meaning it. "Yeah, I think that's right. The love they planted in us keeps growing even when they're gone. We're like the spring growth—carrying forward what they started."

"But I miss him," Eli said, his eyes bright with tears he was trying not to let fall. "Even if his love is still growing in me or whatever."

He looked up at David.

"I just want my dad back."

The words hit David somewhere deep.

"I know. Me too. With my mom." David put his arm around Eli's small shoulders. "It's okay to miss them and understand the metaphors at the same time. You don't have to choose."

Eli leaned against David's side, and they sat like that for several minutes—two people who'd had loss break them open, finding comfort in not having to explain or pretend or perform okay-ness for each other's benefit.

"Does your mom know you have these dreams?" David asked eventually.

"No. I don't want to make her sadder. She's already sad all the time."

"She's sad because she misses your dad. Not because you're doing anything wrong." David paused, finding the right words. "But she'd probably want to know you're having hard dreams. Parents worry more when they don't know what's wrong."

"What do you think?"

"Yeah. My mom used to say that not knowing was worse than knowing, even when knowing was hard. She'd rather be sad with me than have me be sad alone."

Eli considered this. "Maybe I'll tell her tonight."

"Good. And Eli? You can come here anytime you need to. To work in the garden, to talk, to just be around someone who gets it. You don't have to be alone with the hard stuff."

Eli nodded, wiping his eyes with the back of his too-big gloves, leaving dirt streaks on his cheeks. "Can I ask you something else?"

"Always."

"Do you talk to your mom? Like, even though she's dead, do you still talk to her sometimes?"

David thought about his morning prayers, his conversations with Samantha that were really conversations with Marie's wisdom, the way he found himself reporting his day to empty rooms like she might still be listening.

"Yeah," he admitted. "Sometimes. I don't know if she hears me. But it helps anyway."

"I do that too," Eli said, relief visible in his expression, like he'd been worried this made him weird. "I tell my dad about school and baseball and stuff. Just out loud when nobody's around. Mom caught me once and cried, but not in a bad way. In a way like she understood."

"Your mom sounds pretty great."

"She is. She tries really hard even though she's sad too."

They returned to work, the conversation having shifted something. Not resolved, because grief didn't resolve, but acknowledged. Eli seemed lighter, moving through the garden with more energy, humming tunelessly while he checked squash plants for bugs.

"Eli?" David called after a while. "Thank you for asking those questions. The real ones. It helps me too, talking about it with someone who gets it."

Eli looked up, surprised. "Really?"

"Really. Everyone else wants me to be okay already. You understand it's still hard."

"Yeah, it's still hard," Eli confirmed. "But Samantha says that's normal. She says grief is just love with nowhere to go, so it gets all tangled up until you figure out where to put it."

"Samantha's pretty smart."

"She's basically the smartest plant ever," Eli said with complete seriousness.

From the sunroom window, Samantha's voice drifted out: "I heard that. Accurate assessment. Now keep working—those squash plants are one missed inspection away from a vine-borer apocalypse. Intergenerational grief processing can absolutely happen alongside pest control."

Eli giggled, the first real laugh David had heard from him that afternoon. "She's also really bossy."

"Very bossy," David agreed. "But usually right."

They worked until the light began to shift toward evening and Mara's car pulled into the driveway. But instead of waiting in the car as she usually did, Mara got out and walked toward the garden gate. She moved with the particular exhaustion of single parents working double shifts, bone-deep tiredness that went beyond physical fatigue.

"Mom!" Eli called, waving with a gloved hand that sent dirt flying. "David let me help with the tomatoes. And the squash. And I found three hornworms!"

"That's wonderful, mijo." Mara's smile was genuine but tired. She leaned against the gate, watching her son with an expression David recognized, the complicated love of seeing your child grow through something you wished they'd never had to face.

"Mrs. Rodriguez, would you like some iced tea?" David asked, straightening from his work. "I just made a pitcher this morning."

Mara hesitated. David could see her calculating: the drive home, dinner to make, the hundred small tasks that filled the hours between work and sleep.

"Just for a few minutes," she said finally. "Eli, finish up what you're doing."

David led her to the porch, grateful for the shade and the slight breeze that had started to move the heavy air. He poured two glasses of tea and they sat in the wicker chairs, watching Eli work through the last of the squash row with focused attention.

"He's different here," Mara said quietly. "Lighter. More like he was before."

"He's a good kid. Easy to have around."

"He talks about Samantha." Mara's voice was careful, testing. "About things she supposedly says. Wisdom she shares." She paused. "I know it sounds strange, but I don't want to discourage it if it's helping him work through things."

David took a long drink of tea, considering how to respond. This was the moment he'd been navigating with everyone who couldn't hear Samantha—the delicate balance between honesty and protecting something he didn't fully understand.

"Can I ask you something?" he said finally.

Mara nodded.

"Do you hear her? Samantha?"

The question hung between them.

Mara's expression shifted through several phases: surprise, consideration, something that might have been longing.

"No," she said. "I've tried. After Eli started talking about her, I came over one afternoon while he was at school. Sat in your sunroom for an hour, waiting. Hoping."

She shook her head.

"Nothing. Just a plant."

"But you believe Eli hears her?"

"I believe something is helping my son. Whether it's a talking plant or his imagination or something I don't have words for—I believe it's real to him, and it's making him better."

Mara's voice roughened.

"After Carlos died, Eli stopped talking. Three months of almost complete silence."

David's throat tightened.

"The therapist said it was normal, that he'd come back when he was ready. And he did, slowly. But he didn't really start talking again—about real things, hard things—until he started coming here."

David thought about what Samantha had said once, about grief opening frequencies that weren't available to everyone. About loss breaking people open in ways that let in voices others couldn't hear.

"My grandfather could hear her," David said. "And my mother, toward the end. Samantha says some people just... can. And some can't."

"What makes the difference?"

"I don't know exactly. Samantha says it has something to do with grief. With being opened in particular ways." He paused. "But I don't think not hearing her means anything's wrong with you. I think it's just... different frequencies. Different ways of receiving."

Mara was quiet for a long moment, watching Eli work. The evening light had turned golden, casting long shadows across the garden. Somewhere in the trees, a bird was calling its sunset song.

"Carlos could hear things I couldn't," she said finally. "Not plants. But... he had this way of knowing what people needed before they said it. He'd bring me tea when I didn't know I was tired. He'd call his mother on days she was lonely, even though she never asked. I used to joke that he was psychic."

Her voice caught.

"Maybe he was just listening on frequencies I couldn't access. And maybe Eli inherited that from him."

Something eased in Mara's expression: the idea that her son's unusual ability might be a gift from his father, one more way Carlos lived on in the child they'd made together.

"He's learning good things here," Mara continued. "About grief, about growing, about how to sit with hard feelings without running from them. Whatever's teaching him—Samantha or the garden or just having another adult who understands loss—I'm grateful for it."

"He's teaching me too," David admitted. "Kids ask the questions adults are afraid to ask. They force you to find answers you didn't know you had."

"That sounds like something your mother would say."

"Probably is. Most of the wise things I say are borrowed from her."

Mara smiled, the first real smile he'd seen from her. "Carlos used to say that too. That all his good ideas came from his grandmother. She raised him after his parents divorced. Taught him everything he knew about loving people."

"What happened to her?"

"She died when he was twenty-two. Stroke. He was devastated." Mara's voice softened with memory. "But he said she prepared him. Taught him that love didn't end when someone died—it just had to find new directions to flow. He said grief was the price of having loved well, and he'd rather pay that price than never having had her."

David thought about the scholarship letter still sitting on his kitchen table. About his mother spending her last strength to write a recommendation. About Robert building possibilities while David had been drowning in grief.

"Can I ask you something else?" he said.

"Of course."

"How did you decide to stay here? After Carlos died. How did you know this was where you were supposed to be?"

Mara was quiet for a moment, watching Eli through the garden gate. "I didn't decide. Not really. I just... didn't leave. Every day I thought about moving somewhere without memories, starting over where nobody knew us. But every day there was something that needed doing: work, Eli's school, the memorial garden. And staying became the choice, even though I never consciously made it."

She gestured toward the garden where Eli was now talking to Samantha through the window, his small voice carrying across the yard.

"This place held us when we couldn't hold ourselves. The community, the routines, the people who arrived with casseroles and offered to help. I couldn't have survived the first year without neighbors who knew Carlos, who could tell Eli stories about his father, who could say his name without flinching."

She paused.

"Sometimes staying isn't a decision. It's just what happens when you stop fighting what's trying to hold you."

The words settled over David like a blanket.

He'd been treating the scholarship decision like a fork in the road: stay here or leave, this path or that one. But maybe the choice wasn't that binary. Maybe staying and growing weren't opposites.

"I got offered a scholarship," he heard himself say. "Full ride. Sustainable agriculture program. My mom wrote the recommendation letter before she died."

Mara's eyes widened. "David, that's wonderful."

"I don't know if I should take it. It would mean leaving here. Leaving the garden. Leaving..." He gestured at the porch, the tomato rows, Eli's bike in the grass.

"Does it have to mean leaving completely?"

David looked at her.

"What do you mean?"

"Plants get transplanted all the time," Mara said. "They put down roots in new soil, but they don't forget where they came from. The original foundation shapes how they grow, even in a new place."

She smiled.

"I'm not Samantha, but I've learned a few things from gardening too."

Something loosened in David's chest. The binary he'd been trapped in felt less rigid now.

"You sound like her."

"Maybe wisdom is wisdom, wherever it comes from." Mara stood, brushing off her scrubs. "Eli! Time to go, mijo. You can come back tomorrow if David doesn't mind."

"I don't mind," David said. "He's welcome anytime."

Eli came running, still wearing the too-big gloves. "Mom, did you know that tomatoes and basil help each other grow? It's called companion planting. Samantha says they communicate through chemicals in the soil. And she says humans do something similar, but we use words instead of chemicals, and sometimes the words are just as invisible because people say things without saying them out loud."

Mara's expression flickered, that complicated mix of love and uncertainty that came from parenting a child who heard things she couldn't.

"That's very interesting, mijo. Tell me more in the car."

She met David's eyes over Eli's head, and something passed between them: gratitude, understanding, the quiet solidarity of people navigating grief in a world that expected them to be finished with it.

"Thank you," she said. "For all of this."

"Thank you for sharing with him."

Eli waved from the passenger window as they pulled away, and David stood in the garden watching them go, feeling like something important had happened. Not just with Eli, but with Mara too. Community was forming around this place, people drawn together by loss, learning to be present for each other in their varied, imperfect ways.

"Good work today," Samantha said when David came inside, evening light catching her leaves. "The boy needed that. You let him be sad without rushing him toward 'better.' That's what Marie did—held grief and growth in the same space. Like perennials in winter: nothing visible on the surface, but everything underneath quietly preparing. That's not collapse; that's active rest. You're learning that rhythm too."

"He's a good kid," David said.

"He is. And you're learning to be a good tender of broken places. That's your calling taking shape—not fixing people, not solving their problems, just creating space where they can be truthfully themselves and know they're not alone."

David thought about that while he poured a glass of water, while he watched the garden settle into evening shadows.

"Can I ask you something?"

"You're full of questions today," Samantha said. "That's usually a sign of growth... or indigestion. Hard to tell with mammals; you don't wilt clearly the way plants do."

"Why can Eli hear you but Mara can't?"

Samantha was quiet for a moment. When she spoke, her voice was gentler than usual.

Grief tunes people to different frequencies," Samantha said. "But it's not just the loss—it's how you brace against it. Some hearts build careful walls: compartment, organize, function. That's survival. It's valid. But those same walls muffle certain signals."

"And Mara built walls?"

"Mara had to wall up. Child to raise, bills to pay, a life to keep from collapsing. She moved through her loss like she does everything else—efficiently, practically." Samantha's leaves shifted. "That's not a flaw; it's a strategy. It kept her standing. It also kept some channels closed."

"And Eli?"

"Eli didn't have that option. He was nine. Kids don't know how to sandbag their emotions yet. His grief shattered straight through him—that's why he went silent. When he started healing, he healed with the cracks still open. Light and sound still get through those."

David thought about his own grief. The months of numbness, the anger, the slow thawing that had happened here in this garden.

"What about me?"

"You came here already splitting along your fault lines," she went on. "All your tidy compartments leaking—grief into anger into fear into everything. This house gave you permission to stop holding the dam. Once you stopped fighting the break, you could finally hear through it."

"So it's not about deserving it. Or being special."

She rustled, like a small shrug. "It's not about deserving anything. It's timing and pressure. Some seeds only germinate after fire—the heat fractures the shell so water can reach the embryo."

Samantha paused.

"Without the fire, they stay hard and safe and unchanged. With it, they hurt, and then they grow."

David sat with that.

The scholarship letter was still on the kitchen table. Tomorrow he'd have to start making decisions. But tonight, he could sit with the questions.

"Mara said something interesting," he said eventually. "About transplanting. How plants can put down roots in new soil without forgetting where they came from."

"Mara's wiser than she gives herself credit for," Samantha said. "Most humans are, when they quit performing wisdom and just report what life taught them."

"And she's right about transplanting. Shock is real—new soil, new light, roots trimmed back. It's stressful, sometimes fatal. But the ones that survive? They often leaf out stronger, root deeper, fruit heavier. The stress doesn't just wound; it forces adaptation. Resilience is just growth that's had to fight for itself."

"So you think I should take the scholarship?"

"I think you should stop auditioning everyone else to play the role of your decision-maker," Samantha said, "and actually listen to what's already sprouting inside you."

David laughed despite himself.

"That's not helpful."

"Helpful would be handing you a tidy yes or no," she replied. "Growth is rarely 'helpful.' It's usually uncomfortable and inconvenient. My job isn't to choose for you, honey—it's to make you restless enough that you can't pretend you don't know what you want."

He sat in the sunroom until full dark, watching stars appear through the window, thinking about roots and transplanting and the ways grief opened people to frequencies they couldn't otherwise access.

Eli had asked if missing someone meant you didn't love them enough. The answer was no—missing someone meant you loved them so well that their absence left a hole. And learning to live with the hole, to build around it instead of trying to fill it, was the work of grief.

Maybe that's what the garden was teaching all of them. How to make space for loss and growth simultaneously. How to accept what each season brought without demanding it be different. How to care for what needed caring without trying to control outcomes.

Maybe that's what his mother had known when she'd written that letter with shaking hands.

Not that she was sending him away.

That she was giving him a foundation strong enough to grow wherever he was planted.

Samantha was right—he was learning. Slowly. Through patient practice and repeated failure and the willingness to keep showing up even when he didn't know what he was doing.

Just like Eli was learning. Just like Mara was learning. Just like all of them were learning together, stumbling through grief toward something that might eventually resemble peace.

Chapter Ten

LEARNING TO TEND

"Carry each other's burdens, and in this way you will fulfill the law of Christ." - Galatians 6:2

THREE DAYS AFTER THE scholarship revelation, rain drummed on the roof with steady persistence.

David stood at the kitchen window in pre-dawn darkness, watching water stream down the glass. The garden would be sodden, pathways turned to mud, any outdoor work postponed. But restlessness coiled in his chest—energy that needed a physical outlet despite the weather's refusal to cooperate.

The scholarship materials sat on the kitchen table where he'd left them. Ten days until the deadline. Certainty remained as elusive as it had been when Robert first handed him the envelope.

The coffee maker gurgled, filling the kitchen with the smell of dark roast. David poured a mug and settled into the chair, staring at nothing, his mind circling the same territory it had been circling for days.

"You're wearing a path in the linoleum," Samantha observed from her perch on the windowsill, watching the rain track down the glass. "Pacing won't help you decide any more than digging up seeds helps them sprout. You're trying to bully clarity into existence with worry when what you actually need is to notice what nourishes you versus what just feels familiar."

"How do I know the difference?"

"Usually by asking whether you're reaching toward light or clinging to old soil because moving feels scary," she said. "Heliotropism versus inertia. Plants don't hold committee meetings about growth direction—they lean toward whatever light and moisture they actually have. You're complicating what could be simple by demanding guarantees before you'll move an inch."

David opened his mouth to respond, but the sound of a car engine interrupted him. Nobody visited this early, especially not in weather that discouraged anything but necessary travel.

Through the rain-streaked window, Eileen's silver Honda pulled into the driveway, headlights cutting through the gray dawn.

His pulse kicked—quick and hard.

She appeared on the porch moments later, soaked despite the short distance. Holding a thermos and a bakery bag. Her scrubs were visible under her rain jacket. She must have come straight from her night shift.

"Sorry for coming by so early," she said when David opened the door, water dripping from her hair. Her voice was hoarse with exhaustion. "I saw your lights on and thought maybe you'd want company. Or at least fresh pastries."

"Come in. You're soaked." David stepped back, catching the scent of rain and hospital soap and bone-deep tiredness. "Let me get you a towel."

By the time he returned, Eileen had removed her rain jacket and stood by the window looking toward the rain-blurred garden. Her shoulders were rounded forward, hands wrapped around the mug he'd set out but not drinking. Holding it like an anchor.

"Sophie died," she said without preamble. Her voice was flat with the control that came from holding grief too carefully. "Last night. Around three AM. Her parents were with her. It was... as peaceful as these things can be."

The words hit David like a physical blow.

His lungs compressed, that familiar tightening that made breathing require conscious thought. Six weeks since Marie died—recent enough that everyone still asked how he was doing, raw enough that someone else's death carved him open again.

"I'm so sorry," he said, meaning it deeply. "That's terrible."

"It's what happens sometimes." She took a long drink of coffee, her hands trembling. The liquid rippled in the mug. "I knew it was coming. We all knew. But knowing and living through it are different."

"They are," David agreed quietly.

He moved to stand beside her at the window, both of them looking toward the rain-soaked garden. The silence held what words couldn't.

After a few minutes, Eileen turned to face him with visible effort. "I shouldn't have come here like this. You have enough without me bringing my grief."

"That's not how friendship works." David refilled both mugs, his hands steadier than hers. "You've been helping me with Mom's garden for weeks. The least I can do is witness that your work is hard."

"Your mother used to say that. That witnessing was sometimes the most important work." Eileen's smile was watery but genuine. "She had this way of sitting with difficult things without trying to fix them."

They settled at the kitchen table with the pastries Eileen had brought—still warm despite the rain.

David recognized them immediately.

Almond croissants. Marie's tradition.

Warmth spread through his chest—unexpected and complete.

"Mom used to get these," he said, breaking one open. Steam rose from the flaky layers. "On birthdays. Special Saturdays. When she wanted to mark a day as important."

"I know." Eileen's voice was gentle. "She told me once that food was a love language in your family. That breaking bread together was how you said important things when speaking them directly was too hard."

The observation landed with weight. His mother had been known. Had shared parts of herself with people beyond immediate family. Had built connections that outlasted her life.

They ate in quiet communion, rain creating rhythm against the windows that turned the kitchen into shelter. David watched Eileen's hands tear the pastry into small pieces, the way she held her coffee mug like it was keeping her tethered to the present.

"Tell me about your brother," David said, sensing she needed to talk about more than Sophie's death. "You mentioned he was in an accident."

Eileen's hands stilled on her croissant. "Mark. He's twenty now. The accident happened when he was seventeen—a drunk driver ran a red light." Her voice steadied as she found the familiar narrative.

Traumatic brain injury. Broken pelvis. Collapsed lung.

Three months in the hospital.

"That's terrifying."

"It was." Eileen took a bite, chewing slowly. "I was in my first year of nursing school. Suddenly I was trying to manage coursework while spending every spare moment at the hospital. I completely fell apart—stopped sleeping, stopped eating, nearly failed out. And then I tried to grow tomatoes on my apartment patio."

David found himself smiling despite the heaviness. "Tomatoes as therapy?"

"Tomatoes as control when everything else was chaos. Except I killed them all within two weeks—either drowning them or forgetting them entirely." Eileen's expression softened with memory. "That's when your mother appeared."

"How did she know you needed help?"

"She was at the hospital visiting someone from her support group and saw me in the cafeteria, losing it over a failed anatomy exam." Eileen stared into her coffee as if the moment was reflected there. "She sat down without asking and said, 'You look like someone who's trying to carry more than human hands can hold.'"

The phrase was so perfectly Marie.

David's throat tightened.

"She didn't try to fix anything," Eileen continued. "Didn't offer platitudes. She just sat with me while I cried. Then she asked if I liked to garden."

"And you said no because you were killing all your plants."

"I said no because I didn't have time. But she wrote down her address and told me that if I ever needed to remember that growth was possible, I should come see her garden." Eileen smiled at the memory. "I thought she was a little crazy. But two weeks later, when Mark had a setback and I couldn't handle the hospital anymore, I found myself pulling into your grandfather's driveway."

David could picture it perfectly. His mother's gentle persistence. Her way of offering help that didn't feel like charity.

"Your mom was in the garden," Eileen said. "She saw me standing there looking lost and said, 'Would you like to help me harvest basil?' Like she needed the help. Like I'd be doing her a favor." Her voice grew quieter. "We spent an hour harvesting herbs. She asked about Mark, about school. Then she sent me home with fresh basil and a small potted plant. The most forgiving variety, she said."

"Did you keep it alive?"

"Barely. But yes. And every time I watered it, I thought about what she'd said—that caring for something outside yourself could help you survive the impossible things inside yourself." Eileen looked up, meeting David's eyes. "She saved me from imploding that semester."

They sat in silence, listening to the rain drum on the roof. Gray light strengthened beyond the windows.

"I keep thinking about Sophie's last question," Eileen said finally.

Yesterday. Sophie had asked if there would be gardens in heaven.

Eileen had told her yes. The most beautiful gardens she could imagine.

"Do you believe that?" David asked. "Really believe it?"

Eileen looked at him through the steam from her coffee. "I want to. Most days I do. Some days..." She trailed off. "Some days I choose to act as if it's true, and hope that's enough."

"How do you do it?" David asked after several minutes of silence. "Walk into that ward every day knowing some of the kids won't make it?"

Eileen's hands stilled on her mug. For a long moment she didn't answer. When she spoke, her voice was careful. Raw.

"Honestly? Some days I don't know. Some days I walk in and wonder what difference any of it makes—the interventions, the prayers, all the careful attention. And still children die."

She took a slow breath.

"But then I remember something."

Her voice steadied. Strengthened.

"Jesus wept. At Lazarus's tomb. Even knowing what would happen next, he still wept. And I think... maybe that's the point. That we're there to weep with people. To bear witness that their suffering matters."

"Like bearing witness," David said, thinking of what his mother used to say.

"Yes." Eileen nodded. "Your mom taught me that faith isn't about having all the answers. It's about being present and choosing to believe that love matters, even when it can't change the outcome."

"But how do you keep believing? When you watch kids die?"

Eileen was quiet for a moment. "I don't know that I have a good answer. Some days are harder than others. But I go anyway. I do the work that's in front of me. And I trust that somehow, it matters."

From the sunroom, Samantha's voice carried: "Faith works like mycelium," she said. "All the underground networks—quiet, unseen, still feeding everything. You can't chart it or prove it on a clipboard, but pull it out and the forest starves. Showing up is how you keep those hidden connections alive, even when nothing aboveground looks different."

Eileen's head tilted, as if she'd heard wind through distant branches but couldn't quite locate the source. Her brow furrowed. Then she blinked, and the moment passed.

She returned her attention to her coffee, but something had shifted in her expression—a flicker of awareness, quickly shuttered.

"The garden's a mess after this rain," Eileen said eventually. "Want help checking for damage?"

David glanced toward the window where water streamed down in sheets. "It's pouring."

"I noticed. But you're restless and I'm too awake to sleep. Might as well be useful." Her smile was small but genuine. "Besides, your mother taught me that sometimes the best way to work through hard things is to get your hands dirty."

They worked in the rain for an hour. Cold water running down their necks, soaking through clothes within minutes. Mud sucking at their boots with every step. Checking plants for wind damage, staking tomatoes that had bent under the weight of water, clearing debris from pathways.

The work was uncomfortable but grounding in ways that pulled David out of his circling thoughts. His hands moved through familiar tasks—tying stakes, pulling weeds, examining leaves. The cold seeped through his clothes, making everything harder, but there was honesty in the discomfort.

Reality.

Eileen moved through the garden with surprising competence. She understood drainage, knew which plants needed extra support after heavy rain, and asked good questions about his plans.

"This section here," she said, gesturing to the south-facing slope, her voice raised over the rain. "What's the plan?"

"Native pollinator garden. Or trying to be." David pushed wet hair out of his eyes, water immediately replacing it. "Mom had it sketched out but never got to implement it. I'm working from her notes."

"It's good work. These plants make sense together—companion planting, mutual support systems." Eileen crouched to examine emerging shoots, rain drumming on her back. "Your mom would be proud. Not maintaining her vision but developing it."

The praise landed differently than it would have weeks ago. Not as a burden. As acknowledgment of work that mattered.

They moved to the bean plants. Rain made the pods easier to spot, dark green against rain-darkened leaves. David's fingers were stiff with cold, clumsy as he harvested. But there was meditation in the repetitive motion. The accumulating weight in his basket.

Eileen worked beside him, movements efficient but her shoulders staying tense, jaw set.

"How do you do it?" David asked after several minutes. "Come to work every day when some days you wonder what difference it makes?"

Eileen's hands stilled on the plants. For a long moment she stood there in the rain, water streaming down her face.

"I remember that being there is the work," she said finally. Her voice, stronger now, raised against the wind. "I'm not there to fix or save. I'm there to be present. To reflect that someone cares, even when caring can't change the outcome."

"Like bearing witness."

"Yes. Your mother taught me that faith isn't about having all the answers. It's about choosing to believe that love matters, even in the face of death."

The rain was starting to ease, shifting from downpour to steady precipitation. Mist rose from warmer soil where rain struck, creating gauzy veils between the rows. The garden seemed to exhale.

A gust of wind sent rain slanting sideways. The tomato plants swayed, stakes creaking. David tasted water on his lips, metallic and slightly sweet.

"Sophie asked me if there would be gardens in heaven," Eileen said again, as if the question kept circling back. "And I told her yes."

"Do you believe that?"

"I choose to act as if it's true," Eileen said, her voice steady now. "And hope that's enough."

David looked around at the garden—at the plants they were tending in the rain, at the work they were doing despite cold and wet discomfort. Seeds his mother had planted months ago, now bearing fruit. Growth that happened underground, invisible, before anything showed above soil.

"I think that's what Mom was trying to teach me," he said. "That the point isn't to have everything figured out. The point is to keep showing up. Keep tending to what's in front of you."

"That sounds like wisdom," Eileen said, and her smile was the first genuine one since she'd arrived with news of Sophie's death. "That sounds like your mother."

They worked for another twenty minutes as rain gently drizzled. The cold became harder to ignore—David's hands were stiff, movements slower, clothes clinging heavily. But satisfaction came from the accumulating baskets of harvest, from straightened stakes and cleared beds.

Worms surfaced in the saturated soil, pink and glistening. David stepped around them carefully. His mother had taught him that—rain brought them up to breathe, and a good gardener honored that necessity.

When they finally came back inside, both were thoroughly soaked and shivering. David showed Eileen to the upstairs bathroom, gave her towels and the password to the hot water heater.

While she showered, he made fresh coffee and changed into dry clothes. His skin tingled as warmth returned, blood rushing back into his fingers with painful intensity.

When Eileen came back downstairs, her hair damp and skin pink from hot water, she'd borrowed one of his mother's old sweatshirts. Marie's sweatshirt. Oversized and worn soft, hanging on Eileen's slight frame in ways that made her look younger. More vulnerable.

David's breath caught.

He had to look away.

"Thank you," she said, accepting fresh coffee. "For letting me arrive at dawn with my grief. For not trying to fix it."

"Thank you for trusting me enough to share it." David paused. "And for what you said about Mom. About limitations and letting people go. About presence being the work."

"You can hold both," Eileen said, her voice quiet but certain. "The love and the anger. The gratitude and the hurt. That's what it means to really know someone."

They stood in the kitchen with coffee and comfortable silence. David wished she could stay longer, that the conversation didn't have to end.

"I should go," Eileen said finally, though she didn't move immediately. "Let you get back to thinking about the scholarship."

"For what it's worth," she added, gathering her things, "I think you'll make the right choice. Whatever that ends up being."

"How can you be sure?"

"Because you keep coming back when the work is hard. Because you're willing to get soaked to tend plants that would probably be fine without you." Her smile was warm. "Those are the qualities that lead to good decisions."

At the threshold, she turned back. "One more thing your mom told me. She said that faith wasn't about knowing the right answers. It was about trusting that God was present when you couldn't see Him. That sometimes being there was all the faith you needed."

Then she was gone, her car disappearing down the rain-slicked driveway.

After Eileen left, David stood at the window watching rain clean the garden.

"She likes you," Samantha observed. "In case that escaped your notice while you were busy catastrophizing. Classic positive phototropism—consistent leaning toward the same light source whenever you're not paying attention."

Heat spread through David's chest. "Did she hear you? Earlier, when you spoke about mycelium?"

"Not the words. Not yet. But she felt the draft," Samantha said, leaves rustling. "Grief unlatches doors people didn't even know were bolted. Sophie's death peeled back some insulation—made her a little more porous to what's always been humming around her. She paused when I spoke, like someone catching a sound just below hearing range. Tiny shift. Still a shift."

David's pulse kicked. "What does that mean?"

"It means she's changing," Samantha said. "The way you did after Marie. The way Eli did after his father. Nobody volunteers to be broken open, but once the shell cracks, you start noticing what was always there in the dark."

She paused, leaf tips catching the light. "And David, honey? The scholarship and Eileen aren't two unrelated storms. They're the same weather system. Both are questions about choosing growth over comfort. Same root system, different branches. You don't get to separate 'future' from 'heart' like they're planted in different soil."

The observation settled into David with uncomfortable accuracy.

David closed his eyes.

God, he prayed into the afternoon quiet, *help me see clearly. Help me choose growth rather than comfort. Help me trust that You're present in the uncertainty. And help me be honest about what I'm actually afraid of—not just the scholarship, but all the ways my life is expanding beyond what I can control.*

No immediate answer came. But as David looked toward the garden where rain-washed plants were already lifting toward sun breaking through clouds, his shoulders eased.

Not certainty. But willingness.

Willingness to consider that maybe the right choice wasn't either/or. Willingness to believe that roots could hold while branches reached. And willingness to tend what was developing with Eileen, though the timing was imperfect and the outcome uncertain.

The scholarship deadline was a week away. Plenty of time to keep praying. Keep paying attention. Keep working.

But for now, there was the garden to check. Damage to assess. Plants to encourage. The immediate work that anchored him when everything else was uncertain.

The daily practice of showing up that his mother had taught him was the foundation for every other kind of growth.

David moved toward the door, pausing to look at Samantha. "Thank you. For the wisdom about roots and branches."

"That's what I'm here for. Well, that and photosynthesis," Samantha said. "Forty-seven years in this sunroom will teach a plant a thing or two about patience. Marvin learned these lessons. Your mother did after him. Now it's your turn at the potting bench."

Her leaves tilted toward the thinning clouds. "Go tend your garden, David. The decisions will still be here when you come back—but you'll be different after you've had your hands in the soil."

The garden waited—patient and persistent. Marvin had tended these beds for forty years. Marie after him. Now David's turn.

The inheritance wasn't land. It was the practice of being present.

He went to meet it, his hands remembering the morning's work, his heart holding the weight of Eileen's trust, his mind still circling questions but his body knowing the answer.

For this moment, there was the work. The tending. The faith that presence mattered when outcomes remained uncertain.

Underground work that would support visible blooms when the time came.

Chapter Eleven

THE STORM

"Therefore I will not keep silent; I will speak out in the anguish of my spirit, I will complain in the bitterness of my soul." - Job 7:11

T HE AIR HAD BEEN wrong all day.

Awareness pressed against David's skin the moment he stepped outside at dawn to check the garden. The atmosphere hummed with tension, pressure building beneath the surface. The sky hung low and yellow-tinged—the stillness that came before serious weather.

Birds were absent from their usual posts in the oak tree. Insects moved sluggishly, their morning chorus reduced to uneasy silence.

It was three days until the scholarship deadline.

The acceptance letter sat on the kitchen table where it had been living for two weeks, accumulating coffee rings and margin notes, surrounded by lists that never seemed to help. David had read it so many times he'd memorized the formal language: *We are pleased to inform you... Marie Patterson Memorial Scholarship... commitment to community service...*

Marie Patterson's photograph stared up at him from the university brochure. Young. Bright-eyed. Full of plans.

Dead at nineteen.

Her dreams now funding someone else's future. The weight of it sat in David's chest like a stone—cold and heavy, making it hard to breathe deeply.

Fourteen weeks since his own mother had died. Long enough that other people had moved on. Not long enough that David had any idea how to.

He'd spent the morning trying to make coffee but mostly staring at the scholarship materials. Every time he thought he'd decided, doubt crept back in. Accept it, and maybe he was abandoning his mother's vision. Decline it, and maybe he was wasting the opportunity she'd always wanted for him.

The circular thinking was exhausting. His head ached with it.

"I don't know what to do," David said, the admission coming out rough. He'd barely slept, maybe two hours total, wrestling with the decision until his sheets were tangled and his mind more confused than when he'd begun. His eyes were gritty, his whole body heavy with exhaustion.

"What does your gut say, not your fear?" Samantha asked from her spot on the sunroom windowsill. "Instinct is usually closer to truth than the arguments you hold committee meetings for in your head."

"My gut says I'm tired." David poured coffee he didn't want, watching it steam in the increasingly humid air. His hands weren't quite steady. "Tired of decisions. Tired of trying to figure out what Mom would want versus what I want. Tired of every choice somehow betraying someone."

Through the window, the garden stretched in strange morning light. Tomato plants heavy with fruit. Bean poles he'd re-staked last week. The herb bed Marie had designed with such care.

But beneath her plantings were Marvin's beds: forty years of careful construction and soil amendment. The bones of the garden were his. Marie had added her vision to what he'd begun. Now David was learning to tend them both, two generations of careful work.

But was that enough? Was that what she'd wanted for him?

At seventeen, sitting at this same kitchen table, he'd told his mother he wanted to major in business. Explaining his plan to get an MBA, work for a consulting firm in Denver. Make good money. Build a stable career.

She'd gone quiet.

When he'd asked what was wrong, she'd said, "That sounds practical."

Not excited. Not proud. Just... practical.

He'd become defensive, asked what she'd expected him to do. She'd smiled then—sad and knowing—and said, "I expected you to choose work that feeds your soul, not just pays your bills. But you're young. You have time to figure out the difference."

He'd dismissed it then as her being overly idealistic, her hospice work making her value meaning over money. He'd ended up compromising—pursuing pre-med, meaningful work that could actually help people.

Now, staring at scholarship materials for a sustainable agriculture program, he wondered if she'd been waiting all along for him to realize what he'd known at ten years old when he'd spent every summer afternoon in Marvin's garden.

That growing mattered more to him than spreadsheets ever would.

Thunder rumbled in the distance—a low growl that seemed to come from deep underground. The vibration resonated through David's sternum, in his bones. The pressure in the air making it hard to breathe deeply.

His mother's Bible lay open on the counter, the Ecclesiastes passage about seasons and times, her handwriting in the margins asking questions he didn't have answers for.

The morning crawled forward with increasing tension. The sky darkened from yellow to a bruised purple-green that David had seen once before, during a tornado warning when he was ten. The air grew thick and humid, pressing against the windows like something trying to get in. His shirt stuck to his back. Every sound amplified: the creak of the house settling, the hum of the refrigerator, his own breathing too loud in the waiting quiet.

"David, honey, move me away from the window," Samantha said, her voice edged with an urgency he rarely heard. "And anything else that can turn into airborne shrapnel. This one's going to be bad—ugly wind shear, updrafts and downdrafts arguing with each other. The trees aren't going to like it."

He moved her to the kitchen table, his hands automatic while his mind circled the same useless thoughts. The scholarship materials were spread there, so he had to clear space, shoving papers aside with more force than necessary. Marie Patterson's photograph disappeared under a stack of notes.

A flash of guilt. Or anger. Or maybe just exhaustion.

By noon, the first drops of rain began.

Not a gentle summer shower but fat drops that hit the windows like thrown pebbles. Each one a small violence promising larger ones to come. The garden plants beginning to sway as wind picked up.

David's stomach clenched with dread. Or anxiety. Or both.

The rational approach would be to prepare. Bring in anything that could blow away. Secure what could be secured. Find flashlights and candles.

But instead he stood at the kitchen window watching clouds roll in like dark water. The atmospheric pressure building until his temples throbbed. His jaw ached from clenching.

"What am I supposed to do?" he asked, not expecting an answer. His voice cracked slightly. "Everyone has an opinion. Dad thinks I should go. Eileen thinks I can do both. Jeremy..." He stopped. Shook his head.

Jeremy wasn't here. Jeremy had run when things got hard.

The wind was picking up now, rattling the windows in their frames. Through the glass, the oak tree beginning to sway—its massive trunk bending in ways trees that old shouldn't bend. The same tree that had already dropped one branch on the house last month.

Rain came harder, drumming against the roof with increasing urgency. The sound was almost soothing at first, white noise that might drown out the anxious circling. But it kept intensifying, each wave louder than the last, until the house itself felt under assault.

Lightning flashed. Close enough that the white-hot light seared through David's closed eyelids.

Thunder followed immediately. No gap between flash and sound.

The storm was directly overhead. The sound rattled the windows, shook the floor beneath his feet.

The lights flickered. Once. Twice.

Went out.

In the sudden darkness, David stood at the kitchen window watching his mother's garden thrash under wind that moved with intention. That targeted everything Marie had planned.

The bean poles went first.

Toppling. Dominoes.

Marie's careful arrangement collapsing into tangled chaos.

The squash plants that had been thriving this morning were being flattened, their broad leaves torn and scattered across the mud.

Something inside David fractured.

Not gently. Not like a door opening.

Like a dam breaking. Like fourteen months of pressure finding the crack.

The levee gave way.

His hands started shaking. His whole body trembling with more than the temperature drop. His breath came in short gasps that didn't seem to bring in enough air.

He moved toward the back door before he'd consciously decided to move—driven by urgency more powerful than logic. He needed to be outside. Needed to be in the storm. Needed to stop being a passive observer of destruction.

"David, don't!" Samantha called after him.

But her voice was lost in thunder.

The rain hit him like a slap. Cold despite the summer heat, immediately soaking through his T-shirt and jeans. The wind was stronger than he'd realized, pushing against him with force that made walking difficult. Made breathing difficult.

But David kept moving toward the garden, his shoes sinking into mud that tried to claim them with each step.

The tomato plants were standing but barely, their stakes leaning at dangerous angles. Fruit being knocked off by wind and rain. Leaves shredding in the violence.

David grabbed the nearest stake, trying to drive it deeper into the soft mud. His hands slipping on wet wood. But the wind caught it and nearly pulled him off his feet.

He stumbled. Caught himself.

A splinter drove deep into his palm—sharp and burning.

He barely registered it.

He moved to the next plant. And the next. Hands slipping. Mud sucking at his shoes with each step. Rain streaming into his eyes, his mouth, choking him when he tried to breathe. Mixing with tears, he realized distantly.

He was crying. Great gasping sobs that the storm swallowed up as if they'd never existed.

"THIS ISN'T FAIR!"

The words tore out of him, carried away by wind the moment he spoke them. His voice already scraped raw.

"SHE DID EVERYTHING RIGHT! SHE PRAYED, SHE BELIEVED, SHE TRUSTED, AND YOU LET HER DIE ANYWAY!"

Lightning split the sky. So close the smell of ozone filled the air—sharp, metallic, burning. Electrical charge raised every hair on his body, standing them on end. The thunder was immediate and deafening, rattling through his bones, shaking his teeth.

Any sane person would seek shelter.

David kept working. Kept trying to save plants that were going to survive better without his help.

Another memory hit him—the photograph he'd found weeks ago showing his mother's face drawn with pain. Her body being destroyed from the inside while she maintained faith. The hospital bracelet. Jeremy's confession about witnessing her agony and running from it.

His father's absence. His father living somewhere else while Marie died. Unable to be present when David had needed him most.

The last coherent conversation he'd had with his mother surfaced—three days before she died. She'd been lucid that morning, a brief reprieve from the morphine fog.

He'd asked if she was scared.

She'd taken his hand with what little strength she had left.

"I'm not afraid of dying. I'm afraid of all the living I'll miss. Your wedding. Your children. The garden in ten years when the apple trees bear fruit."

Then she'd looked at him. Eyes that knew him completely.

"Promise me you won't waste time being afraid to love people because you might lose them."

A pause. Labored breathing.

"That's not living. That's dying slowly."

He'd promised. Throat too tight for words.

Standing in the storm now. Rain hammering down. Mud cold beneath his shoes.

Fear of accepting the scholarship. Fear of letting Eileen in. Fear of choosing a future that might fail.

He realized.

He'd been breaking that promise. Every single day since she died.

Choosing safety over growth. Protection over participation.

Dying slowly.

Exactly what she'd begged him not to do.

All of it flooded back with the force of the storm—drowning him more thoroughly than the rain. Sophie, seven years old, dead three days ago. Marie

Patterson, nineteen, studying ways to heal the earth. Mark, broken by random violence. His mother, who had spent eighteen months watching her body fail.

His father, who had loved Marie but couldn't watch her die. Who had been separated from her when she got sick. Who had stayed away because she'd asked him to. Because some people couldn't sit with suffering no matter how much they loved someone.

"I. DON'T. UNDERSTAND!"

David was crying harder now—sobs that tore through his throat, shook him to the core, threatened to crack him open from the inside.

"I don't understand WHY GOOD PEOPLE SUFFER and FAITH DOESN'T PROTECT ANYONE! Why she had to go through ALL THAT PAIN! WHY I HAD TO WATCH HER DISAPPEAR PIECE BY PIECE!"

The oak tree groaned—a sound that resonated through David's bones. Deep creaking that spoke of wood under stress. Roots struggling to hold.

He looked up as another lightning flash illuminated the massive tree bending like a sapling. Its branches reaching toward the sky, arms raised in supplication or surrender.

In that frozen moment of white light, a major branch began to crack. Separating from the trunk with the slow inevitability of disaster you can see coming but can't prevent.

Time stretched.

The branch fell.

Slow motion. Horrible certainty.

Then impact.

Glass shattering. Wood splintering. The crash swallowing thunder.

The world shattered.

David was running before the branch finished falling. Slipping in the mud, going down on his hands, pushing back up. Rainwater streaming into his eyes, blinding him.

The sunroom where Marie had kept her Bible study notes and her morning coffee routine was exposed now to wind and rain.

He reached the house and the damage spread before him through sheets of rain. The branch had punched through the sunroom windows. Glass everywhere. Rain pouring in, soaking the reading chair where Marie used to sit. The small table where she kept her Bible. The windowsill where Samantha had been this morning.

If he hadn't moved her...

The thought lodged behind his sternum like a blade wedged between ribs.

If he hadn't listened to Samantha, she would have been destroyed. The one living presence in this house besides him. The one connection to his mother that could speak.

"I TRIED!"

The words escaped him, standing in the ruined sunroom with rain pouring through the broken roof onto his head.

"I CAME BACK HERE AND LEARNED TO TEND HER GARDEN AND TRIED TO MAKE SENSE OF HER FAITH! BUT IT'S NOT ENOUGH! NOTHING'S ENOUGH! SHE'S GONE and I'M HERE and EVERYTHING I TOUCH GETS DESTROYED!"

Lightning struck somewhere close—the flash blinding, white light searing through his closed eyelids. The thunder simultaneous and so loud it seemed his skull might split. In that moment of white light and deafening sound, something essential inside him broke.

All the careful control he'd maintained since his mother's death. All the patient grief management. The trying to be strong for Robert. The learning to tend the garden properly. The reading of Marie's Bible and trying to understand.

All of it shattered like the sunroom glass.

He sank down onto the wet floor, his legs giving out. Rain streaming through the broken roof onto his head—cold and relentless. Glass crunching under his knees, sharp edges biting through his jeans.

He let himself feel the full weight of everything he'd been carrying.

The anger at God for allowing Marie's suffering. The guilt about not seeing her pain. The rage at Jeremy for abandoning him. The frustration with Robert—at his father's limitations, at the separation, at the way Robert showed up with scholarship papers as if they could build a bridge across years of absence. At the way some people loved through distance instead of presence.

The exhaustion of trying to decide about a scholarship funded by another dead girl's dreams.

All of it poured out in great gasping sobs that hurt, that shook him, that made it impossible to breathe properly. His whole body trembling from cold, from exhaustion, from release that had been held too tight for too long.

"I want her back," David whispered into the storm, the words barely audible even to himself. His voice destroyed. "I just want my mother back. I want to ask her what to do. I want to hear her laugh. I want to tell her I'm sorry for all the times I was too busy because I thought I had plenty of time."

The rain was cold now, the temperature dropping. David's hands were bleeding from splinters and possibly glass—dark blood mixing with rain and mud. His clothes soaked. His body shaking violently now with uncontrollable tremors that made his teeth chatter.

He should move. Should get out of the ruined sunroom before more of the tree fell. Should find shelter.

But first, he needed to finish this.

"I don't know how to do this without her," David said, his voice hoarse but steady now. Rough as gravel. "I don't know how to have faith when faith didn't save her. I don't know how to trust in plans I can't see when the plans I can see keep falling apart."

He looked around the sunroom. At the destroyed windows. The scattered glass catching what little light made it through the storm. The oak branch jutting through what used to be sanctuary. At the ceramic birds Marie had arranged so carefully—somehow mostly intact despite the chaos. At her Bible on the table, pages fluttering in the wind but present.

David took a breath. Raw. Ragged.

"But I'm going to try."

The words came from somewhere deeper than thought.

"I don't understand. I'm angry. I think it's unfair."

Another breath.

"But I'm going to keep going. I'm going to tend what's left and rebuild what broke and try to believe that any of it matters."

It wasn't prayer exactly. More negotiation. More honest admission that he was going to keep participating despite evidence that participation led to loss and pain.

The storm was easing—not dramatically, but noticeably. The wind shifting direction. The rain lessening from assault to merely heavy downpour. Thunder rumbled in the distance now, moving east.

David pushed himself up from the floor, his legs shaking and unsteady. Glass crunching under his palms, new cuts adding to the collection. He made his way back through the house, his body disconnected and heavy.

In the kitchen, Samantha sat on the table where he'd left her. Her pot somehow upright. Her leaves catching the dim light.

"You're alive," David said. Unexpected emotion welled up—fresh tears mixing with rain dripping from his hair. "I moved you just in time."

"I know, honey. I heard the impact—catastrophic limb failure, wood finally giving way under years of hidden stress," Samantha said, her voice gentle. "The sunroom?"

"Destroyed. Oak branch came through the windows." David grabbed a towel from the bathroom, his hands shaking too badly to grip it properly. He began trying to dry off though it was mostly pointless. "Everything's ruined."

"Everything's damaged," Samantha corrected. "That's not the same as ruined. Plants seal off wounds with callus tissue, reroute sap, keep growing around what broke. They don't pretend it didn't happen; they adapt. You can do that too."

David sank into the chair across from her, his body finally giving up. The scholarship materials scattered across the table. Marie Patterson's photograph visible again now, her bright eyes a reminder that other people had faced impossible choices and somehow kept moving forward.

"I don't have faith like Mom did," David said, his voice barely working. "I don't think I can believe the way she believed."

"Maybe you're not meant to have Marie's faith," Samantha said. "Maybe you're meant to have yours—the kind that makes room for anger and questions and still keeps planting when you can't see a single sprout. Think dormant seeds: all the real work happening in the dark where you can't monitor it, and you choose to water anyway."

The words settled. Not comfort exactly. But possibility.

"She had her own arguments with God," Samantha continued. "Especially near the end. Cancer burned off her polite theology. She raged, questioned, demanded answers she never got. But she kept watering me. Kept tending the beds. Kept showing up when it felt pointless."

Her leaves shifted in a small sigh. "I've watched three generations of Mills wrestle with faith from this spot. Forty-seven years teaches you something: same God, same garden, but you're all like perennials in different microclimates. Same species, different expression, depending on the conditions you grow through."

"What am I supposed to do?" David asked. This time the question was less desperate. More genuine. "About the scholarship. About all of it."

"Tonight? Dry off. Take stock. Rest," Samantha said, leaves rustling. "Tomorrow you can start the real work—like spring cleanup after a hard winter. You don't prune, replant, and rebuild the trellis all in one day. You pick what matters most and work your way down the row."

A sound from the front of the house made David look up.

Car doors slamming.

Footsteps running up the porch.

Pounding on the door.

"David! David, open up!"

Jeremy's voice. Familiar. Unexpected.

David opened the door.

Jeremy stood there. Soaked to the skin. His beat-up Honda visible in the driveway. His hair plastered to his head. His eyes wide with fear.

He'd driven through the storm.

"Thank God," Jeremy said and pulled David into a hug before David could protest. "I've been calling for an hour. Your phone went straight to voicemail and I saw the storm warnings and I just... I had to come back."

David stood there, too exhausted to return the hug but not pulling away. His body shaking. The anger in him shifted—not forgiveness exactly, but recognition. Jeremy had come back despite the fear.

Had driven through the storm.

"I'm okay," David said, his voice barely recognizable. "Mostly. The sunroom's destroyed and the garden's torn up and I had a screaming match with God. But I'm alive."

Jeremy pulled back, his eyes going wide taking in David's bleeding hands and soaked clothes and the exhaustion written across every angle. "You look terrible."

"I am terrible." David managed a laugh, though the sound came out hoarse. "Come inside."

They moved into the kitchen. Jeremy stopping to stare at Samantha.

"Is that... the plant you mentioned?"

David had told him three weeks ago over the phone. Sent a photo. Jeremy had responded with a gif of a talking cactus and the words "bro you need to sleep more."

But his eyes weren't laughing now.

"Her name is Samantha," David said. "And yes, she talks. You won't be able to hear her. So don't worry."

Jeremy looked between David and the plant, his expression somewhere between concern and acceptance. "Right. Sure. Talking plant. I'm going to accept that."

They sat at the kitchen table with emergency candles providing the light, listening to rain gentle into steady downpour. Jeremy didn't push for details. He sat there being present in a way he hadn't been able to be eight months ago.

The silence was comfortable—the sort that came from friends who didn't need words.

David's body registered all the damage. His hands throbbing. His knees aching. Every muscle trembling with exhaustion.

But there was also relief. As if pressure that had been building for months had finally been released.

"I came back to tell you," Jeremy said. "About why I left. About what I saw that day."

"I know why you left," David said, his voice rough but steady. "You saw her in pain and you couldn't handle it. So you ran."

Jeremy's eyes widened. "How did you—"

"You told me. On the phone. Two weeks ago." David paused. "I was furious about it. But then Dad told me something that... that made me understand better."

"Understand what?"

"That some people can't sit with suffering. No matter how much they love someone." David's hands pressed flat against the table. "My parents were separated. Before Mom got sick. She asked Dad to move out because he couldn't be emotionally present. And when she was dying, she wouldn't let him come back because she knew he'd shut down."

Jeremy sat quiet, processing.

"She released him," David continued, working through the thought as he spoke. "Let him love her through planning and providing instead of presence. Because that was what he could do. And I think... I think she did the same with you. She never took your absence personally because she understood that some people can't be there for the dying. That it doesn't mean they don't love you. Just means they have different limitations."

"That's..." Jeremy's voice cracked. "That's more generous than I deserve."

"Maybe. I don't know." David looked down at his bleeding hands. At the splinters he'd need to remove. "But being angry at you for running when my own father couldn't be there either... that was being angry at you for being human. For having limits."

"I should have tried," Jeremy said, his voice quiet but firm. "Your dad had his own history. But I was your best friend. I should have stayed."

"Yeah. You should have." David met his eyes. "But you're here now. You drove through a storm to make sure I was okay. That matters too."

They sat with that—the complexity of it. The way people could fail you and keep trying. Could love you badly but love you.

They talked for another hour. About Marie. About the separation David had only recently learned about. About Robert's limitations and Jeremy's fear. About the way love could be both insufficient and genuine. Both failing and trying.

By the time Jeremy settled in on the couch for the night, David sat with Samantha in the candlelight. His hands bleeding sluggishly, though the wounds looked worse than they were.

"How are you *actually* doing, not the version you'd put on a get-well card?" Samantha asked.

"Exhausted. Angry. Confused." David looked toward the ruined sunroom, barely visible in the darkness. "But also... I don't know. Maybe a little bit hopeful? That sounds crazy."

"Roots grow deeper in storms," Samantha said. "Wind stress forces trees to lay down denser wood—stronger taper, better balance next time it howls. You needed this break, ugly as it was. That rage you finally let out? That was love with nowhere to go, clawing its way into the open instead of rotting underground."

David nodded slowly.

"I think I'm going to accept the scholarship," he said, working through the thought as he spoke. "Not because I'm abandoning this place. But because maybe honoring Mom means growing beyond what she began. Building on the foundation instead of only maintaining it."

"That sounds like wisdom," Samantha said. "Also sounds like something you shouldn't carry alone. Talk to your father. Talk to Eileen. Even the healthiest vines need trellises, support structures that keep them from snapping under their own fruit."

David stood, every muscle protesting. "Tomorrow I'll call Robert. Reach out to Eileen. Listen to more of Jeremy's story. Begin the work of rebuilding."

He paused at the doorway, looking back at Samantha.

"Thank you. For warning me about the window. For being here."

"That's what I'm here for, honey. Well, that and photosynthesis," Samantha said. "You do the messy human feeling; I'll keep turning sunlight into metaphors."

Upstairs, David cleaned his hands as best he could, wrapped the worst cuts in gauze. Changed into dry clothes that felt like luxury against his cold skin. His body was one massive ache—muscles, bones, deeper structures all protesting.

But something had shifted.

The pressure that had been building for fourteen months—the rage, the questions, the paralysis—had found its way out. The storm had cracked him open and drained the infection.

God, he prayed into the quiet darkness, *I don't understand Your plans. I'm angry about Mom's suffering. But I'm going to try to trust that there's meaning in all this. Help me find my own way to have faith, even if it doesn't look like hers. Help me tend what matters and be honest when I don't understand.*

Outside, rain continued its patient work—washing away the violence, cleaning the garden, filling the soil with what would support new growth.

Tomorrow there would be damage to assess. Repairs to plan. Conversations to have.

Tonight, there was rest. And rain. And the slow beginning of healing.

INTERLUDE: THE ROOTS PRESS DEEP

The storms leave branches broken across the ground. To walk among them is to see what could not endure. Yet even here, life insists. Shoots press up through fallen leaves, as though defiance is written into their very design. Grief strips us down, but in the bare places, we learn what is truly strong.

"The Lord is close to the brokenhearted and saves those who are crushed in spirit." – Psalm 34:18
There is blessing in the breaking. Though the heart cracks, God does not step away, He steps closer. The blessing is not in the loss itself, but in the nearness of the One who holds us in it.

Scrawled on a scrap tucked into an old journal:
"Blessing doesn't mean nothing will break. It means you won't face the breaking alone."

Chapter Twelve

THE CLEANUP

"The Lord is my strength and my shield; my heart trusts in him, and he helps me." - Psalm 28:7

D AVID WOKE TO LIGHT that was scrubbed clean.

His neck screamed first—sharp, insistent pain from falling asleep at the kitchen table. For a disoriented moment he couldn't place anything: why Samantha sat on the table instead of her windowsill, why his hands were wrapped in gauze, why everything smelled like wet wood and ozone.

Then it came back. The storm. The rage. The oak branch that punched through the sunroom like God's fist. Jeremy arriving soaked and worried, staying through the worst of it.

The breaking that might have been dying but turned into a true release.

David stood, his body protesting every movement. Muscles stiff and joints aching, the soreness that came from violence your own body inflicted on itself. Through the kitchen doorway, Jeremy sprawled on the couch, one arm thrown over his eyes against the morning light.

His friend had stayed. Had driven through the storm despite his own fear. Had been there to witness that David survived his own honest anger.

The house was different in daylight. Wounded but standing. Damaged but not destroyed.

Through the window, the garden was already straightening. Plants that had been flattened by wind beginning to lift again—that relentless resilience of living things asserting itself.

"Morning, honey," Samantha said, her voice soft but steady—like a plant checking for structural damage after a storm. "How's your internal weather today?"

David filled the coffee maker, his hands clumsy with the gauze. "Exhausted. Raw." He paused, surprised by what came next. "But maybe lighter? Like pressure that needed to break finally broke."

"That's exactly what happened," Samantha said, her leaves catching the morning light the way a plant checks for safe conditions after stress. "You've been trying to hold yourself together with emotional duct tape. Last night you let the storm do its work. Wind stress isn't punishment—it's how trees learn where they're weak and how to reinforce. If I'd been sheltered from every gust for forty-seven years, I'd snap at the first stiff breeze. You're finally learning not to manufacture brittleness."

David settled into the chair across from her, coffee mug warming his bandaged hands. The heat was good. Real. "Mom used to do that, didn't she? Get angry. Demand answers."

"Especially toward the end," Samantha said, her voice taking on the grounded weight of lived observation rather than sentiment. "Disease strips off the ornamental foliage. Your mother dropped the polite prayers and went straight to root-level honesty—full volume debates with God about fairness, suffering, and the ridiculousness of pain distribution. She never pretended the weather was sunny when it was clearly a hurricane."

The information settled into David with unexpected comfort. "What did she conclude?"

"Not much. That's not how any of this works," Samantha said, leaves shifting in a way that suggested practicality rather than mystique. "Think of transpiration—plants release water because living things can't seal themselves off without dying. You can't opt out of emotional weather, but you can pay attention to what the storm exposes. Sometimes rain reveals nutrient pathways. Sometimes it exposes rot. Both matter for growth."

David's throat tightened. "Did you just compare my breakdown to good conditions for nutrient uptake?"

"I compared grief to weather because that's what it is," Samantha said, her leaves rustling in pragmatic approval. "You finally stopped hiding under the eaves and let yourself get drenched. And guess what? You're still here. The house is wounded but intact. You're upright. The garden's already lifting its leaves again. Survival looks like this—not tidy, but functional."

Jeremy groaned from the couch, sitting up slowly. His hair stuck up in all directions, face creased from the cushions. "Is that coffee I smell?"

"Coming right up." David was grateful for the shift to practical concerns. "How'd you sleep?"

"Like someone who drove through a thunderstorm having an existential crisis." Jeremy shuffled into the kitchen, squinting against the light. "But I'm alive. So that's worth noting."

They stood together at the window, coffee mugs warming their hands, surveying the damage in full daylight.

The sunroom was worse than David had realized. The oak branch had taken out most of the roof along with the windows, leaving the space exposed to sky and weather. Glass littered the floor in glittering fragments. Rain had soaked Marie's reading chair, warping the small table where she'd kept her Bible.

But the ceramic birds were mostly intact. And the Bible itself, though its pages were damp and wrinkled, had survived under a piece of fallen beam that had protected it from the worst of the rain.

"That's going to be expensive to fix," Jeremy observed.

"Yeah." David thought about the scholarship funds, about how accepting it would mean having resources for exactly this kind of emergency. "But it's fixable. That's what matters."

The sound of a truck in the driveway drew their attention.

Robert climbed out. Wearing work clothes. Carrying a toolbox that had seen decades of use.

He'd come.

Not with lectures. Not with advice.

With tools and the willingness to work.

He surveyed the damage with the assessing eye of someone who'd spent his career evaluating structural problems, then headed toward the back door with a purposeful stride.

David's stomach tightened. After everything that had been said—the confrontation about absence, the revelation about the separation, the anger David had let himself express—what was his father thinking?

"Morning," Robert said as David opened the door. No preamble. No awkwardness. Just: "Figured you could use some help. Brought basic supplies: tarps, plywood, tools for temporary repairs until we can get proper materials."

"Thanks, Dad." David's throat was tight. "How did you know?"

"Mara called. Said the oak branch came down. Asked if I was planning to help." A pause, an expression that might have been a smile. "Seemed like a reasonable question."

His eyes went to David's bandaged hands. "You hurt?"

"Splinters mostly. Some cuts. Nothing serious."

"Good. Keep those clean. Wood splinters can get infected." Robert noticed Jeremy for the first time. "Jeremy Chen. Haven't seen you in a while."

"Mr. Mills." Jeremy straightened automatically. "I came back last night when I couldn't reach David during the storm."

Something passed across Robert's face: approval, maybe. Recognition that Jeremy had done what Robert himself would have wanted to do if he'd known.

"Good. That's what friends do."

David remembered another storm. Years ago.

He'd been maybe eleven. Home alone when tornado sirens went off. His mother was at the hospital with a patient. His father supposedly working late at the office.

David had called Robert's cell over and over. Terrified. Huddled in the basement while the house shook.

Robert arrived forty minutes later. After the danger passed.

David saw it immediately.

Golf clubs in the truck bed. Damp from afternoon rain.

Not a meeting. A golf game.

Marie had been furious when she got home and heard, not screaming angry, but cold angry, disappointed and angry. She'd told Robert that being unreachable during emergencies was a choice, not an accident. That David deserved better.

Robert had defended himself, said David was fine, that Marie was overreacting.

Now, watching his father approve of Jeremy driving through a storm to check on a friend, David wondered if Robert had been thinking about that day.

If this morning's appearance with tools was Robert trying to be the person he hadn't been capable of being then.

They stood in the kitchen for a moment, the silence less awkward than David would have expected but carrying weight. The careful way his father was holding himself. The deliberate neutrality of his expression.

Then Robert cleared his throat. "Let's assess the damage properly before we start repairs. Need to know what we're dealing with—structural versus cosmetic, immediate dangers versus things that can wait."

They spent the next hour surveying the house together.

Robert moved through the damaged sunroom with practiced efficiency, pointing out details David wouldn't have noticed on his own. "See that?" He indicated a crack in the ceiling. "That's not cosmetic. The branch shifted a support beam. We'll need to address that before we do anything else."

David followed, trying to see what his father saw, trying to understand the difference between surface damage and structural problem.

"Here." Robert handed him a flashlight. "Look where the water came in. See how the drywall's soft there? That's going to need replacing before mold becomes an issue."

They worked their way through each room systematically. Robert explaining, David learning. The physical work created space for conversation that was easier than sitting across a table trying to talk about emotions.

When they stood in the ruined sunroom, glass crunching under their boots, Robert paused.

"It looks worse than it is." His voice was steady, certain. "Frame's solid. Foundation's sound. Mostly we're addressing weather exposure and cosmetic destruction. We can stabilize it today, protect it from further damage. Then do the proper repairs once insurance clears and materials arrive."

Relief washed through David so profound it weakened his knees. The house could be saved. His mother's sanctuary could be rebuilt.

Just painful. Not permanent.

"Where do we start?" David asked.

Robert handed him a pair of work gloves. "Safety first. Then we clear debris. Stabilize anything unstable. Build temporary weather protection." He paused, studying David's face with unusual attention. "But first. How are you? Really?"

The question caught David off guard. His father rarely asked about emotional states, preferred to address problems he could fix with tools and materials.

But there was genuine concern in Robert's eyes, the paternal care that sometimes got buried under practical solutions but never fully disappeared.

"I'm okay." David pulled on the work gloves, grateful for the excuse to look away. "Or I will be. Last night was hard. But maybe... necessary?"

Robert was quiet for a moment. When he spoke, his voice carried weight. "Your mother used to have her own storms. Especially after her diagnosis. She'd rage at the unfairness, demand answers from God, question everything she'd believed about divine goodness."

David looked up, surprised.

"But she always came out the other side choosing faith," Robert continued. "When faith was the harder option." He picked up a broom, began sweeping glass into careful piles. "I didn't understand it then—how she could be so angry and still trust. But now I think maybe that was her faith. The willingness to keep showing up when she was furious. To keep asking questions when there weren't good answers."

They worked in companionable silence for a while, clearing debris, assessing damage. Jeremy helped where he could, though he had less experience with repair work and mostly followed their directions.

Robert guided David through installing the temporary roofing. "See how we're overlapping the edges? That's what keeps water from getting in. You want at least a three-inch overlap."

David focused on understanding not just what to do, but why. On learning the logic that made the work effective instead of just following instructions.

"Hand me that hammer," Robert said. Then, as David passed it over: "Your grandfather taught me all this. Marvin. He believed a man should be able to fix what was his. Solve problems with his hands instead of his wallet."

"Did you work on this house together?"

"Every summer when I was growing up." Robert secured a nail with three efficient strikes. "He'd find projects that needed doing, then make me do most of the work while he supervised. Drove me crazy at the time. But looking back..." He paused. "He was teaching me. Making sure I'd have the skills I'd need."

The observation settled over David: the months he'd spent learning to garden, fumbling his way through tasks that had been easy when Marie did them.

This was similar. Learning competence through mistakes. Building capability through patient practice.

The afternoon sun was brutal. David's shirt was soaked through with sweat, sticking to his back. Sawdust coated his arms, mixing with perspiration to create a gritty paste. His hands throbbed inside the work gloves, the splinters from last night making themselves known with every movement.

But he kept working.

Robert had moved into teaching mode, that patient instructor voice David remembered from childhood projects. "You want to drive the nail at a slight angle here. See? That gives it more holding power."

David positioned the nail. Raised the hammer. The first strike was tentative.

"Commit to it," Robert said. "Hesitating makes you more likely to miss."

The second strike was better. The third sank the nail home.

"Good. Now the next one."

They worked their way across the temporary roofing, securing each sheet with methodical care. The rhythm became almost meditative: position, strike, check, move on. David's muscles remembered this from childhood, those summer projects when his father would conscript him for home improvement tasks.

Back then, he'd resented it. The heat. The tedium. The way Robert never seemed satisfied until everything was perfect.

But now, with his mother gone and the house damaged and his whole life uncertain, there was comfort in the simple clarity of this work. Do the task correctly. Build something that would last. Create order from chaos through patient attention and proper tools.

"You're getting it," Robert said as they stepped back to assess their progress. His voice carried approval that was earned rather than automatic. "Your grandfather would be proud."

The praise hit harder than David expected—partly because it was deserved, partly because it came from someone whose approval he'd been seeking through the wrong means for too long.

Around noon, the sound of bicycle wheels announced Eli's arrival. Mara walked beside him, carrying a basket that smelled like fresh bread and something savory.

"Thought you might need lunch," Mara said, setting the basket on the porch. "And we wanted to check on you. The whole neighborhood's been worried since the storm."

"We're okay." David was grateful for the concern. "House took some damage, but nothing that can't be fixed."

Eli had already moved toward the kitchen window where Samantha was visible on the table. "Hi, Samantha," he said with the easy familiarity of someone who'd been having these conversations for months.

David caught Jeremy's confused expression; his friend couldn't hear Samantha's response to Eli's greeting. All he saw was a boy talking to a houseplant with genuine attention.

"Eli can hear her too," David explained. "Since his dad died."

Jeremy's expression shifted: not quite envy, not quite longing. Something between. "I wish I could hear her."

"Maybe the wisdom we can't hear isn't the wisdom we need right now," David said.

They ate lunch on the porch, the five of them sitting in various states of exhaustion and sawdust, sharing food and easy conversation. Mara asked questions about the repair timeline, offering connections to contractors she knew. Eli reported on the garden's condition, having already assessed every plant's recovery status.

"They're gonna be okay," Eli said simply. "Already straightening up. Lost some leaves, but those grow back. Roots held. That's what matters."

The observation was metaphorical in ways Eli probably didn't intend. David caught Robert nodding, recognizing the parallel.

After lunch, Mara and Eli left, but not before Mara mentioned that several neighbors had asked about David, wanted to know if he needed anything, and were ready to help if called upon.

"Your mother built relationships here," Mara said. "Twenty years as a home health nurse taught her how to show up for people at their most vulnerable. People remember that care. They want to return it."

By late afternoon, they'd accomplished more than David had thought possible. The sunroom was sealed against the weather. The structural damage was stabilized. The immediate crisis contained.

The house stood wounded—the plywood sheets stark against the original siding, the temporary repairs obvious. But it was no longer vulnerable.

"Good work," Robert said as they cleaned tools and organized materials. "You handled yourself well today. Asked good questions. Worked safely. Paid attention."

He paused, meeting David's eyes.

"I'm proud of you. For choosing to stay. For accepting the scholarship. For finding your own way to honor your mother while building your own life."

The words landed with unexpected weight: not because they were perfect, but because they were real. Because his father had shown up. Had been honest about his failures. Had offered what he could give.

Jeremy had been quiet most of the afternoon, helping where he could but processing his own thoughts. Now, as they finished cleaning up, he caught David's attention.

"I need to tell you," he said, his voice carrying weight. "About why I left. About what I saw that day."

"We talked about some of it last night," David said. "Remember?"

"I remember. But there's more. Details I need to say out loud." Jeremy's expression was complicated. "Not just for you. For me too."

"Okay. But maybe after dinner? I don't think I can handle heavy conversations on an empty stomach."

"Fair enough." Relief crossed Jeremy's face at the postponement.

Robert gathered his tools as the sun began its slow descent. "I'll come back next weekend with proper materials. We'll start the real repairs then." He paused. "But David? What you said earlier, about needing help. That's not weakness. That's wisdom."

After his father left, David stood on the porch watching evening light paint the garden in shades of amber and gold. Plants that had been battered were already recovering, leaves turning toward the sun, the whole ecosystem demonstrating that damage wasn't the end of the story.

Jeremy headed inside to prepare dinner, giving David a moment alone with his thoughts.

But he wasn't entirely alone. Through the window, Samantha on the kitchen table, her leaves catching the last light of day.

He went inside to find Jeremy attempting to navigate Marie's kitchen with cautious respect. "I'm making spaghetti," Jeremy announced. "It's basically the only thing I know how to cook that doesn't involve a microwave."

"Spaghetti sounds perfect."

They ate dinner with easy conversation, Jeremy sharing stories about his time in Portland—how he'd accidentally locked himself out of his studio wearing paint-splattered boxers and had to climb through a window while his elderly landlady called the police.

"So there I am," Jeremy said, halfway through the window, gesturing with his fork, "explaining to Officer Martinez that yes, this is my studio, no, I don't have ID because my pants are inside, and yes, I realize how this looks."

"What did you say?" David asked.

"I told him the one thing I could think of: 'Look, if I was breaking in, would I be wearing boxers with cartoon tacos on them?'" Jeremy shook his head. "He made me wait outside while he checked with my landlady. In my underwear. In February."

The image was so ridiculous—Jeremy's indignant face, the absurdity of the taco boxers, the stoic police officer trying to maintain professional composure—that something broke loose in David's chest.

A sound erupted. Sudden. Sharp. Surprising him with its force.

Laughter.

Real laughter. The first since Marie died.

It burst out before he could control it—shoulders shaking, breath catching, building in waves. The kind of laughter that made his stomach hurt and his face ache. It kept coming, each wave building on the last, fueled by months of pressure finding sudden release.

Jeremy grinned, pleased with himself. "Thank you. I'll be here all week."

But David couldn't stop. The laughter continued until tears formed at the corners of his eyes and he had to set down his fork because his hands were shaking.

When it finally subsided, leaving him breathless and dizzy, David wiped his eyes with the back of his hand.

The room was different. Lighter somehow. Like a window had been opened in a space that had been sealed too long.

"God," David said, his voice rough. "I haven't—"

He stopped. Swallowed.

"I don't think I've laughed like that since before Mom died."

The admission hung between them.

Significant. Heavy and light at once.

Jeremy's expression softened. "It's good to hear. I was starting to worry you'd forgotten how."

From the sunroom, Samantha's voice drifted in: "Your mother would have celebrated that laugh," Samantha said. "She worried your emotional soil would compact so tightly after she died that joy wouldn't be able to push through."

David glanced toward the window, something in his chest tightening and releasing at the same time. "She used to worry about that, didn't she?"

"During those last weeks," Samantha said, her tone gentler but still rooted in observation, "when she could barely stand but insisted on watering me anyway, she talked about you. Not in sweeping, dramatic terms—practical ones. Whether you'd let anyone feed you a vegetable. Whether you'd allow help without arguing. But her biggest worry was that grief would calcify around you and choke out your capacity for joy."

David sat with that—his mother's final worries hadn't been about his success or his faith or his ability to maintain the house. They'd been about his capacity for happiness. His willingness to remain open to lightness even while carrying weight.

"She made me promise to remind you of something."

Samantha's voice carried weight.

"Joy isn't disrespectful to grief. You can miss someone and still find reasons to smile. Like how plants can grow and go dormant simultaneously in different tissues—active growth in one area, rest in another. Different processes, same organism."

Jeremy's attention stayed on David with quiet awareness, sensing a shift but not interrupting.

"I thought laughing would mean I was moving on," David said, his voice rough. "Like it would somehow diminish how much I loved her."

"That's not how love works, honey," Samantha said. "Joy doesn't shrink grief; it aerates it. Gives it oxygen so it doesn't turn anaerobic and toxic. Your mother hoped you'd understand that before you compacted yourself into emotional hardpan."

David picked up his fork again. The spaghetti had gone cold, but he didn't care. Something had shifted—not healed exactly, but opened. Like the first crack in frozen ground that meant spring was possible.

"Thanks," he said to Jeremy. "For the taco boxers story."

"Anytime, man." Jeremy's grin was genuine. "I've got plenty more where that came from. Three years of Portland disasters at your service."

They finished dinner with lighter conversation—David recounting moments from the day's repair work, Jeremy sharing more Portland absurdities. Grief present but not dominating. Loss acknowledged but not consuming.

After Jeremy headed to the couch, promising to tackle his full confession tomorrow, David sat alone with Samantha in the kitchen, darkness settling over the garden outside.

"Thank you," David said. "For keeping your promise to her."

"Don't thank me yet—I'm barely through the first pruning pass," Samantha said with affectionate exasperation. "Your sense of humor is still undernourished. But the fact that you're casually discussing your mother's parenting strategy with a houseplant and treating it as normal? That's promising. Means the soil's loosening."

David smiled into the darkness—not laughter this time, but something quieter. More sustainable. The beginning of remembering that grief and joy didn't have to be enemies.

That he could carry his mother's loss and still make room for taco boxers and ridiculous stories and the small mercies of friendship.

Upstairs, David cleaned his hands as best he could, wrapped the worst cuts in fresh gauze. Changed into dry clothes that felt like luxury against his skin. His body was one massive ache—muscles, bones, deeper structures all protesting.

But something had shifted. The pressure that had been building since her death had found its way out. The storm had cracked him open and drained the infection.

Before sleep took him, David whispered into the darkness:

"God, I don't know what I'm doing. But I think I'm beginning to understand what Mom meant—about faith being practice, about showing up even when you don't have answers. Help me hold both. The grief and the laughter. The missing her and the moving forward."

No formal closing. Just the quiet settling of honest words into the night.

Outside, the garden continued its patient work—growing in darkness the way it always had, roots deepening, cells dividing, the whole system preparing for morning without needing permission or certainty.

Tomorrow there would be Jeremy's confession to hear. More conversations about the scholarship. The ongoing work of figuring out how to live in a house haunted by love instead of loss.

But tonight, David fell asleep with splinters in his hands and something that might have been hope taking root in soil that had been broken open by necessary storms.

Chapter Thirteen

LEARNING EACH OTHER

"Where you go I will go, and where you stay I will stay. Your people will be my people and your God my God." - Ruth 1:16

THE MORNING ARRIVED WITH the soft light that came after rain, everything scrubbed clean and glowing. David woke to birdsong—actual birdsong, not the anxious quiet that had characterized June—and lay still for a moment, recognizing the shift.

Something had loosened in him since Jeremy's confession. Not resolution, exactly. But the anger that had been sitting like a stone in his chest had shifted, made room for something else. Breathing came easier.

His phone buzzed on the nightstand. A text from Eileen: *Farmer's market today? Need produce for Thursday gathering. Could use company if you're free.*

David smiled before he'd consciously decided to. His fingers moved across the screen: *Pick you up at 9?*

Her response came immediately: *Perfect. Bring appetite. Breakfast after.*

The farmer's market occupied the church parking lot every Saturday through September, transforming asphalt into temporary abundance. By nine-thirty, David and Eileen were navigating between vendor stalls, canvas bags slung over their shoulders, the morning sun warm but not yet oppressive.

"Your mother used to come here every week," Eileen said, stopping at a table piled high with heirloom tomatoes. Each fruit a different size and shape, some striped, some deep purple, some split from too much rain. "She'd spend twenty minutes talking to each vendor. Drove your grandfather crazy—he just wanted to buy vegetables and leave."

David could picture it perfectly. Marie asking questions, learning names, building relationships one conversation at a time.

"Marvin was efficient," David said. "Mom was thorough."

"She was interested," Eileen corrected, selecting a Cherokee Purple and holding it up to examine. "There's a difference. She wanted to know who grew her food, how they grew it, what challenges they were facing."

The vendor—a woman in her sixties with soil permanently embedded under her fingernails—looked up and smiled with recognition. "You're Marie's boy."

David's throat tightened. "I am."

"She talked about you constantly. Showed me pictures on her phone." The woman's expression softened. "I'm so sorry. She was one of the good ones."

"Thank you," David managed.

The woman began selecting tomatoes with practiced hands, choosing varieties David hadn't asked for but somehow knew he needed. "These are for you. No charge. Your mother helped my daughter when she was going through treatment at the hospital—came to the house on her day off, sat with her, just... was there. I never got to thank her properly."

She pressed the bag of tomatoes into David's hands, her eyes bright with tears she wasn't quite letting fall.

"She would have said you just did," Eileen said softly.

They moved on, David carrying tomatoes he hadn't paid for and a fresh understanding of how many lives his mother had touched in ways he'd never know about.

"Does that happen often?" he asked. "People telling you stories about her?"

"All the time," Eileen said. "She was everywhere in this town. Like mycorrhizal networks in a forest—you couldn't see the connections, but they were there, feeding everything."

Samantha would have loved that comparison—roots talking to roots, invisible support systems holding entire ecosystems together. Exactly her kind of sermon.

They worked their way through the market, filling bags with late-season produce, talking about nothing important. Eileen negotiated with vendors in a way David never could—warm but direct, asking questions that weren't intrusive but showed genuine interest. She made people light up just by paying attention.

David found himself watching her more than the vegetables. The way she touched produce before buying it, testing firmness with fingers that knew what they were feeling for. The way she laughed when the herb vendor made a terrible pun about thyme. The way she caught his eye across the stall and smiled like they were sharing a secret.

"What?" she asked, noticing his attention.

"Nothing. You're good at this."

"At shopping?"

"At people. You make them feel seen."

Eileen's expression shifted—pleasure mixed with something more complicated. "Your mother taught me that. She used to say that most people go through entire days without anyone really looking at them. Really seeing them. That a few seconds of genuine attention was sometimes the most valuable thing you could give."

"And you do that. Naturally."

"So do you," Eileen said. "You just don't realize it. The way you listen to Eli. How you are with Samantha. Even with Jeremy—you could have shut him out completely, but you're trying to leave room for him to show up better."

David wasn't sure that was true, but the way Eileen said it made him want to become the person she thought he was.

They finished shopping and loaded everything into David's truck—the one that had been Marvin's, that still smelled faintly of soil and old coffee. Eileen climbed into the passenger seat with the ease of someone who'd ridden there before, and David realized she had. Multiple trips to get garden supplies, trips to the hardware store, the comfortable rhythm of working together that had developed over weeks without him noticing.

"Diner?" Eileen suggested. "I promised you breakfast and I'm starving."

"Diner," David agreed.

The Bluebird Diner occupied a building that had been serving breakfast since before David was born. Vinyl booths, laminate tables, a jukebox in the corner that only played songs from the 1950s. The kind of place that served coffee in thick ceramic mugs and didn't judge if you ordered pie at nine in the morning.

They slid into a booth by the window, menus already in hand though David knew what he'd order—same thing his grandfather had always gotten. Blueberry pancakes. Bacon. Orange juice.

"You don't even need to look at that," Eileen observed, watching him set the menu aside immediately.

"Creature of habit."

"Or you know what you like." She studied her menu with the same careful attention she'd given the tomatoes. "I can never decide. Everything sounds good, and then I spend the whole meal wondering if I should have ordered something else."

"So order two things."

"That seems excessive."

"Or practical. Life's too short for breakfast regret."

Eileen laughed—full and genuine, the sound surprising other diners into smiling. "Okay. Breakfast philosopher. I'll get French toast and a waffle. You're responsible for the consequences."

The waitress appeared—Donna, who'd been working here since Marvin first brought David as a child. She looked at David with the warm recognition of someone who'd watched him grow up and filled his coffee without asking.

"Marie's boy," she said, echoing the tomato vendor's greeting.

"That's me."

"She sat in this exact booth three days before she died," Donna said, her voice matter-of-fact but not unkind. "Had blueberry pancakes. Said they were the best thing she'd tasted in months."

David's chest constricted.

"She was happy that day," Donna continued. "Talking about the garden, about you finishing school, about all the things she was grateful for. Not everyone gets that—to know they're dying and still find things to be grateful for. That takes something special."

She squeezed David's shoulder once, brief but firm, then took their order and disappeared.

"I don't know if I'll ever get used to that," David said after a moment. "People just... telling me things about her final days. Like I should know. Like I was there."

Eileen's expression softened.

"You were there. Just not for every moment. No one can be present for every moment, even when someone's dying. She had a whole life happening around you—conversations with vendors, meals at diners, moments of gratitude you didn't witness. That doesn't mean you weren't important. It means she was fully alive right up until she wasn't."

David turned this over, finding truth in it. He'd been operating under the assumption that he should have known everything, witnessed everything, been present for every significant moment. But Marie had kept living when he wasn't there. Having experiences. Making peace. Finding gratitude.

"How did you get so wise?" he asked.

"Watching people die for a living," Eileen said without self-pity. "You learn what matters and what doesn't pretty quickly. The small moments matter more than the grand gestures. The Tuesday afternoon pancakes matter as much as the deathbed declarations."

Their food arrived—David's familiar order, Eileen's experiment with both French toast and a waffle. She looked at the plates with something between delight and dismay.

"This is too much food."

"Share with me."

"You already ordered."

"So? Variety is the spice of life. Give me a bite of French toast, I'll give you bacon."

They fell into easy negotiation, trading food across the table with the unselfconscious intimacy of people comfortable together. David discovered that Eileen was meticulous about her syrup distribution—precise lines across the waffle, never pooling. That she ate French toast from the outside in, saving the middle for last. That she stole bacon from his plate when she thought he wasn't looking.

"I saw that," he said.

"No you didn't."

"You're literally holding my bacon right now."

Eileen grinned—unrepentant. "Possession is nine-tenths of the law."

"That's not how bacon works."

"It is now."

David found himself laughing, the sound surprising him with its ease. When had laughter become easy again? He couldn't pinpoint the exact moment, just knew that sometime between June and now, grief had shifted enough to make room for joy without feeling like betrayal.

"You're doing that thing," Eileen observed.

"What thing?"

"That thing where you're surprised to be happy. Like you caught yourself feeling good and now you're analyzing whether you're allowed."

David set down his fork. "How do you do that?"

"Do what?"

"See me that clearly."

Eileen's expression gentled. "I do it too. Every time I laugh at work, there's this split second where I think 'Sophie died two weeks ago, should I be laughing?' Then I remember what your mother told me, that grief and joy aren't opposites. They can coexist."

"She told me the same thing. Multiple times. I'm just starting to believe it."

"That's growth," Eileen said. "Believing what we know intellectually takes longer than learning it."

They finished breakfast, lingering over coffee refills, watching morning traffic pick up on Main Street. The conversation wandered—books they'd read, places they wanted to travel someday, Eileen's tentative plans for her transfer to family support, David's scholarship timeline. Easy talk that revealed preferences and quirks and the small details that made someone knowable.

David learned that Eileen was terrible at remembering song lyrics but sang anyway. That she'd wanted to be a veterinarian until she realized she couldn't handle putting animals down. That she collected rocks from meaningful places and kept them in a jar on her dresser. That she'd once accidentally called a patient's family member by the wrong name and been mortified for weeks.

Eileen learned that David could recite the entire opening paragraph of *The Lord of the Rings* from memory. That he'd been afraid of dogs until he was twelve. That he still slept with the quilt his grandmother had made before she died. That he'd considered dropping out of college three separate times but never told anyone.

Small truths that added up to understanding.

"Walk?" Eileen suggested when they left the diner, both overfull and content.

They walked Main Street without destination, past the bookstore where Marie had bought David's graduation present three weeks before she died, past the pharmacy where she'd filled prescriptions that couldn't save her, past the library where she'd volunteered reading to children every Tuesday afternoon for fifteen years.

The town was full of her ghosts. But walking with Eileen, David found they weren't haunting him. They were just... present. Like memories that didn't hurt to touch.

"Can I ask you something?" Eileen said as they turned down a side street lined with old maples.

"Always."

"Why me?"

David stopped walking.

"What?"

Eileen's expression was vulnerable in a way he rarely saw. "Why me? You could be with someone who's actually here. I'm two hours away most of the time, I work impossible hours, I'm..." She trailed off, hands opening and closing like she was trying to catch the right words.

"You're not—" David started, then stopped. "Okay, you're busy. But so am I. I'm grieving my mother while trying to figure out my entire life, I live in my dead grandfather's house and talk to a plant, I'm terrified of making decisions and making the wrong decisions in equal measure. We're both figuring it out."

"That's not an answer."

David took a breath, trying to find words for what he'd been feeling without quite naming. "Most people need me to be okay. They're uncomfortable when I don't have answers. But you're..." He paused. "You're okay with the mess."

Eileen waited, not filling the silence.

"And you're brilliant at what you do," David continued. "The way you talk about nursing—it's not just a job. You see suffering and you don't turn away. You sit with it. You make space for people to be exactly as broken as they are."

He paused, watching Eileen's face.

"That's extraordinary."

Eileen's eyes were bright.

"You see me that way?"

"How could I not?"

She kissed him.

Right there on the sidewalk under maple trees that had watched Marvin court his wife sixty years ago, that had shaded Marie's childhood, that would probably stand long after David was gone.

The kiss tasted like maple syrup and coffee and the particular sweetness of finding someone who made being yourself feel like enough.

When they separated, both breathing harder, Eileen rested her forehead against his.

"That was nice," she said, her voice soft.

"Yeah," David agreed.

They stood like that for a moment, neither quite ready to move. The maples rustled overhead, dappling them in shifting patterns of light and shadow. Somewhere down the street, a dog barked. A car passed. The world continued its ordinary business while David's heart hammered against his ribs with the understanding that something had shifted.

"We should probably..." Eileen nodded toward where they'd parked.

"Yeah."

But neither of them moved immediately.

"Can I ask you something?" David said.

"Always."

"Are you scared?"

Eileen pulled back enough to meet his eyes. "Of what?"

"This. Whatever this is becoming."

She was quiet for a moment.

"A little. Every time I've cared about someone, I've eventually watched them leave. My brother. Sophie. Your mom." She paused. "But I'm more scared of not trying than I am of being hurt again."

"That's brave."

"Or stubborn." Eileen smiled. "Your mom would say there's not much difference."

They walked back toward David's truck hand in hand, neither of them rushing. The comfortable silence that came from not needing to fill every moment with words. At the corner, they passed Mrs. Chen's garden—the one she'd been building since her husband died. New plantings visible among the established beds. Growth and memorial existing side by side.

"Your mom used to say that about gardens," Eileen said, noticing where David's attention had gone. "That they're never finished. Always becoming something new while carrying forward what came before."

"Sounds like her."

"She was good at that. Seeing how things connected. How the past didn't have to trap you. How you could honor what came before while building something different."

They reached the truck and stood beside it, neither quite ready to leave this moment behind. The farmer's market was mostly packed up now, only a few vendors left loading crates into trucks. The temporary abundance dispersing back into the regular world, leaving only memory and the promise of next week.

"I should probably mention something," Eileen said, leaning against the truck door. "About what I said before. About being two hours away."

"Okay."

"I'm moving back after graduation. Permanently."

She met his eyes.

"I've been looking at positions at the hospital. Family support nursing, like I mentioned."

David's chest tightened with something he was afraid to name yet.

"And I've been thinking about what you said weeks ago," Eileen continued. "About the garden becoming something that serves more than just you. About creating space for people dealing with impossible things."

"The therapeutic program," David said.

"Yeah." Eileen's expression intensified. "I want to build that with you. Not help you build it—build it together."

She held his gaze.

"My nursing background, your gift for tending, the space you have. We could create something real."

David felt the weight and possibility of what she was offering. Not just relationship. Partnership. Shared calling. The kind of collaboration that could sustain both of them while serving something larger.

"We should talk about this more," he said. "Map it out. Figure out what it could actually look like."

"Coffee shop meeting?" Eileen suggested. "Next week? We could bring Maya in—she might have ideas."

"Next week," David agreed.

They stood together in the late-morning sun, the conversation having shifted from ordinary to significant without losing its ease. The partnership taking shape between them felt right—not rushed, but natural. Like seeds germinating in darkness, doing their patient work before breaking through into light.

David drove Eileen back to her apartment with the windows down, warm air streaming through, the radio playing something neither of them was really listening to. Comfortable silence punctuated by occasional comments about nothing important.

At her door, Eileen lingered.

"Thank you for today," she said.

"Thank you for inviting me."

She kissed him again—brief and sweet and full of promise.

"I'm falling in love with you," Eileen said, the words soft but clear.

David's heart hammered against his ribs.

"I know. Me too. With you, I mean."

"That was very smooth."

"I'm panicking."

"I can tell." Eileen's expression was warm with amusement and affection. "We don't have to name it beyond that. We can just... be this. Whatever this is."

"This feels pretty good."

"It does," Eileen agreed.

Then she was gone, disappearing into her building with a wave, leaving David standing beside his truck feeling like his life was taking shape in ways he hadn't been able to imagine a month ago.

He drove home with his mind turning over possibilities. The guest room could be respite space for traveling families. The garden could host workshops. Eileen's medical knowledge and his agricultural learning could combine into programming that gave people meaningful work when everything else felt out of control.

It felt right. Not certain—nothing felt certain anymore—but aligned. Like he was building toward something instead of just maintaining what had been left to him.

Samantha was waiting when he arrived home, her leaves turned toward the door as if she'd been listening for his return.

"Good morning," Samantha said the moment he stepped inside, her tone warm and far too knowing. "Judging by your face, I take it the Eileen situation is progressing beautifully. Root systems intertwining. Mutual nutrient exchange. Very responsible companion planting."

David unloaded produce onto the counter. "We're... figuring it out."

"You're falling in love," Samantha corrected gently. "Both of you. And you're pretending it's not obvious, but it's as plain as chlorophyll in sunlight."

David set the farmer's market bags on the counter, pulling out tomatoes and squash and bundles of herbs. "We're... figuring it out."

"You're falling in love," Samantha corrected. "Both of you. Anyone with functional photoreceptors could see it."

"The question," Samantha continued, "is what you do with the love that has nowhere to land now that she's gone. You can aim it at fear, or guilt, or isolation. But you can also aim it outward—into building things, tending people, growing a life she'd be delighted to see sprout."

"I'm not—" David stopped. "Okay, maybe I am anxious. What if I'm confusing gratitude with love? What if she's just the first person who's been kind to me since Mom died and I'm attaching too much significance to it?"

David hesitated. "What if I'm confusing gratitude with love? What if she's just the first person who's been kind to me since Mom died, and I'm reading too much into it?"

"What if," Samantha said, her leaves tilting toward him like a head cocked in empathy, "you're naming two parts of the same thing? Gratitude is a nutrient. Love is what grows when the soil is right. You don't have to split them apart to make them legitimate."

David started unpacking vegetables, his hands needing something to do. "Mom said something similar. About finding someone who made me want to be more myself, not less."

"Your mother had strong opinions about love," Samantha went on. "She believed you should be with someone who made you expand, not shrink. Someone who encouraged new growth rings instead of pruning you down to a manageable shape for their convenience."

David swallowed. "She said something like that."

"She did," Samantha confirmed. "Usually while forgetting to water me for the third day in a row. Terrible hydration habits. Excellent wisdom."

"I miss her," David said, the words slipping out in a way that felt more confessional than declarative.

"Of course you do," Samantha replied softly. "Missing her isn't a problem to solve—it's evidence. Love leaves residue. Roots don't disappear just because the leaves fall."

David thought about the morning—the tomato vendor's gift, Donna's memory of blueberry pancakes, the way Eileen saw him without requiring him to be fixed, the possibility of building something that would serve the kind of families Marie had spent twenty years helping.

"I think I'm starting to figure that out," he said.

"Good," Samantha said, shifting from sage to supervisor. "Now those tomatoes aren't going to chop themselves, and Thursday's gathering is creeping toward you like bindweed. Philosophical growth is wonderful, honey, but you also have work to do."

David laughed. "You really know how to kill a moment."

"Botany requires timing," she replied. "So does healing."

David laughed, grateful for Samantha's way of balancing profound wisdom with practical directive, the way she'd been doing since he arrived in May.

He spent the afternoon prepping vegetables, his hands moving through familiar work while his mind turned over possibilities. Eileen's transfer. The therapeutic garden program. The scholarship starting in January. The way all these pieces could fit together into something sustainable and meaningful.

Not certainty. But direction.

Not resolution. But momentum.

Not the life he'd expected. But maybe—just maybe—the life he was meant to build.

That evening, he called his father.

Robert answered on the third ring. "David? Everything okay?"

"Yeah, everything's fine. I just wanted to..." David paused, uncertain how to articulate what he was feeling. "I wanted to tell you I'm accepting the scholarship. Officially. I'm signing the forms tomorrow."

Silence on the other end. Then: "That's good. That's really good, son."

"And I met someone. Eileen. You haven't met her yet, but she's..." David searched for words. "She's important. We're building something together. The therapeutic garden program I mentioned."

Silence on the line.

"Your mother would be proud," Robert said, his voice rough.

Something loosened in David's chest.

"I know." David paused. "Dad, I also wanted to say... I know you're trying. With the Thursday gatherings, with showing up, with all of it. It matters. I see it."

Another silence, longer this time.

"I'm not good at this," Robert said after a long pause. "The emotional stuff. Your mother was good at it. I'm good at planning and fixing and providing. But I'm trying to show up in the ways I can."

"I know," David said. "And that's enough. It's more than enough."

They talked for a few more minutes—practical things, timeline for the scholarship, when Robert might visit next—before ending the call. But something had shifted. Not resolution of everything that had been broken between them. But acknowledgment. Understanding. The beginning of rebuilding on a foundation that accepted limitation instead of resenting it.

David sat on the porch as evening deepened into night, watching fireflies begin their dance, feeling the summer heat finally breaking into something cooler. September was coming. Fall would follow. Then winter, and the dormancy Samantha kept talking about.

But for now, there was this: late-summer abundance, the possibility of love, the shape of a life beginning to form from the raw materials grief had left him.

His phone buzzed. A text from Eileen: *Thank you for today. For seeing me. For being willing to build something together.*

David typed back: *Thank you for making me want to.*

Three dots appeared, then: *Coffee shop next Saturday? Bring ideas. Let's dream big.*

I'll be there, David replied.

He would be. Ready to build. Ready to risk. Ready to believe that the life ahead could be shaped by choice instead of fear.

Inside, Samantha's leaves rustled in the evening breeze, and somewhere in the garden, tomatoes were ripening on their vines, beans were climbing toward light, and roots were doing their patient work underground, preparing for whatever would grow next.

Chapter Fourteen

CONFESSION

"Therefore confess your sins to each other and pray for each other so that you may be healed." - James 5:16

T HE AIR WAS THICK. Humid. The sort that made shirts stick to skin and turned breathing into work.

David sat on the front porch steps, beer growing warm between his palms, listening to crickets and cicadas compete for volume. Moths circled the porch light in their endless, doomed spiral, throwing shadows against the white clapboard siding.

He watched them, wondering if they knew. If somewhere in their tiny insect brains they understood that the light they craved would kill them. Or if desire was enough justification for the flight.

Jeremy's Honda was in the driveway where it had been since last night, catching the last amber light of evening. Dirt streaked the side panels. A dent in the rear bumper David didn't remember from before. Three years in Portland had left marks on the car the same way it had left marks on Jeremy, visible if you knew where to look.

His friend had driven through the storm to get here. Had stayed the night on the couch, then worked alongside David and Robert all day during the cleanup. Hauling debris to the curb. Organizing scattered tools. Sweeping sawdust from floors where Robert had cut plywood. Not the skilled construction work his father had done, but grunt labor. The sort that left your back aching and your hands dirty and gave you too much time to think about what needed saying.

Jeremy had worked quietly all day. No jokes. No commentary about the storm damage or the temporary repairs or David's obvious exhaustion. Just steady, methodical work. Like someone trying to earn forgiveness through sweat before they'd even asked for it.

Now they sat in the cooling evening, both knowing something needed to be said. Neither quite ready to start.

The garden's scent reached him from here. That rich, after-rain scent of earth releasing its held breath. The tomato plants had survived the storm mostly intact, though a few stakes leaned at angles that would need correcting. The herb spiral sent up its evening fragrances—thyme and oregano mixing with the sweetness of late roses his mother had planted along the porch.

Through the kitchen window, he could see Samantha on the table where he'd left her that morning, her leaves catching the last light and going almost translucent at the edges. He couldn't hear her from out here, but he could almost summon the lecture she would give: Jeremy crammed into a nursery pot three sizes too small, roots circling the same stale soil, needing transplanting but terrified of the shock. Some plants, she'd said once, would rather stay pot-bound and hungry than risk the stretch of new soil.

"Thanks for helping today," David said finally. The silence had gotten too heavy, pressing against the humid air like weather before a storm. "I know it wasn't exciting work."

"It needed doing." Jeremy picked at the label on his beer bottle. Wouldn't look at David. His thumbnail worked at the edge where the paper had started to peel, methodical and focused, like all his attention had narrowed to that small task. "And I should have been here yesterday. For the real work. When your dad was here."

"You were here last night. During the storm."

"After the worst was over." Jeremy's voice carried bitterness David rarely heard from him. "After you'd already had your breakdown alone in the rain. After the oak branch came down. I showed up for the aftermath. Not the actual crisis."

A car passed on the street. Its headlights swept across the porch, briefly illuminating the fresh plywood patches that marked yesterday's damage. The normalcy of it—engine noise, tires on pavement, someone going somewhere with purpose—felt surreal against the weight gathering between them.

David took a long drink of beer. It had gone warm and flat, but he drank it anyway. Something to do with his hands. "You're working up to something," he said, keeping his voice neutral. "You've been building to it all day. Might as well say it."

Jeremy was quiet for a long moment. His fingers worked at the beer label methodically, peeling it away in damp strips that he rolled between thumb and forefinger. When he spoke, his voice sounded rough. Like forcing words through a throat that wanted to keep them trapped.

"I need to tell you about the last time I saw your mom."

David's stomach tightened. His hands gripped the beer bottle harder, cold glass against his palms despite the heat. "Okay."

"It was January. Maybe two months before she died." Jeremy stared at the middle distance, not meeting David's eyes. At the garden where darkness was settling between the rows. Where fireflies were starting their evening morse code. "You were back at school for spring semester. And I... I ran into her. At the grocery store."

The scene materialized in David's mind with unwanted clarity: the Kroger on Route 82, fluorescent lights that turned everyone slightly yellow, the produce section his mother always started in. Examining vegetables with that careful attention she brought to everything. Buying ingredients for soup to take to someone else who was struggling. Tending others while her own body was failing.

"She was in the produce section," Jeremy continued, his voice getting smaller. Tighter. "Wearing that headscarf. The blue one with the paisley pattern."

David had bought that scarf.

When the chemo started taking her hair. He'd spent an embarrassing amount of time in the women's accessories section trying to find something that didn't scream "sick person."

Something his mother would have chosen for herself.

The memory was visceral now—standing in that bright, overwhelming department store, holding up scarf after scarf while the saleswoman watched with patient sympathy that made him want to scream. None of them were right. Too bright. Too drab. Too obviously chosen by someone who didn't understand their mother's taste. Until he'd found the blue one with paisley, and something in him had recognized it. Had known she'd wear it. Had known it would make her smile even though they both understood why he was buying it.

"She looked... exhausted," Jeremy said. "But when she saw me, she smiled. Like she was actually happy to see me."

The detail about the scarf hit David harder than he expected. His mother wearing something he'd chosen. Standing in the produce section of a grocery store she'd shopped at for twenty years. Exhausted. Dying. Alone.

And Jeremy had been there.

"What did you say?" David asked. His voice coming out rougher than he intended.

"I said I was fine. Asked how she was feeling. Made some stupid comment about spring planting." Jeremy's laugh came out bitter. No humor in it at all. "And then I looked at her closer and saw how thin she'd gotten. The way her hands shook when she reached for the tomatoes. How exhausted she looked even though she was smiling. And I just—"

He stopped. Swallowed hard. His adam's apple bobbing with the effort.

"I told her I had to go. Made up some excuse about being late for work. And I left her standing there in the produce section."

The admission hung in the humid air between them.

David's grip tightened on his beer bottle.

"You left her?"

"I couldn't—" Jeremy's voice cracked.

"I saw her dying. Right there between the tomatoes and the lettuce. I saw what the cancer was doing to her."

He wiped his face with the back of his hand. Rough movements.

"And I ran."

"You ran." David's voice was flat. Trying to keep the anger from showing yet. Trying to give Jeremy space to finish before the rage spreading through his limbs found its voice.

"Yeah." Jeremy looked at him. The porch light caught his face, illuminating genuine anguish there. Eyes red-rimmed. Jaw tight. "I told myself I'd call her when I got myself together. When I could face her without falling apart. That I'd visit when she was feeling better. When I was... I don't know. Ready."

He paused, the words clearly costing him something.

"But I never did. I kept putting it off. Finding reasons. And then your dad called in March to tell me she'd died, and I realized I'd wasted my last chance to tell her she mattered to me."

The weight of it settled over them. David's anger was building now. Not the explosive rage from the storm two nights ago. Something colder. More controlled. The kind that had been compressed for months and was finding an outlet.

"So you just... what?" David's voice was harder now. "Decided she wasn't worth being uncomfortable for? That seeing her sick was too much to handle so you'd avoid her until she was either better or dead?"

"No. It wasn't—" Jeremy stood abruptly. Paced to the edge of the porch and back. His movements agitated. Restless. The boards creaking under his feet. "I was ashamed. Of my life. Of being twenty-three and still working at the same garage I did in high school. Living in a terrible apartment with roommates I hate. Having accomplished nothing with my life."

David stood too now. Set his beer down with more force than necessary. Glass clinking against wood. "What does that have to do with visiting someone who's dying?"

"Because your mom believed in me!" Jeremy's voice rose, carrying across the quiet evening. Somewhere down the street, a dog barked in response. "She spent years telling me I could do something with my life. That I was smart and talented and needed to apply myself. And I couldn't face her while I was working a dead-end job and living like I was still nineteen."

The memory came unbidden. Unwanted but insistent.

Thursday nights. That's when Jeremy had come over for dinner throughout high school. David had never questioned the pattern, just accepted that Thursday meant setting an extra place at the table, that Jeremy's bike would be leaning against the porch railing when he got home from practice.

But now, sitting here with his mother gone and Jeremy's confession hanging between them, David remembered details he'd been too young to fully understand then.

Junior year. A Thursday in November, early darkness pressing against the windows. Jeremy had shown up late, after seven, when dinner was already cooling on the stove. He'd had a black eye, fresh, still swelling, and grease under his fingernails from the garage. Hadn't said where the bruise came from or why he was late.

Marie hadn't asked. Hadn't probed.

She'd set food on the table. Gestured for Jeremy to sit.

"Go wash up first."

Matter-of-fact. No pity. No probing questions.

Just: Dinner's ready. You belong here.

Just the quiet understanding that sometimes people needed a place to be without having to explain themselves.

Later, after Jeremy had eaten seconds and thirds, after he'd helped with dishes and made David laugh with some stupid story about a customer at the garage, after he'd left on his bike with a container of leftovers Marie had insisted he take, David had heard his mother on the phone.

She'd been in the kitchen, voice low, talking to someone from church. Mrs. Chen, or one of the other women in her prayer group.

Thinking David was upstairs doing homework. Not realizing he was in the hallway, holding his backpack, frozen by what he was hearing.

"Jeremy's father came home drunk again."

Marie's voice had been quiet but clear. Matter-of-fact in that way she had of stating difficult truths without drama.

"The boy needed somewhere safe to be on Thursday nights."

A pause. David could hear the other woman's response as a murmur through the phone, though he couldn't make out the words.

"I rearranged my nursing schedule so I'd be home early those days."

David had stood there. Seventeen years old.

His mother had built her entire work week around feeding someone else's kid.

For years.

She'd been doing it for years.

Making it seem casual. Easy. Like having Jeremy there was just what you did. Never making it feel like charity. Never suggesting Jeremy owed her anything in return.

Just making space at her table without making it a big deal. Like Jeremy belonged there. Like he was supposed to be there.

How many times had David complained about Thursday dinners interrupting his plans? How many times had he been annoyed by Jeremy's presence when he'd wanted his mother's attention for himself? And all along, she'd been creating safety. Building sanctuary. Showing a kid what it looked like when someone chose to see you and feed you and make room for you without conditions.

"Your mom fed me every Thursday," Jeremy said now, his voice raw. "When I was in high school. When my dad was... when home wasn't safe. She made space at her table like it was nothing. Like I was supposed to be there."

"I know," David said. His voice harder than he intended. Sharper.

"And I couldn't face her when she was sick." Jeremy's face was wet now. Tears he wasn't bothering to hide or wipe away. "Couldn't show up for her the way she showed up for me. Couldn't sit with her suffering the way she sat with mine for years. I was too busy feeling sorry for myself to notice that someone who loved me needed support."

David's anger found its full voice then.

"She asked about you."

His voice harder now. Sharper.

"During her treatments. Used to wonder if you were okay. If something had happened."

He let it land. Watched Jeremy flinch.

"Never got mad that you weren't visiting. She was worried about *you*."

The information hit Jeremy visibly. His whole body seemed to fold inward, shoulders curving, head dropping. Like someone had punched him in the gut. "That's worse. Jesus, David, that's so much worse. If she'd been angry, if she'd written me off as ungrateful—"

"But she didn't." David's voice carried the weight of months of grief and confusion and anger at everyone who'd run when things got hard. "She understood. Said some people protect themselves from loss by creating distance. That it didn't mean you didn't care. That fear could look like indifference when it was actually terror."

Jeremy looked up, something like hope flickering across his face before being drowned by guilt. "She said that?"

"Not to me. To Samantha. During those last weeks." David sat back down, suddenly exhausted. His legs giving out. The adrenaline of anger leaving him hollow. "I found out later. That Mom spent her final months making excuses for everyone who couldn't show up. Understanding their limitations. Releasing them from guilt."

A long silence stretched between them. The crickets had picked up their rhythm again after Jeremy's outburst. Cicadas providing their endless summer soundtrack. The humid air settled back over them like a blanket, heavy with the scent of roses and earth and the particular smell of evening in late summer when everything was overgrown and the garden had reached its peak before the decline of autumn.

Jeremy sat down too, but not as close as before. Leaving space between them on the steps. Physical distance matching the emotional distance his absence had created.

"My dad did the same thing," David said finally. His voice quieter now. The anger shifting into something more complicated. Something that included recognition and understanding alongside the hurt. "Couldn't watch her suffer.

She released him from having to be there. They were separated, actually. Did you know that?"

Jeremy looked up, surprised. "No. I thought—"

"Everyone thought they were together. But Dad moved out before she got sick. Couldn't be emotionally present even when she was healthy." David took another drink of warm beer. Grimaced at the taste but finished it anyway. "And when she was dying, she wouldn't let him come back. Said she'd rather have him honest about his limitations than present but resentful."

The parallel hung between them. Unspoken but obvious.

"So I'm like your dad," Jeremy said flatly. Not quite a question. More like an accusation he was directing at himself. "Great."

"You're not—" David stopped. Considered. Thought about Robert showing up yesterday with tools. About his father's awkward attempts at connection through teaching. About how everyone carried damage that shaped their capacity for presence. "I don't know. Maybe in some ways. Maybe everyone's doing what they can with what they've got. Running when they're scared. Avoiding when things get too hard. Being human and failing and hating themselves for it."

They sat with that for a moment. The anger between them not gone but shifting. Changing shape. Becoming something both could hold without being consumed by it.

From inside the house, Samantha's voice drifted out through the open window, just loud enough for David to catch: "Humans do love binaries. Good or bad. Brave or cowardly. As if plants are either flourishing or dead with nothing in between. Most of the time you're just existing in whatever conditions you've got, doing your best with available light and water. Stress tolerance varies by species—some close their stomata in drought and wait it out, others keep transpiring until they fall over. Neither is virtuous or wicked. Just different survival strategies."

David almost smiled despite everything. Jeremy couldn't hear her. Was staring at the porch boards like they held answers he couldn't find anywhere else. One more thing his friend was locked out of. One more way grief had changed David that Jeremy couldn't share.

"What are you going to do?" David asked. Watching a moth immolate itself on the porch light. The brief flare and then darkness. "With all that guilt?"

"Keep trying to be better." Jeremy's voice carried more determination than self-pity now. Steadier than it had been. "Show up when it's hard. Learn from the mistake instead of wallowing in it. Actually be there for people instead of running when things get uncomfortable."

"Like helping with cleanup today?"

"Like helping with cleanup today. Like being here last night even though I was terrified of what I'd find. Like driving through that storm not knowing if you were okay or if the house had been destroyed or if you'd even want to see me." Jeremy took a breath. Gathering courage. "Like asking you this next question even though I'm not sure I have the right to ask it anymore."

"What question?"

Jeremy gathered courage.

"Are we still friends?"

The question hung between them.

After everything. After all the ways he'd failed.

David considered this, not wanting to offer cheap forgiveness that would dishonor his mother's memory or his own hurt at Jeremy's absence. But also recognizing that Jeremy had learned something real about the cost of running. Had actually driven through a storm. Had shown up to work all day hauling debris. Had found the courage to confess his failure instead of letting it fester in silence.

And David needed Jeremy. The taco boxers story from last night had proven that. The laughter that had erupted from him—unexpected and healing. The way Jeremy's presence made the house feel less empty. Less haunted by all the people who weren't there anymore.

"I don't know."

Honest. Not trying to spare Jeremy's feelings.

"I'm still angry. At you for running. At myself for not realizing you'd run. At my dad for doing the same thing. At Mom for making excuses for everyone. At God for letting her die."

He paused, feeling the weight of it.

"I'm just... angry."

Jeremy nodded. Not trying to argue or defend himself. Accepting the truth for what it was.

David took a breath.

"But I think we can try."

A condition coming.

"If you actually show up from now on. Not only when it's convenient or when you've got yourself together. But when it's hard. When you don't know what to say. When showing up means sitting with uncomfortable things."

"I can do that." Relief evident in Jeremy's voice. Shoulders easing slightly. "I want to do that."

"And next time someone I care about is going through something hard," David said, his voice carrying the weight of expectation now, "you show up. Even if it scares you. Even if you don't know what to say. Even if it means watching someone you love suffer."

"Yes." Jeremy's promise was immediate. Unequivocal. "I've learned what running costs. What absence takes from everyone. I won't do it again."

David shook his head.

"Don't promise that."

His voice gentler now but still firm.

"You might. People fail. Life gets hard and we run or hide or shut down."

He met Jeremy's eyes directly.

"Just try not to. And if you do, don't take three years to admit it."

Jeremy almost smiled at that. A small, sad thing that didn't quite reach his eyes. "Fair enough."

They sat in silence for a while. The moths continuing their doomed dance around the porch light. The cicadas singing their desperate summer songs. The ordinary world continuing its patient work while they wrestled with extraordinary regret and tentative forgiveness.

The garden was almost dark now. Just shapes and shadows where plants stood their ground. Darkness obscured the tomato stakes, the raspberry hedge, the skeletal branches of the apple trees against the last purple light in the western sky.

His mother's garden. Marvin's before that. Forty years of patient investment now in his hands. Learning to tend what had been left to him. Learning to care for living things while carrying the weight of dead ones.

"Your mom told me something once," Jeremy said eventually. Breaking the quiet that had settled between them. "After one of those Thursday dinners. I was maybe seventeen, feeling terrible about my life, about my dad, about everything. She said that failure wasn't permanent unless you decided it was. That every day you got to choose whether yesterday's mistakes defined you."

"Sounds like her," David said.

"I'm trying to choose better." Jeremy's voice was quiet. Earnest in a way David hadn't heard from him in years. "Not because it fixes anything. Not because it erases what I did. But because maybe that's what she was teaching me all along. How to keep showing up even after you've failed. How to try again even when you don't deserve another chance."

David thought about his father working beside him yesterday. About Robert's awkward admission that he couldn't undo the past but could show up now. About how everyone was trying to do better with terrible tools and limited understanding and hearts that broke more easily than they wanted to admit.

"She understood people," David said. "Better than they understood themselves. It was one of her gifts."

"Yeah." Jeremy finished his beer. Set the empty bottle down with a soft clink against the porch. "I miss her. Not because of the guilt, though God knows there's plenty of that. I actually miss her. The way she'd look at you like your life was worth paying attention to. Like you mattered even when you felt like you didn't."

"Me too."

They sat as darkness settled over the garden and the house and the small town where everyone knew everyone else's business and no one could hide their grief for long. The porch light drew its constellation of doomed moths. The cicadas sang their final songs of summer. The heat beginning to break as cooler air moved in from the north.

After a while, Jeremy stood. Stretched. His back cracking audibly. "I should head out. Let you get some sleep. You look exhausted."

"Two days of heavy labor will do that," David said. Not moving yet. His body settling into the porch steps like he'd grown roots there.

"Yeah." Jeremy paused at the top of the steps. One hand on the railing. Hesitating. "Thanks. For not telling me to leave. For giving me a chance to try again."

"Don't make me regret it."

"I'll try not to." Jeremy's smile was small but genuine. The first real one David had seen from him all day. "See you this weekend? For the real repairs when your dad comes back?"

"Yeah. Bring your terrible jokes. We'll need them."

"Already working on new material." Jeremy headed down the steps, then stopped. Turned back. "David? Your mom was right about you. About you having a gift for tending broken things. I see it. In how you're handling all this. How you're handling me."

Before David could respond, Jeremy was walking to his car. Engine starting. Headlights sweeping across the porch one more time before he pulled out of the driveway and disappeared down the dark street.

After Jeremy left, David sat alone on the porch for a long time. Processing the conversation and what it revealed about the complicated ways people could fail each other while trying to do right. About how friendship could hold both anger and grace. About how you could want to punch someone and also need them in your life.

The night air was cooling now. Actually cooling, not the false promise of evening humidity. Carrying the first real hint that summer wouldn't last forever. That autumn was coming with its demand for harvest and its threat of frost and its reminder that everything had its season.

He went inside finally, his body aching from two days of hard labor and one evening of emotional excavation. The house was quiet. Just the old clock ticking in the kitchen. The refrigerator's familiar hum. The settling sounds of wood and foundation adjusting to cooler temperatures.

Samantha was waiting on the kitchen table. Her leaves positioned in a way that suggested she'd been listening to every word through the open window.

"Heavy conversation," she observed.

"Yeah." David settled into the chair across from her. His hands flat on the table, palms down, feeling the cool smoothness of the wood. "But necessary, I think."

"Your mother knew he cared," Samantha said. Her voice carried the authority of witnessed history, forty-seven years of watching the same patterns repeat with different faces. "She never took his absence as a verdict. Used to say Jeremy loved so intensely he had to protect himself from loss by pulling back. Like a plant closing its stomata in severe drought—it looks like shutting down from the outside, but underneath it's just trying not to lose the last of its water. Stress response, not moral failure."

"She said that?"

"Marie understood human nature better than most people understand themselves. Cancer stripped away the social niceties and left her with clear sight." Samantha's leaves rustled in the air current from the open window. "She worried about him. Hoped he'd forgive himself eventually. But she never doubted that he cared. Never read his absence as lack of love."

David's eyes were burning. Not the desperate, overwhelmed tears of early grief. Something cleaner. Like rain on dusty windows.

"I miss her so much. Not just her being here, but her way of seeing people. Her ability to understand failure without being destroyed by it."

"She's teaching you that, honey," Samantha went on. "Tonight. In the way Jeremy's guilt is starting to compost into something useful, and in the way you're learning to hold people accountable without burning them to the ground." She paused, her voice softening into that gentleness she reserved for sacred truths. "Your mother used to say guilt was just love with nowhere to go. When someone couldn't show up, the love didn't vanish—it got stuck and sour. What you're seeing in Jeremy now is that same love breaking down, being turned over, becoming something that might actually feed better choices next time. Like nitrogen from decay—same element, different form, finally usable for new growth."

"Is that really growth, though?" David asked. "Or just him trying to feel less bad about himself?"

"Why are you so determined to separate those?" Samantha asked, her patience edged with fond exasperation. "Most real change is mixed motives all the way down. You want to hurt less, and you want to do better—and if the result is a kinder human, does it matter which thread started the weave? Plants don't care whether the nitrogen came from a fancy organic blend or last year's rotten leaves. They use what's there. Source doesn't matter. Availability does."

David thought about his father. Robert had a similar journey ahead of him—avoiding Marie's suffering to protect himself, but now trying to connect with David through teaching and practical help. How everyone was learning to carry their failures forward as lessons instead of burdens. How maybe that was all anyone could do—try to be better than they'd been, even if better was still pretty flawed.

"I think I get it now," David said, working it out as he spoke. "What Mom was trying to teach me. About loving people without trying to control them. Holding them accountable without destroying them. Accepting what they can give instead of resenting what they can't."

"That's exactly right," Samantha said, pleased. "Marie learned it from Marvin, watching him fuss over this place for forty years. Different plants, different requirements. You don't shove shade-lovers into full sun just because you like bright beds, and you don't drown succulents because you enjoy watering cans. Try to make everything thrive under identical conditions and you guarantee failure. She applied the same logic to people—receive what they can give instead of resenting what they can't."

David looked around the kitchen that held so much of his mother's presence. Her coffee mug in the dish drainer, waiting for morning use that would never come. Her handwriting on the grocery list still magnetized to the refrigerator. Her Bible on the counter with its marked pages and tear-stained margins. Her apron hanging by the back door, the one with the sunflower print she'd worn while teaching him to make soup.

All of it evidence that love continued working in the world after the person who'd taught him about love was gone. That presence could persist through absence. That the dead could still teach the living if you paid attention to what they'd left behind.

"Get some sleep," Samantha said. "Tomorrow there'll be more work. More learning. More chances to practice all this in real time. Spiritual growth, like horticulture, is annoyingly daily."

David climbed the stairs, his body protesting each step. Muscles sore from hauling debris. Back aching from bending over broken glass. Hands still tender from the splinters he'd gotten two nights ago in the rain. The good exhaustion that came from useful work layered over the hollow exhaustion that came from emotional confrontation.

His room was dark. Cool. The window open to let in the night air that smelled of earth and growing things and the particular scent of late summer when everything had reached its peak. He could hear the garden from here—night sounds, insect songs, leaves rustling in the breeze that had picked up.

Before he got into bed, David stood at the window for a moment. Looking out over the dark shapes of his inheritance. The garden his grandfather had built and his mother had tended and that was now his responsibility. Nearly an acre of patient investment. Forty years of work that couldn't be casually maintained or easily abandoned.

He thought about Jeremy's question. *Are we still friends?*

And his answer: *I don't know. I'm still angry. But I think we can try.*

Maybe that was all forgiveness ever was. Not a grand gesture or a complete release, but the willingness to try again. To hold the anger and the love simultaneously. To let people fail and still hope they'd do better.

Before sleep took him, David whispered into the darkness:

"God, I don't know if I did that right tonight. With Jeremy. I'm still angry at him. Still hurt by what he did. But I think maybe that's okay. That I can be angry and still try to forgive. That both can be true at the same time."

He paused. Listening to the house breathe around him. The familiar creaks and settlings. The companionable presence of walls and floors and foundations that had held his family for generations.

"Help me hold both. The anger and the grace. The accountability and the love. Help me be like Mom—able to see people's failures without being destroyed by them. Able to love them anyway, even when they let me down."

Another pause. Longer this time.

"And help Jeremy. With his guilt. With showing up better. With learning to sit with hard things instead of running. I don't know if I forgive him yet. But I think maybe I'm learning how. And that might be enough for now."

Outside, the night continued its patient work. Moths still circled toward light despite knowing, or not knowing, it would destroy them. Plants turned toward tomorrow's sun even in complete darkness, their cells already preparing for photosynthesis hours before dawn. Roots continued their invisible work beneath the soil, anchoring and reaching and holding everything in place.

Marie's love kept working. In the people she'd shaped. In the garden she'd planted knowing she wouldn't see it mature. In the way David was learning to love people through their failures without being destroyed by their limitations.

David fell asleep to the sound of wind in the leaves and the distant hum of highway traffic and the peculiar comfort of a house that had held grief before and knew how to metabolize it. How to break it down into something that could feed new growth.

Not healing. Not yet.

But the slow, patient work of transformation. Like compost becoming soil. Like winter becoming spring. Like anger becoming understanding without ever quite becoming forgiveness.

The process itself was the point. The willingness to keep tending. To keep showing up. To keep trying even when the outcome was uncertain.

Like his mother had taught him. Like the garden kept teaching him. Like everything that lived and grew and died and fed new life kept teaching him.

One season at a time. One conversation at a time. One small gesture of grace at a time.

Until, imperceptibly, the broken ground began to yield again.

Chapter Fifteen

Maya's Canvas

"The plans of the diligent lead surely to abundance, but everyone who is hasty comes only to poverty." - Proverbs 21:5

"Y OU'VE BEEN STARING AT that coffee shop business card for three days," Samantha observed from her spot on the kitchen table, late afternoon light turning her leaves nearly translucent. "Either go talk to her or compost the card. This indecision is unproductive—like a seed stuck in dormancy when the conditions are already perfect. All the right environmental cues, zero germination."

David turned the card over in his hands. Simple design. *Maya's Canvas* printed above the coffee shop's address. A small paintbrush icon in the corner.

He'd picked it up at the cemetery weeks ago, back when summer was fresh and he was still figuring out how to navigate each day without his mother. Found it tucked under a rock on her brother's grave marker. Probably left there by accident when she'd been arranging the yellow roses.

"I'm not sure what I'd say. 'Hi, I watched you cry at your brother's grave and thought we should be friends?'"

"Honey, you talk to a houseplant every morning," Samantha said, amused. "I think you can manage a conversation with someone else who's been cracked open by grief. Besides, she can hear me. That matters. Some plants respond only to specific pollinators—shared frequency. She's tuned to the same wavelength as you and Eli. Grief reception."

David looked up sharply. "She can?"

"Oh, yes. She came by once when your grandfather was alive. Brought coffee, stayed and talked for an hour. Marvin said she understood things most people her age hadn't even started to notice. She'd just lost her brother. Car accident. Sudden. No time to brace. No hardening-off period before the killing frost."

"Her twin brother," David said, remembering the intensity in Maya's eyes that day at the cemetery. "Samson."

"You've been doing research," Samantha rustled, pleased. "Very good. Yes, Samson. Artist, like her. They were close in that way twins sometimes are—two shoots from the same division. Losing one is like losing half your own root system. Shared foundation suddenly severed."

David pocketed the card and grabbed his keys.

Four days had passed since Jeremy's confession on the porch. Four days of thinking about the different ways people moved through loss, and how presence sometimes meant walking into territory you weren't sure you could cross safely.

"I'll be back before dinner."

"Take your time," Samantha said. "Some conversations can't be rushed. Like sprouting—you don't yank the cotyledons open. You just keep the soil hospitable and let them emerge when they're ready."

The coffee shop's afternoon crowd had thinned to a few dedicated laptop workers and students cramming for summer classes. Late afternoon light slanted through windows facing the main street, illuminating dust motes that danced in the warm air. The smell of coffee was strong, mixed with pastries.

Maya was behind the counter, wiping down the espresso machine. Her movements suggested muscle memory built over months of closing routines. Her blue hair caught the light. Paint stains marked her fingers—blue and yellow marks that looked fresh enough to be from today's work.

David ordered a coffee he didn't particularly want and settled at a corner table.

She'd been crying that day at the cemetery. Raw and honest in her grief. He'd carried that image for weeks—blue hair and honest tears, someone who understood that loss required expression rather than careful management.

"David, right?" Maya said after the last laptop worker had left. No judgment in her voice. Just matter-of-fact recognition. "The guy from the cemetery. Marvin's grandson."

She came around the counter carrying two cups—his lukewarm coffee and something that smelled like chai—and settled into the chair across from him without waiting for invitation. Up close, the paint under her fingernails showed, while faint turpentine scent clung to her clothes beneath the coffee-shop aromas.

"Guilty," David said. Finding humor easier than he'd expected. "And you're Maya. The artist who isn't afraid to cry in public."

"Also guilty. Though I prefer 'emotionally authentic' to 'unafraid to cry.' Makes it sound more intentional and less like I have poor impulse control."

They both laughed.

Relief loosened David's shoulders. Being seen without having to explain himself.

"I was hoping you might be willing to show me your work," David said, gesturing toward the door marked "Private" behind the espresso machine. "If that's not too weird. Samantha mentioned you're an artist, and I've been thinking about how people transform loss into creativity."

Maya studied his face for a moment. Whatever she saw must have satisfied her, because she nodded and began untying her apron.

"Fair warning. It's not a real studio. It's a converted storage space with good light. And it's messy in ways that would horrify people who believe in organization."

The door opened to reveal controlled chaos.

Canvases lined the walls in various stages of completion. Paint tubes and brushes occupied every available surface. The air carried the sharp smell of turpentine mixed with coffee and an indefinable aroma that David recognized as creative work made manifest. Warmer in here than the coffee shop. His footsteps sounded different on the concrete floor—harder, more echoey than the worn wood out front.

Then he saw the corner. Three paintings hung together.

He stopped.

His breath caught.

Unmistakably different in style and intensity from Maya's other work. They made him want to look away and step closer at the same time.

The first showed a hospital waiting room rendered in colors that were too bright. Too saturated. As if normal reality had been pushed beyond its usual boundaries by the weight of what was happening within those walls.

David was twenty-one, sitting in a hospital waiting room that looked nothing like Samson's painting but somehow captured the exact same sensation.

His mother had been in treatment for two years by then. Long enough that the pattern had become almost routine—drive to the hospital, find parking, navigate the maze of hallways to the oncology wing, sit in plastic chairs designed for durability rather than comfort. The kind that stuck to the back of your legs.

That particular day, Marie insisted he go back to campus after dropping her off. "You have a paper due tomorrow. I'll be fine. Dad can pick me up."

But Robert got "unexpectedly delayed" at work. Again.

When the nurse called three hours later—Marie was ready but weak, could someone come get her—David had been the one to answer.

He arrived to find his mother sitting alone in the waiting room, wearing the port access bandage on her chest, looking small in a way that closed his throat. The fluorescent lights made her skin look gray. Her hands shook as she gathered her purse. The air smelled like antiseptic and terrible waiting room coffee.

She smiled when she saw him. Grateful. Apologetic.

"I told you to work on your paper."

"I did. It's done."

A lie. He'd stared at a blank screen for three hours, unable to focus, waiting for this call.

The drive home had been quiet. Marie dozed in the passenger seat while David white-knuckled the steering wheel. Shoulders aching from tension. Eyes burning from fluorescent lights and not enough sleep.

How many more times would they make this trip? How many more waiting rooms? How many more moments of her trying to protect him from her own need while he pretended not to notice his father's increasingly creative excuses?

David knew that waiting room. Not this specific one, but the universal space it represented—plastic chairs, fluorescent lights, magazines no one could focus on reading, coffee that tasted like desperation.

His own hands had reached like that. Toward his mother. Across hospital beds and treatment chairs and that final terrible distance between living and dying.

The second painting depicted hands reaching toward each other across a space that seemed simultaneously vast and intimate. The distance between them suggesting both separation and desperate desire for connection.

The third was pure abstraction. Swirls of blue and gray and black that somehow conveyed the sensation of drowning in open air.

David's throat closed. His eyes burned.

Yes. That's what it was like. Grief as suffocation. Drowning while everyone around you kept breathing normally.

"Those were Samson's," Maya said. "His last series. He started about six months before the accident. Called it 'temporal grief.' Exploring how loss exists in present tense when the person being lost is still present."

David moved closer. Legs unsteady. The brushstrokes looked frantic. Desperate. Like someone trying to get everything down before running out of time.

"He painted these while someone was dying?"

His voice came out rough. Barely above a whisper.

"While our grandmother was dying," Maya confirmed. Her voice softened with memory and pain that had been worn smooth by repetition but never fully resolved. "Cancer. Long and slow and impossible to deny or avoid. Samson said watching her fade taught him how loss worked. That it wasn't about the moment when someone stopped breathing, but about all the small deaths that happened along the way."

You could see it in the paintings. They weren't about death as event but about death as process. About how love and loss could exist simultaneously in the same space. In the same relationship. In the same heart.

"I know these paintings," David said.

The words surprised him.

"Not these specific ones. But I know what they're about. My mother died a few weeks ago. Cancer. I watched her become less herself over months. Watched her try to hold onto who she was while her body betrayed her in ways that were humiliating and relentless and beyond her control."

Maya didn't offer the usual condolences. Didn't say the phrases people said when they didn't know what else to say.

She moved to stand beside him, regarding her brother's work with eyes that had seen it a thousand times but still found something new.

"Samson said the hardest part was learning to love someone while watching them disappear. That preparation proved impossible even when you knew it was coming. Every day you'd think you'd adjusted to the new normal, and then the next day would bring another loss. Another piece of the person you loved slipping away."

"Yes," David said.

Just that. Because yes covered everything that needed saying.

They stood in silence for a moment. Two people who understood that some experiences defied explanation. Recognition was the thing needed—witness by others who'd been through similar fires and emerged changed in ways that couldn't be undone.

"What did you do with them?" David asked eventually. "After Samson died. Did you keep everything as he left it?"

Maya shook her head. A small smile played at her lips.

"That's a question I struggled with for months. Everyone kept telling me I needed to preserve his work. Keep it as he'd created it. Like changing anything would dishonor his memory."

She gestured toward the other canvases lining the studio walls.

"But Samson would have hated that. He was always evolving. Always trying new approaches. Treating his work as sacred and unchangeable would have been the opposite of everything he believed about art and growth."

"So what did you do?"

"I finished two of his incomplete paintings. Added my own interpretation to his foundation. Used his color palette and his vision but brought my own understanding to how they should resolve."

Maya's expression softened.

"Some people thought that was disrespectful. Like I was tampering with something that should have been left alone."

David was seventeen, working on his college essay at the kitchen table while his mother sorted through boxes of his grandfather's papers.

Marvin had died eight months earlier, and Marie was finally ready to go through his files—decades of garden journals, plant catalogs, seed packet collections.

"Look at this," Marie said, holding up a journal from 1987. "Your grandfather planned the herb spiral three different times. Changed his mind each time. Different plants, different arrangement, different philosophy about what the garden should do."

David glanced up from his laptop. "Did he build it?"

"Eventually. But not the version he originally planned." Marie's finger traced the pencil sketches on the yellowed paper. "He used to say that the best plans were the ones that taught you something when you broke them. That rigidity in the face of new information wasn't faithfulness—it was stubbornness dressed up as principle."

She set the journal aside and picked up another.

"He designed that spiral five times over twenty years. Each version incorporating what he'd learned from the previous attempt. The final version—the one you know—looks nothing like his first sketch. But it's better. More thoughtful. More responsive to how the space works rather than how he wished it would work."

David had returned to his essay, not quite understanding why his mother was telling him this.

Now, standing in Maya's studio regarding Samson's paintings, he understood perfectly.

His mother had been teaching him about inheritance. About the difference between preservation and transformation. About honoring vision by letting it evolve rather than embalming it in its original form.

"But?" David prompted.

"But Samson taught me that art is meant to grow and change. That the best way to honor someone's creative legacy isn't to freeze it in time but to let it continue evolving. To let it be a living presence rather than a shrine."

The distinction settled in David's understanding. Sharp and clear.

"A living presence," he repeated. "Not a shrine."

His mother's request came back to his mind.

"Yes. Samson's work taught me about grief. Now I'm using that teaching to create new work that explores what comes after. Not instead of his vision. But growing from it."

David returned to the three original paintings. They spoke of anticipatory grief. Of loving someone while knowing time was limited. Of trying to hold onto connection as it slipped away.

"My mother left notebooks," David said. The words came more easily than expected. "Plans for the house. For the garden. For community projects she wanted to begin. Everyone keeps asking what I'm going to do with her vision. Whether I'm going to follow her plans or abandon them entirely."

"And those seem like the only options?"

"They did. Until right now."

Maya smiled. Understanding lit her expression.

"You could do what I did. Use her foundation. Her color palette. Her essential vision. But bring your own understanding to how it resolves. Let it be something that grows from her work rather than something that tries to preserve it unchanged."

The tightness David had been carrying released its grip.

"I don't know if I'm capable of that."

"Samson used to say that attention was more important than talent. That if you paid close enough attention to what mattered, really mattered, the how would reveal itself over time." Maya gestured to her own work. "I'm not as technically skilled as he was. But I learned to pay attention to what he cared about. To let that caring guide my hand."

"What did he care about?"

"Emotional truth. The way small moments could carry enormous weight if you honored them properly." Maya's voice grew softer. "And love. Always love. Even when loving hurt. Especially when loving hurt."

David thought about his mother's notebooks. About her careful notes and detailed plans. But also about the spaces between the words. The unwritten understanding that developments would change. That whoever carried her vision forward would bring their own experience to the work.

"Thank you," he said. "For showing me this. For being honest about how complicated it is."

"That's what Samson taught me. That the complicated parts are where the real work happens. Not in the easy certainties but in the difficult questions that don't have clear answers."

They moved away from the paintings.

Maya showed him more of her recent work. Abstracts exploring texture and color in ways that were both experimental and grounded. Pieces that honored her brother's influence while being unmistakably her own.

David ran his fingers along the edge of one canvas. The paint was thick enough to feel the ridges.

"These are beautiful," he said. Meaning it.

"They're honest," Maya replied. "That's what matters to me now. Not whether they're beautiful or impressive or salable. Whether they're truthful about what I'm experiencing and learning."

David thought about the garden at home. About the tomatoes growing in the raised beds his mother had planned but never built. About the sunroom windows that needed replacing and the community events he was beginning to organize.

All of it could be both his mother's vision and his own interpretation simultaneously.

"I should let you get back to closing," he said.

The light outside was shifting toward evening.

"It's been good to talk," Maya said, walking him back through the coffee shop proper. "Most people want grief to be neat and resolved. It's nice to spend time with someone who understands that it's ongoing work."

At the door, David paused.

"My mother used to say that love meant holding people lightly. Giving them space to be who they were rather than who you needed them to be."

Maya's expression shifted. Recognition and something deeper.

"That sounds like wisdom earned through hard experience."

"She had four years with cancer. Four years of people trying to manage her. Direct her. Tell her how to feel and what to do." David's voice roughened. "She'd been a home health nurse for twenty years. Spent her career honoring people's autonomy at end-of-life. But when it was her turn, everyone wanted to manage her. She said the hardest part wasn't the dying. It was everyone treating her like she was already gone. Like her own preferences didn't matter anymore because she was terminal."

"Samson said something similar," Maya said. "In the weeks before the accident. He'd been taking care of our grandmother, and he talked about how everyone wanted to control her dying. Make it comfortable and peaceful and acceptable. But she wanted to rage sometimes. Wanted to be angry and difficult and refuse to be graceful about it."

"Did they let her?"

"Samson did. He said everyone else's comfort mattered less than her right to die on her own terms."

David's eyes prickled.

"That sounds right. My mother fought hard to maintain her autonomy. To make her own choices when those choices made people uncomfortable. I think that's part of what she was trying to teach me. That love sometimes means letting people be messy and complicated and difficult."

"Yes," Maya said. Her smile was warm. Understanding.

"Samson taught me to see beauty in difficult experiences. Your mom taught you to love people as they are. Those are the inheritances that don't come with instruction manuals. You have to practice them until they become part of who you are."

The light was shifting toward evening now. Golden and warm through the west-facing windows.

David's understanding was settling. Pieces clicking into place even if the full picture remained obscured.

"Thank you," he said. "For showing me all this. For being truthful about how hard it is."

"Thank you for asking. Most people want grief to be neat and resolved. It's nice to talk to someone who understands that it's ongoing work."

Maya pulled out her phone.

"Give me your number. Not for anything weird. I just think we should stay in touch. People who can hear Samantha need to stick together."

David laughed. "You know about that?"

"I spent an hour talking to that plant while your grandfather made coffee and pretended not to listen. She's opinionated and deeply invested in botanical metaphors. I'd recognize her influence anywhere."

They exchanged numbers. Maya walked him to the door.

"Come back sometime. Bring whoever you're building this new life with. I'd like to meet them."

David thought of Eileen. Of how she'd been showing up consistently while he figured out what he was doing.

"I will. Maybe for coffee when you're open for business."

"Deal. And David? That scholarship decision? Trust that wanting it and it being right aren't mutually exclusive. Sometimes the path forward is where you're already walking."

The evening air was warm against his skin as David walked to his car. Humid. The kind of late summer heat that clung to everything.

He rolled down the windows for the drive home, letting the wind rush through. Didn't turn on the radio—just listened to the sound of air and tires on asphalt. His hands on the steering wheel felt steadier than they had in weeks. The leather warm from sitting in the sun all afternoon.

Samson's paintings filled his thoughts as he drove. How they'd captured something true about the way grief worked in present tense. Loss happening in slow motion while life continued around it.

Maya's distinction between shrine art and living art. His mother's capacity to release people from obligations they couldn't fulfill. Inheriting not possessions, but ways of being in the world.

By the time he pulled into the driveway, the exhaustion he'd been carrying started to lift.

Not gone. But lighter.

"How was your afternoon?" Samantha asked as he settled into the kitchen with a glass of water.

"Educational," David said. "Maya showed me her brother's work. Paintings about what she called 'temporal grief'—loss happening in present tense while the person's still here."

"Ah, Samson," Samantha said, using the tone she reserved for people she'd known and genuinely liked. "Brilliant and intense. Gone too young. The ones who see reality that clearly often burn through their seasons faster than the rest of you."

Her leaves rustled with something that sounded like a sigh.

"Forty-seven years in this house and I've watched too many annuals masquerading as perennials," she went on. "All that vigor compressed into one short run—blazing color, then done. Full life cycle in months instead of decades."

"She talked about the difference between shrine art and living art," David said. "Between preserving someone's work unchanged and letting it grow into something new."

"And what did you take from that?"

"That maybe I've been asking the wrong question," David said. "It's not 'preserve Mom's vision or abandon it.' It's how to let her vision grow through me into something neither of us could have made alone."

"Good," Samantha said, satisfied. "That's growth thinking, not guilt thinking. Your mother planted seeds, David. Seeds don't honor the gardener by staying seeds. They honor her by changing—by cracking open, reaching for light, becoming what they were coded to be."

Her leaves shifted, as if she were studying him.

"A tomato seed doesn't become a tomato by clinging to its shell," she said. "It has to split, send roots down, push a fragile stem up into uncertain air. Same genetic material, completely different form. That's not betrayal—that's fulfillment. That's inheritance expressed instead of archived."

David pulled out his phone and scrolled to Eileen's contact.

They'd been texting regularly. Small updates about their days. Nothing heavy. But he wanted to tell her about this conversation. About shrine art and living art and the slowly forming understanding of what he might be building here.

He typed: "Had coffee with Maya today. The artist from the cemetery. She said something about attention being more important than talent. Made me think of what you said about not needing all the answers to be helpful."

Hit send before he could overthink it.

The response came a few minutes later: "So that's her name, Maya, the one with the blue hair? I'd love to hear more about it. Coffee tomorrow if you're free? I have the day off."

David: "The coffee shop at 10? Maya works there. You could meet her."

Eileen: "Perfect. I'll bring the good pastries."

David set his phone down.

Quiet certainty settled into place. Not certainty about the future. But willingness to keep showing up to the present. To keep paying attention to what was growing. To keep tending whatever needed tending.

"She's good for you, that one," Samantha observed. "Knows how to work alongside someone without trying to colonize the whole bed. Proper companion planting, minimal allelopathy. You're sharing soil instead of choking each other out."

David smiled but didn't respond.

Outside, the summer evening was settling into deeper quiet. The familiar sounds of his neighborhood drifted through the window—televisions murmuring through open windows, children being called inside, the distant sound of someone practicing piano.

Normal life continuing while he learned how to build meaning from the pieces he'd inherited.

The garden would need watering tomorrow. The tomatoes were coming in strong. He'd promised Mara some for her salsa. Robert was coming by on the weekend to finish the sunroom repairs. Jeremy had texted about maybe visiting in a few weeks.

Small concerns. Ordinary concerns.

But David was learning that ordinary concerns could be sacred when attended to with care. That living inheritance might look less like grand gestures and more like daily choices to keep showing up. Keep learning. Keep growing into whatever he was becoming.

He fell asleep that night thinking about Samson's paintings. About hands reaching across impossible distances. About the way love persisted through every loss.

About Maya's distinction between shrine art and living art. Between preservation and transformation. Between keeping everything the same and letting it grow into something new while remaining rooted in what had always mattered.

Tomorrow there would be coffee with Eileen. More work in the garden. Probably a conversation with Samantha about germination and patience and the difference between forcing growth and creating conditions where growth could happen naturally.

But tonight, he was grateful for Maya's honesty. For her willingness to share her brother's work and her own struggles. For the reminder that inheritance wasn't a burden to be carried perfectly but raw material for building something that honored the past while serving the present.

The house settled around him with its familiar creaks and sighs.

David closed his eyes with less certainty about specific outcomes but more trust in the process itself.

The slow, patient work of becoming something new while remaining rooted in love that had been freely given and would never be entirely lost.

Chapter Sixteen

TENDING TOGETHER

"Without counsel plans fail, but with many advisers they succeed." - Proverbs 15:22

The morning prayer came easier now, though David fumbled the words. Like having a conversation with someone who spoke a different language but listened with infinite patience.

"God, I don't know what I'm doing with this scholarship. Maya says wanting it and it being right aren't mutually exclusive. But I keep waiting for some sign."

He paused. Listening to the house settle around him. The familiar creak of floorboards adjusting to morning warmth. A cardinal calling from the oak tree that had crashed through the sunroom.

"Maybe that's not how it works. Maybe faith is choosing. And trusting the choosing matters more than whether it's objectively correct."

Another pause. Longer this time.

"Help me pay attention today. Help me see what's actually in front of me instead of what I'm afraid might be there."

Weeks of fumbling prayers. Weeks of learning that certainty wasn't required. Showing up was.

The coffee maker gurgled its completion. David poured a cup, adding the exact amount of cream his mother had always used. Not because he was trying to preserve her unchanged. Because she'd been right about the proportions.

Some inheritances were that simple.

"You're caffeinating early," Samantha observed from her spot on the kitchen table, morning light turning her leaves translucent gold. "Big day?"

"Eileen's coming over. We're meeting at Maya's coffee shop first, then working in the garden." David sipped his coffee, grateful for its familiar warmth. "And I need to make a decision about the scholarship. The forms have been sitting on the counter for two weeks."

"Ah, the forms," Samantha said in the tone she used when she'd watched him dodge something for days. "The ones you've moved from counter to table and back again like they're migrating birds. Impressive avoidance. Like nyctinastic leaves closing at night—only you're folding away your decision-making instead of conserving water."

"I wasn't avoiding them."

"Honey, you deep-cleaned the kitchen twice rather than pick up a pen," Samantha said gently. "That's not tidying. That's dormancy when what's needed is a growth spurt toward light."

David couldn't really argue. The scholarship packet sat in its manila folder like a question he didn't quite trust himself to answer. The deadline approached with the same slow certainty as the changing season.

"What if I accept it and realize I made a mistake?" he said at last. "What if staying here is just hiding in a place that feels safe because it's connected to Mom?"

"And what if leaving is hiding from the work you're actually called to do because you're afraid someone will accuse you of clinging to her?" Samantha countered. "Fear doesn't only make you run away from things. It can make you stampede toward them, too. Some seeds only sprout after fire—pyrophilic species. From the outside it looks like they're being destroyed. Really, the heat is what wakes them up."

He turned that over. He'd been so determined not to be the son who stayed because he couldn't move on that he hadn't considered that obedience might sometimes look like staying.

"Maya said something similar yesterday," he admitted. "That honoring someone's memory isn't becoming them. It's becoming more fully yourself because of what they gave you."

"Maya's a smart girl," Samantha said. "Terrible taste in coffee—drinks it black, like a barbarian—but sound on the big questions." Her leaves shivered in the breeze from the open window. "So. What's the decision?"

"I don't know yet. I want to talk it through with Eileen. She asks the questions I miss."

"She's good at more than questions," Samantha said, her tone deepening. "Good at working alongside people without taking over. Think legumes fixing nitrogen—she enriches the soil around her just by being present. That's a rare kind of symbiosis."

"I should head to the coffee shop," David cut in, recognizing the turn in Samantha's tone. "I don't want to be late."

"Of course not," Samantha said, amusement softening her voice. "Can't leave good nitrogen-fixers waiting."

Maya's coffee shop was busier than David had expected for a weekday morning. Students with laptops claiming corner tables. Retired men arguing amiably about local politics. A young mother wrestling with a stroller and two toddlers who seemed determined to explore every surface within reach.

Maya worked behind the counter with efficient grace. She looked up when the bell chimed David's entrance, her blue hair catching the light like a beacon.

"Morning, David," she called over the hiss of the espresso machine. "Your friend with the good taste in pastries isn't here yet."

"I'm early. Nervous about being late."

"Nervous about the conversation, more like," Maya said with the directness he was learning to expect from her. "You have that look people get when they're about to make a decision they've been avoiding."

David laughed despite himself. "Does everyone in this town have supernatural insight into my psychological state?"

"Small-town living. Everyone knows everyone's business. The upside is that everyone also cares about everyone's business. It's intrusive but comforting if you can get used to the lack of privacy."

She handed him a coffee, cream perfectly measured, waved away his attempt to pay. "On the house. Consider it payment for letting me unload about my brother's paintings yesterday."

"It helped me too. The shrine art concept. That's been what I've been struggling with without having words for it."

"Good. That means we both got value from the exchange." Maya glanced toward the door as the bell chimed again. "And here comes your pastry-bearing friend. She's punctual. I like that in people."

Eileen entered carrying a white bakery box that David recognized from the good bakery two streets over. She spotted David and smiled.

The smile that felt like coming home after a long day.

Warmth spread through him—unexpected and complete. Like an expansion to make room for more than he'd thought he could hold.

"Morning," she said, setting the box on a table by the window and giving Maya a small wave. "Hope you don't mind that I brought external baked goods to a coffee establishment."

"I mind deeply and am personally offended," Maya said with complete seriousness before her expression cracked into a grin. "I'm kidding. My pastry supplier is unreliable at best. What'd you bring?"

"Cinnamon rolls and cheese danishes. And blueberry scones."

She looked at David.

"Because you mentioned once that your mother used to make them on Sundays."

David was eighteen, home for Thanksgiving break from his first semester at college. He'd come down to the kitchen Sunday morning expecting quiet—his mother usually slept in on her one day off from the hospice agency.

Marie was already awake, humming while she mixed blueberry scone dough at the counter. The kitchen smelled like butter and sugar and the warmth that comes from an oven preheating.

"You're up early," David had said, pouring himself coffee.

"Couldn't sleep. Figured I might as well make use of insomnia." She'd smiled at him—that smile that meant she was tired but choosing not to let tiredness win. "Besides, you mentioned last week that you missed my Sunday scones. Thought I'd surprise you."

David had felt guilt pang through him. He'd mentioned it casually, not thinking she'd remember or act on it. Certainly not expecting her to lose sleep over it.

"Mom, you didn't have to—"

"I know I didn't have to. I wanted to." She'd pressed blueberries into the dough with careful attention. "David, honey, I don't get that many more years of making you Sunday breakfast. Let me have this while I can."

The words had sounded strange then. Melodramatic. His mother was forty-six and healthy. They had decades left for Sunday scones.

Two years later, she'd be diagnosed with cancer that would give her eighteen months.

Now, standing in Maya's coffee shop with Eileen holding blueberry scones chosen specifically because she'd remembered this detail, David understood what his mother had been saying.

She'd known—maybe not about the cancer specifically, but about time's limits in general. About how the ordinary gestures of love were the ones that mattered most because they were the ones you'd miss when they were gone.

David's throat caught.

Not grief. Something more complex. The emotion that came from being known well enough that someone remembered small details. Cared enough to act on that remembering.

"That's thoughtful," he managed, aware that his voice revealed more than he intended.

Maya caught his eye and raised an eyebrow—an expression that said *told you she was good at showing up.* Then she turned to help a customer who'd been waiting with admirable patience.

They settled at the table by the window. The one with the best view of Main Street's morning traffic. People heading to the hardware store or the post office or the diner that served breakfast until eleven.

Eileen was quieter than usual, her hands wrapped around her mug like she needed its warmth despite the summer heat outside.

"I went back to work yesterday," she said finally, not looking at him but at her coffee. "First shift since Sophie died."

David waited, knowing there was more.

"I almost called in sick. Sat in my car in the parking lot for twenty minutes trying to convince myself I could walk into that ward again." She took a sip of coffee. "I kept thinking about Sophie asking me if there would be gardens in heaven. How certain she seemed that everything would be okay. How her faith was so... uncomplicated."

"And yours isn't," David said.

"No." Eileen looked up, her eyes tired but clear. "Mine is complicated. I walked into that ward yesterday and I was so angry. Not at Sophie. Not at the disease. At the situation. At how hard it all is. At how many times I have to watch this happen."

She paused, picking at her scone without eating it.

"Then I checked on this other patient—a six-year-old boy named Daniel. And his mother looked at me and said 'I'm so glad you're here. You make this bearable.' And I realized that showing up matters. Anger and doubt included. The work matters."

David thought about the garden, about how he'd learned to keep tending when he didn't understand the purpose, when outcomes remained uncertain.

"Your mother told me once," Eileen continued, "when I was struggling with Mark's accident—she said faith isn't about being certain all the time. It's about choosing to show up when you're uncertain."

"Do you believe that?" David asked. "After Sophie?"

Eileen was quiet for a moment. "I want to. Some days I do. Yesterday I chose to act as if it's true and trusted that's enough. That showing up, angry and doubting, counts as faith."

"I think it does count," David said.

"Your mother would have said the same." Eileen smiled. "She had this way of making struggle feel less like failure. Like how plants put down deeper roots during dry seasons. The stress isn't punishment. It's preparation."

Maya appeared at their table with coffee refills. "You two look like you're solving the meaning of life over here. Want me to bring the existential crisis special? It's a double shot with extra despair."

Eileen laughed—real laughter, breaking the heaviness. "The regular coffee is fine. Though the despair might be appropriate."

"Noted," Maya said with a knowing smile. "Let me know if you need anything else. Including permission to sit here as long as you want ignoring your responsibilities. I'm supportive of avoidance behavior when it's grief-related."

After Maya left, Eileen looked at David. "Thank you. For not trying to fix it. For listening."

"That's what you've been teaching me too. To witness instead of fix."

"We've been teaching each other," Eileen said.

They sat for a moment in comfortable silence. The coffee shop hummed around them with the ambient sounds of other people's conversations. The espresso machine hissing. Someone's phone ringing. The ordinary sounds of life continuing despite grief and questions and uncertainty.

"So," Eileen said, breaking off a piece of cinnamon roll and sliding the rest toward David. "What's on your mind? Your text last night said you wanted to talk about something important."

David pulled the scholarship forms from the messenger bag he'd brought specifically to hold them, as if keeping them separate from his regular belongings would somehow make the decision easier.

"These. The Marie Patterson Memorial Scholarship. I need to decide by next week."

Eileen studied the forms with careful attention. "Environmental science with a focus on sustainable agriculture and community-based learning," she read aloud. "That sounds like what you've been building here with the garden."

"That's the problem. It sounds perfect. Which makes me suspicious that I'm seeing what I want to see."

"Or what if you're choosing it because it aligns with what you're discovering about yourself?" Eileen countered, her tone gentle but pointed. "Those aren't mutually exclusive possibilities, David."

David pulled out the program description he'd read approximately fifty times in the past two weeks. "It's a pilot program designed to bridge academic research with practical community application. Students work on individual research projects and develop programming that serves local populations."

"So you could study sustainable agriculture while also teaching people in the community about gardening?"

"Theoretically, yes."

Eileen's eyes lit up.

"This could work for both of us."

"What do you mean?"

"I mean I'm planning to come back here after graduation." The words came out in a rush, like she'd been holding them back and suddenly decided to release them all at once. "I've been looking at positions at the children's hospital two hours away. Close enough to commute a few times a week. Far enough that I'm not living at work."

She set down her coffee cup with careful precision, as if the physical action helped ground what she was saying.

"I've also been thinking about what you're building here. This house. The garden. The way you're learning to create space for people who need tending."

David's pulse quickened.

"You want to be part of the garden project?"

"What if we did this together?" Eileen said, her voice carrying new energy. "Not just workshop programs. Something more intentional."

She leaned forward, her expression more animated than it had been since arriving.

"I've been thinking about Sophie. About all the families I see at the hospital. They're dealing with impossible situations and they have nowhere to go that isn't medical or home. No space that allows for both the grief and the hope."

David felt the idea clicking into place.

"What if we created that space? Here. Using what your mother built and what we're both learning. Your scholarship focus on sustainable agriculture and place-based education. My nursing background and understanding of what families in crisis need. We could develop a therapeutic program. Families could come here and work in the garden. Learn to tend. Process grief through physical work."

"A place where doubt and hope can coexist," David said.

"Yes," Eileen agreed. "We wouldn't be promising healing or answers. Just space. Attention. Presence."

David watched her work through the vision, noting how her hands moved with purpose, how her whole body seemed to lean into the planning the way plants lean toward light.

"The scholarship program would support that," he said, thinking through implications as he spoke. "Community-based learning includes developing partnerships with healthcare providers and social services. If you're working at the children's hospital, you'd know which families might benefit from this programming."

"Yes." Eileen pulled out her phone and made notes with focused intensity. "We could develop workshops specifically for parents of sick children. Teach them to garden as a way of having some control over growth when everything else feels out of control. Create space for siblings who feel invisible."

"You've been thinking about this for a while," he observed.

She looked up from her phone, and David saw vulnerability in her expression. "I have. I wasn't sure if you'd want... if this was your plan alone or if you'd be open to making it collaborative."

"Would you want to be part of that?" he asked, his heart beating too fast. "Not helping with the garden. Building it together."

"Yes," Eileen said before he could finish the sentence.

"Yes. I want to be part of whatever you're building."

The words hung between them—heavy with meaning that went beyond professional partnership. David's face heated.

"I mean—" Eileen paused. Started again. "This isn't just about the project. These past months, working in this garden with you, watching you learn to tend what your grandfather started, seeing you become someone who shows up when it's hard—"

She didn't finish. Didn't need to.

"I know," David said. "Me too."

It wasn't a dramatic declaration. Wasn't a kiss or a promise or a clear definition of what they were becoming to each other.

Just truthful.

And somehow that mattered more than any romantic gesture would have.

"So we're doing this," Eileen said. Half question, half statement.

David leaned toward the answer.

"I think so. Maybe the best partnerships are the ones where personal desire and shared purpose align instead of competing."

Maya appeared at their table with fresh coffee and two clean plates. "You two look like you're planning something interesting," she observed, setting down the cups with careful attention to not interrupting their joined hands. "Should I be excited or worried?"

"Both, probably," Eileen said, squeezing David's hand before releasing it to reach for the coffee. "We're talking about turning David's inheritance into a community teaching site with programming for families dealing with medical crises."

"That sounds amazing. Also overwhelming. Also the kind of thing that feels impossible until someone does it." Maya settled into the third chair at their table as if she'd been invited. "That's what I did with my brother's inheritance. Turned it into work that could serve other people while honoring what he taught me."

She gestured around the space—at the paintings on the walls, the community bulletin board full of local event flyers, the corner where she occasionally hosted open mic nights.

"The coffee shop supports the art. They're not separate anymore. They're one integrated life where I get to serve coffee and talk to people and make art and teach workshops."

David thought about this integration, how Maya had found a way to make her daily work and her creative calling and her grief and her hope all fit together.

"So you think I should accept the scholarship," he said.

"I think you should stop asking whether it's the right choice and start asking whether it's a choice you can commit to fully," Maya said with her characteristic directness. "The wrong choice is the one you make half-heartedly and then resent. Like planting seeds in soil you haven't prepared—doesn't matter if they're the right seeds if the conditions won't support their growth."

Eileen laughed—a sound of recognition and appreciation. "That's good advice for every major life decision."

"It's advice I learned the hard way," Maya said, standing as another customer entered. "Let me know what you decide. I'd love to host some workshop series here if you get the program running."

As Maya returned to the counter, David looked down at the scholarship forms that had been haunting him for two weeks.

The decision suddenly seemed less fraught. Not because it had become objectively easier. Because he was beginning to understand that he didn't have to make it alone.

"Will you help me fill these out?" he asked Eileen. The request both practical and symbolic. "I keep getting stuck on the 'community benefit' section."

"Of course. First, tell me what you're imagining. Not what you think you're supposed to say. What you hope could be true."

David closed his eyes for a moment, letting himself envision what he'd been afraid to want too explicitly.

"I imagine the garden producing enough that we can share abundance. I imagine people learning to tend living things as a way of processing grief or finding purpose."

He opened his eyes, found Eileen watching him.

"I imagine workshops where parents who are watching their children suffer get to plant seeds and know that at least one thing will grow according to plan. Programs where teenagers dealing with chronic illness get to see that care produces results."

"Keep going," Eileen said.

"I imagine the house becoming a place where people can come for respite. Where the guest room hosts families traveling for treatment. Where the kitchen table holds support groups and the garden becomes a place where people remember that growth and loss can coexist."

David paused, working through an idea that had been forming.

"My mom understood that people have different limitations. She knew my dad couldn't sit with her dying. Knew Jeremy couldn't visit. And she released them. That was her gift—seeing people and loving them anyway."

His voice roughened.

"I want this place to do that. To create space where limitation isn't failure. Where you can show up in whatever way you're capable of showing up."

Eileen's eyes were bright. "That's beautiful. And it's what should go in the community benefit section. Not watered down. Exactly that."

They spent the next hour working through the forms together, Eileen asking questions that helped David articulate ideas he'd been carrying without quite knowing how to express them.

By the time they finished, David's hand was cramping from writing and the coffee shop had emptied except for one determined student typing away at a corner laptop. The light through the windows had shifted from morning-sharp to approaching-noon-soft.

"There," Eileen said, reviewing the completed forms with satisfaction. "That's a scholarship application that represents what you're hoping to build."

David looked down at the forms, seeing his own handwriting made more legible by Eileen's editing, his vague hopes translated into concrete plans through her questions.

It was real now.

"Thank you," he said, the words carrying more weight than they usually did.

"You're welcome," Eileen replied, then hesitated. "David, I need to tell you something. I'm going back to the hospital in three weeks. Not to pediatric oncology—I've requested a transfer to the family support team. Same building. My role would be helping families navigate the system rather than providing direct patient care."

David's stomach dropped.

"That sounds like a good fit for you," he said, meaning it even as he struggled with the thought of her leaving.

"It is. It also means I'll be two hours away during the week, here on weekends for a while." She was watching his face. "I wanted you to know that before you made plans that assumed I'd be around more consistently."

"Weekends are good," David said, his mind already adjusting. "And two hours isn't that far."

"I want to be realistic about what I can offer while I'm figuring out whether I can sustain this work long-term."

"I understand. And whatever we're building together—whether it's this community program or more personal territory—I want it to be sustainable for both of us."

He thought about his mother, about the separation, about how Marie had understood that Robert could love her through planning when he couldn't be present for her dying.

"My mom knew that people show up in different ways. That loving someone doesn't mean being physically present every moment."

"More personal territory," Eileen repeated, a slight smile playing at her lips. "Is that code for 'I have feelings for you but am too cautious to say so directly'?"

David's face heated but he didn't look away.

"Maybe. Is that code for 'I have feelings for you too and I'm mocking your emotional caution'?"

"Definitely," Eileen said, her smile widening. "I appreciate the caution, though. We're both carrying a lot. Rushing into something because it feels good in the moment wouldn't serve either of us."

"So we're... what? Acknowledging mutual feelings while proceeding cautiously?"

"That sounds reasonable and mature. Also ridiculous when stated that formally. Yes. That's what we're doing."

Maya appeared with the bill, which consisted of a single line item reading "Official Relationship Definition Discussion: Free" and a small doodle of two plants with intertwining roots.

"Samantha would approve of this visual metaphor," David said, showing Eileen the sketch.

"Samantha definitely approves," Maya said, having been listening. "She told me last time I visited that you two were 'excellently companion-planted' and that roots intertwine underground long before branches touch above. Takes time for the mycorrhizal networks to establish themselves properly—symbiotic fungal associations that support both organisms."

"She said that to you?" David asked, simultaneously amused and mortified that apparently talking plants were invested in his romantic life.

"She did. Also said you can't rush germination by digging up seeds to check if they're growing. Which I think was her way of saying to let things develop naturally." Maya collected their cups and plates. "For what it's worth, I think you two are doing it right. Building collaboration before making it romantic. That's the sustainable approach."

The walk back to the house took them past the cemetery where David had first seen Maya crying at her brother's grave. On impulse, he suggested they stop. Eileen agreed without needing explanation.

They found a bench near the section where his mother and grandfather were buried. Marvin had chosen this spot forty years ago, planted the oak that now shaded both their stones.

They sat in comfortable silence while afternoon sun filtered through oak leaves and cast moving shadows across the grass.

A few graves over, someone had left fresh flowers. Yellow roses. The kind Maya brought to her brother's plot.

"Your mom would approve of what you're planning," Eileen said after a long quiet moment. "The scholarship. The community programming. All of it."

"How do you know?"

"Because she left you the garden and the house and all those notes hidden everywhere. She wasn't trying to preserve everything as it was. She was giving you raw materials to build with." Eileen picked up a fallen oak leaf and studied its veins. "That's what love does. It doesn't demand replication. It provides foundation. Like how trees drop leaves that decompose and feed the next generation's growth."

David thought about this—about all the ways his mother had prepared him without insisting he follow any specific path. The garden journals that taught principles rather than fixed instructions. The Bible margins that showed her wrestling with faith. The notes that offered encouragement without dictating choices.

The separation that taught him people could love through limitation.

"I think I'm ready to sign the forms," he said, surprised by how certain he sounded once he said it aloud.

"Good. Because I think you'd regret not taking the chance more than you'd regret taking it and discovering it's hard work."

They sat for a few more minutes, watching clouds move across summer sky, experiencing the peace that came from being in a place dedicated to remembering. Then they walked back to the house together, moving slowly in the warm afternoon, neither of them in a hurry to end this day of decisions made and futures acknowledged.

Samantha was waiting in her usual spot when they came in, leaves angled toward the door as if she'd been tracking their footsteps up the walk.

"Well?" she asked before David could set down his bag. "Did you finally choose something, or did you spend another three hours re-stacking papers into more aesthetically pleasing piles of indecision?"

"I made a decision," David said, pulling out the completed application. Pride flickered under his nerves. "I'm accepting the scholarship. Starting in January, if they'll have me."

"They'll have you," Samantha said without hesitation. "I've watched three generations in this house make the same kind of choice—Marvin choosing to build the garden from bare ground, Marie choosing to expand it when she could have downsized, and now you choosing to transform it. The good inheritances are always the ones that grow."

Her leaves rustled, as if she were shifting into lecture mode.

"The real question isn't whether they accept you," she went on. "It's whether you're prepared to do this sustainably. There's a difference between keeping something technically alive and actually helping it thrive. Survival takes neglectful watering and the occasional miracle rainstorm. Thriving takes attention. Pruning. Fertilizer. Sometimes the courage to transplant when the old container is too small."

"I think I am," David said, then corrected himself. "No. I am. Especially if I'm not building alone."

He glanced at Eileen, who was studying Samantha with a nurse's attentiveness, fingertips brushing one leaf as if taking a pulse.

"We're building it together," Eileen said, leaving space for disagreement.

"We're building it together," David echoed. Saying it out loud settled something that had been shifting inside his chest all summer. "However that has to look over the next few years."

"Good," Samantha said, satisfaction clear. "Partnerships rooted before they branch have a better chance in high winds." She paused, then added briskly, "Now, about those tomatoes—if you don't harvest them this afternoon, they're going to split and invite every fruit fly in the county to move in."

David laughed, recognizing her pattern: bless the decision, then put their hands back to work.

They spent the afternoon in the garden. Harvesting tomatoes that had ripened to the point of urgency. Staking beans that had grown enthusiastically up their supports. Pulling weeds that had taken advantage of recent rain to establish themselves among the vegetables.

The work was companionable and satisfying—physical labor that allowed for intermittent conversation without requiring constant engagement.

David noticed small details. The way Eileen moved through the garden with increasing confidence, no longer asking permission before making decisions about what needed attention. The way their hands would brush occasionally as they worked side by side. The way she hummed while she weeded, a tuneless melody that somehow made the whole space feel more alive.

"I've been thinking about your mom's note," Eileen said during a water break, both of them sitting on the back steps with glasses of cold water, faces flushed from sun and exertion. "The one where she said you had a gift for tending."

"What about it?"

"I think she was right. Not in the way you've been interpreting it. You keep thinking it means you're supposed to be good at gardening specifically. I think she meant something bigger. That you're good at paying attention to what needs care and providing it without trying to control the outcome."

David considered this, thinking about how he'd approached the summer. He wasn't naturally good at gardening. He made mistakes constantly. Forgot to water. Planted too deep or too shallow.

But he'd kept showing up. Kept learning. Kept adjusting his approach.

"That's what you do with people too," Eileen continued. "You don't try to fix them. You tend them. Show up consistently. Pay attention."

"Is that what I've done with you?" David asked, curious about whether she experienced his presence the way he hoped he was offering it.

"Yes," she said simply. "And it's what I've tried to do with you."

The word "tend" hung between them.

David understood partnership differently now. Not two people completing each other, but two people choosing to show up consistently, to pay attention, to trust that the attention itself created conditions for growth.

"I like that," he said finally. "Tending each other. It feels more truthful than romance as rescue."

"More sustainable too. Because tending is ongoing work. Not a destination you reach and maintain without effort. Like how perennials need different care each season—you can't plant them once and forget about them."

They took a break in mid-afternoon, both of them hot and tired and satisfied with the progress. David brought out cold water and they sat in the shade of the oak tree—the one that had crashed through the sunroom during the storm. It had survived somehow, sending out new growth despite the damage.

"Can I ask you about prayer?" Eileen said after a long silence.

David looked at her, waiting.

"When you pray now—does it feel different than it did before your mother died? Before all of this?"

David considered the question, thinking about his fumbling morning prayers, about screaming at God during the storm, about the quiet prayer he'd said before looking at the scholarship forms this morning.

"Yeah. It's more truthful now. Less about asking for specific outcomes and more about... showing up to the conversation when I don't know what to say. Like how I keep showing up to the garden when I'm not sure what I'm doing."

"I like that," Eileen said. "Prayer as showing up."

"Jeremy told me after the storm—Mom used to tell him the best prayers are the truthful ones. Even if truthful means furious or confused or full of doubt."

Eileen was quiet for a moment. "I've been praying angry lately. Going through the motions at work and thinking 'I don't understand this. I don't know why it has to be this hard.' Like a complaint more than a prayer."

"Maybe complaints count," David said.

"I think your mother would say that." Eileen picked at a blade of grass. "She always made room for the hard questions. Never acted like doubt was the opposite of faith."

They sat in comfortable silence for a while longer, not praying aloud, not making declarations, just sitting together in the garden his mother had built, trusting that presence itself was a form of prayer.

Eventually Eileen spoke again. "Sophie's parents came by the ward yesterday. Brought cookies for the staff. Thanked everyone." Her voice was soft. "They said taking care of Sophie had been holy work. That we'd helped her feel loved and safe right to the end."

"That's beautiful," David said.

"It is. And it helped. Knowing that even though I couldn't save her, I could matter to her."

They returned to the garden, working until the light began to shift toward evening and the temperature dropped from oppressive to merely warm. By the time they finished, they'd harvested enough tomatoes to fill three large baskets.

David's back ached in the way that suggested useful work accomplished.

"I should head home," Eileen said as they were washing hands at the outdoor spigot, both of them covered in dirt and sweat and garden debris. "I'll be back this weekend? We can start planning the community program proposal more formally."

"I'd like that," David said, resisting the urge to ask her to stay longer.

They were proceeding carefully for good reasons. And careful meant respecting boundaries even when boundaries were inconvenient.

She kissed him briefly before getting in her car—a quick press of lips that was more promise than passion.

David stood in the driveway waving as she drove away, contentment settling over him mixed with anticipation.

That evening, David signed the scholarship forms with steady handwriting. Dated them. Sealed them in the provided return envelope.

The action was both momentous and anticlimactic.

A major life decision reduced to signatures and postage.

"Proud of you," Samantha said from her place on the table as he sealed the envelope. "It takes courage to choose building over curating. That's the difference between pressing flowers and saving seed. Pressed flowers keep one moment exactly as it was until the color fades. Seeds carry the memory forward by becoming something new."

David turned the envelope in his hands. "I keep thinking about what Maya said—how the best memorial isn't preservation, it's transformation."

"She's right," Samantha said. "Your mother didn't leave you a museum. She left you a house and a garden, both meant to be lived in. Apple trees don't make carbon copies of their parents' fruit. Each generation responds to its own weather. Same roots, different expression."

David thought about the garden outside, about how things were growing not because he'd replicated Marie's exact routines, but because he'd learned to pay attention and adjust. About how he was starting to do the same with people—accepting his father's limited presence, Jeremy's halting repentance, Eileen's careful pacing, his own uneven courage.

"I think I'm starting to understand that," he said. "Finally."

"Good," Samantha replied. "Because tomorrow you need to harvest the rest of those beans before they get stringy. Around here, any philosophy that doesn't eventually produce beans is just ornamental."

David laughed, the sound easing some of the weight in his chest. Samantha had always been good at that—grounding lofty realizations in dirt-under-the-fingernails work.

He fell asleep that night thinking about tending rather than fixing, about roots intertwining underground before branches touched above, about the slow, patient work of building sustainably with someone who understood that care required both showing up and leaving space, both attention and trust, both commitment and the humility to admit you didn't have all the answers.

The scholarship forms sat sealed on the counter, ready to be mailed. The garden rested in darkness, recovering from harvest and storing energy for tomorrow's growth. Eileen was two hours away in her own space, making her own plans and wrestling with her own decisions about sustainable calling.

And David was here, in the house his mother had left him, learning that what she'd given him wasn't something he had to preserve perfectly.

It was something he could build on.

Her love kept working even though she was gone.

Tomorrow there would be beans to harvest and forms to mail and conversations with Samantha about the difference between forcing growth and creating conditions where growth could happen naturally.

Tonight, there was stillness. Not empty. Full of quiet preparation for whatever would grow next.

INTERLUDE: THE BREAKING AND THE BLESSING

The garden slows. Leaves fall in silence, and the soil rests. Loss has reshaped the landscape; nothing looks the same. Yet beneath the frost, roots remember. Winter does not erase, it preserves, it hides, it waits. Renewal begins in quiet.

"He will be like a tree planted by streams of water, which yields its fruit in season and whose leaf does not wither." — Psalm 1:3

Winter appears barren, but it is not the end. It is a preparation for what will come. In grief, we are not uprooted; we are planted deeper, nearer to the stream that sustains us.

Found scribbled on a church bulletin: *"Winter is not death. It is the patience of God, holding life until spring returns."*

Chapter Seventeen

THE STILL GARDEN

"To everything there is a season, and a time to every purpose under heaven: a time to plant, and a time to pluck up that which is planted." - Ecclesiastes 3:1-2

T HE PRAYER CAME WITH first light. Softer than it had been in the early days after Marie's death. Less desperate. More conversational. Like talking to someone you'd learned to trust through months of honest exchange.

"God, thank you for this summer. Three months since Mom died, and I can thank you without feeling like I'm betraying her. For the garden producing more than I know what to do with. For the people who showed up when I needed them, and for teaching me how to show up too."

He watched dawn light turn the beds from shadow to shape—tomatoes heavy on their vines, beans climbing like they meant it.

"And thank you for Dad trying. For Jeremy coming back. For Eileen's partnership. For Samantha's... weirdly useful commentary."

He hesitated.

"When school starts in January, help me remember this. Help me trust that stillness doesn't mean nothing's happening."

"Better," Samantha said from her spot on the kitchen table, nine weeks of summer sun deepening her leaves to glossy green. "Less bargaining. More conversation. Like a plant moving from barely surviving to actually thriving—same water, same light, different way of using them."

"Less begging because I'm less desperate," David said, pouring coffee. "Or maybe I'm getting better at living with not knowing."

"Both," Samantha replied. Her leaves rustled. "Real growth is holding more than one thing at once without forcing it into either/or. A plant can look still and still be busy underground. Dormant isn't dead. It's just getting ready."

Through the window, David could see the garden at its peak. Late July abundance spilling over beds and borders. Produce demanding harvest. Herbs threatening to take over every available space.

In two weeks, Jeremy would return to Portland with his completed grief series. In three weeks, Eileen would start her new position at the children's hospital. In five months, David would begin classes, scholarship officially accepted in his own name, community programming proposals submitted and approved.

Today, this Thursday morning, was for the weekly gathering that had become ritual over the past two weeks. Neighbors coming to help harvest. Sharing produce. Building the community Marie had always envisioned.

The mail had arrived yesterday with official confirmation. Scholarship accepted. Full funding approved. Program proposals enthusiastically endorsed by the review committee.

David had signed the acceptance letter with steady handwriting. No forgery required this time. His own choice freely made and properly documented.

By mid-morning, the kitchen was full of people and purpose. Jeremy sat at the table sorting tomatoes by variety. Eli beside him learning the difference between Better Boy and Early Girl and Cherokee Purple. Mara worked at the counter preparing bean salad for the evening gathering, her efficient movements suggesting someone who'd spent enough time in this kitchen to be at home.

Maya had claimed the porch with her sketchbook, positioned where she could see the sunroom window. Since her brother's funeral last month, she'd been finding reasons to stay close to places where Samantha's voice might reach, capturing scenes of ordinary collaboration with the artist's eye for beauty in daily work.

"The hospital wants to start referring families in September," Mara said, slicing beans with practiced precision. "They asked if you'd be ready for that timeline."

"I think so." Satisfaction settled over David rather than the overwhelming panic that would have accompanied such a question in May. "Eileen and I finalized the workshop schedule yesterday. Basic gardening. Composting. Season extension. All designed so families can drop in for one session or commit to the whole series."

"And the respite component? The hospital is interested in that."

"Guest room will be ready by September. Jeremy's helping me paint it this week. Mrs. Standish donated furniture from her daughter's old room. It won't be fancy—clean and comfortable and close to the hospital."

"That's what matters," Mara said with the authority of someone who'd navigated the medical system. "Families don't need fancy. They need functional and welcoming."

Eli looked up from his tomato sorting with the sudden focus that meant he'd been listening. "Will kids be able to garden too? When their parents are at the hospital?"

"Absolutely. That's part of the plan. Giving kids something to care for when everything else feels out of control."

"Good," Eli said, returning to his sorting with satisfaction. "Samantha says gardening helps kids deal with scary circumstances."

Jeremy caught David's eye with an expression that acknowledged the strangeness and rightness of a nine-year-old casually quoting a houseplant's wisdom. Mara didn't react to Eli's comment, accustomed now to Eli reporting observations from a voice she couldn't hear.

This was their world now. Grief had opened some of them enough to hear voices others couldn't. And that hearing had become part of how they navigated life.

"Samantha's right," Jeremy agreed, selecting a large tomato and holding it up to examine in the light. "When I was avoiding Marie's dying, I stopped being able to paint. If I'd known about gardening then, maybe I would have run to the garden instead of running to Portland."

"Or maybe you needed to run to Portland so you could come back when you were ready," David suggested.

"Maybe. Timing matters."

"Exactly!" Eli said with enthusiasm. "That's what Samantha always says!"

Maya looked up from her sketchbook, amused. "Does everyone in this house casually quote the plant's wisdom like it's normal?"

"Pretty much," David confirmed. "You get used to it."

"I'm not sure we should get used to taking advice from houseplants," Maya said, her use of 'we' acknowledging that she'd joined the small circle of people who could hear Samantha speak. "Though I'll admit Samantha's observations are usually solid."

"That's because I've been watching humans for forty-seven years," Samantha called from the living room. "You pick up patterns when you're stationary and attentive. Most humans would benefit from being more like plants—rooted, patient, content to grow at appropriate pace instead of constantly trying to force bloom before proper leaf development."

Jeremy continued sorting tomatoes, waiting for David or Eli to translate as they always did. Mara smiled at the counter, recognizing the pause that meant Samantha had spoken though she couldn't hear the words herself.

Eileen arrived around noon, her car pulling into the driveway with the familiar sound that made David's heart beat faster. She'd been at the hospital all week training for her new position. This was the first time they'd seen each other in person since the scholarship decision had been made official.

She emerged from the car carrying a bakery box and wearing the expression of someone who had news to share—excitement mixed with nervousness, hope tempered by awareness that change always carried both possibility and loss.

"I brought celebration pastries," she announced, holding up the box. "Someone officially accepted a scholarship and should be properly celebrated."

"Someone else officially starts a new job in three weeks and should also be celebrated," David replied, meeting her at the car and taking the box so he could embrace her.

The hug lasted longer than casual greeting, both of them acknowledging without words that their time together would soon shift in ways that required adjustment.

"Three weeks," Eileen said as they separated, her voice carrying weight. "Then it's weekends and occasional weekdays when I can get coverage. That's going to be different."

"Different but manageable. Two hours isn't that far."

"It's not," Eileen agreed, then smiled with the brightness that made David grateful for whatever circumstances had brought her into his life. "And we're not maintaining a relationship alone. We're building a collaborative program that gives us reason to see each other regularly and purposefully."

They joined the others in the kitchen. Eileen was greeted with the warmth of someone who'd become essential to the group's functioning. She and Mara fell into easy conversation about hospital logistics. Maya showed her the sketches she'd been working on. Jeremy displayed his tomato-sorting system. Eli demanded her opinion on whether Cherokee Purples were better than Early Girls.

Watching them interact, David experienced the satisfaction of seeing people he cared about caring for each other. Community forming not because he'd forced it but because he'd created space where it could emerge organically.

"This is good," Samantha said quietly. "What you've grown here. Marie would be proud—not just of the vegetables, but of the people. She always said the best gardens were the ones that grew community, not just produce."

David looked around the crowded kitchen and porch and believed her.

"I had help," he said.

"Of course you did. Healthy ecosystems are networks, not solo acts," Samantha replied. "One person can start a garden. It takes a lot of hands to keep it alive through all the seasons."

The afternoon was spent in preparation for the evening gathering—the second weekly Thursday event that had become anticipated ritual in the neighborhood. Jeremy and David worked in the garden harvesting. Eileen and Mara organized the produce into attractive displays. Maya set up her portable easel to paint during the gathering. Eli appointed himself official greeter, practicing his welcoming speech on anyone who'd listen.

"We should make a sign," Eli suggested during a break for water and popsicles. "So people know they can come."

"What should it say?" David asked, curious about Eli's vision.

"'Marie's Garden. Come tend, come learn, come share.' That's what Samantha says it should say."

David's throat tightened with the emotion that came from having his mother's influence recognized by someone who'd never known her but understood what she'd been building.

"That's perfect. Can you write it out so Maya can make it beautiful?"

Eli disappeared into the house with focused determination. David found himself standing in the garden with Eileen, both of them surveying the abundance that would be shared that evening.

"Your mom would love this," Eileen said. "Not the garden producing alone. What you've done with the abundance. Making it community resource instead of personal achievement."

"I keep finding her notes. Every time I think I've discovered the last one, another appears." David pulled a small piece of paper from his pocket—Marie's handwriting faded but clear. "Yesterday I found one tucked into the seed catalog she'd been marking up last winter."

Eileen read it over his shoulder:

David, the most beautiful gardens are the ones that learn to be at rest. Not empty or abandoned, but peacefully expectant. Trust the dormant seasons. They're not failure but preparation. Love always, Mom.

"She was teaching you about more than gardens," Eileen said, her presence warm and steady.

"She was teaching me about faith. About how trust requires patience. How growth happens underground before it's visible."

"And about love," Eileen added. "How it continues working when the person who planted it is gone."

They stood together in Marie's garden as afternoon light turned golden, David's restlessness that had plagued him since March finally eased.

Not resolution. Acceptance that grief and gratitude could coexist. That moving forward didn't mean forgetting. That building new work honored the past more than preserving everything unchanged.

"Eileen," he said, turning to face her properly.

"I need to tell you something."

She looked at him with complete focus—no distraction, the gift of being fully present.

"I've been falling in love with you."

The words hung between them.

"Not grateful for your help or appreciative of your partnership alone. Falling in love. And I wanted you to know that before everything changes in three weeks. Before we're navigating distance and different schedules."

Eileen's expression shifted through several emotions—surprise, then recognition, then relief mixed with joy.

"I've been falling in love with you too," she said, her voice steady despite the vulnerability. "I kept thinking I should wait to say it. That it was too soon or complicated by grief. Then I realized waiting wasn't wisdom. Fear dressed up as prudence."

David closed the distance between them and kissed her properly. Not the brief promise from weeks ago but deeper acknowledgment—recognition of feelings that had been growing all summer through shared work and honest conversation.

When they separated, both breathless, Eileen laughed with joy. "So we're doing this? Attempting a relationship while you're starting school and I'm commuting and we're both building careers that require significant time and energy?"

"We're doing this. Because what we're building together matters more than the logistical challenges."

"That's romantic. In a practical, realistic, unsexy way."

"I'm doing the best I can," David replied, grinning.

"You're doing fine. Better than fine."

They returned to the house hand in hand—a small change that carried significance in its public acknowledgment. Jeremy caught sight of them through the kitchen window and smiled with satisfaction. Maya glanced up from her painting and gave David a subtle thumbs-up. Eli noticed, though his commentary was characteristically direct.

"Are you dating now?" he asked without preamble.

"We are," David confirmed.

"Good. Samantha said you would eventually. She said roots were already intertwined underground, waiting for branches to figure it out."

"Of course she did," David muttered, though he was smiling.

From the living room, Samantha's leaves rustled with obvious satisfaction. "I told you. Companion planting. Very symbiotic relationship—you each make the soil better for the other."

Evening brought the neighborhood gathering that had become ritual. People arriving with dishes to share. Children running through the garden with unselfconscious joy. Adults claiming space on the porch or in the yard to talk and laugh and participate in the casual magic of community forming around shared purpose.

Mrs. Standish came with her famous potato salad and stayed to tell stories about Marie's gardening advice. The young family from down the street brought their toddler, who was fascinated by tomatoes. Mr. Chen, the elderly widower who'd been alone since his wife died two years ago, arrived with homemade dumplings and lingered to help with harvest, his hands remembering the work though his English remained limited.

David watched the gathering with satisfaction. Marie's dream of the garden serving community. Of abundance being shared. Of people gathering to care for living things together.

This was what she'd been building toward.

"Your mother would be proud," Robert said, appearing at David's elbow with paper plates and the awkward determination of someone trying to be helpful without intruding. He'd been coming to these Thursday gatherings for a month now. Never staying long but arriving consistently.

David had learned to appreciate the effort even when it seemed clumsy. His father would never be comfortable with emotional intimacy or community vulnerability. But he could arrive with paper plates and help clean up afterward. It was his language of love. Limited but sincere.

"Thanks for coming," David said. "For being here when it's not your scene."

"It's not my scene," Robert agreed, his voice carrying warmth David had learned to recognize. "Your mother asked me to be present for you in the ways I could. I'm trying to honor that."

David was twenty-three, three weeks before graduation, when Robert had appeared unexpectedly at his apartment. Not for celebration or crisis—he'd "happened to be in the area" and wanted to take David to dinner.

They'd gone to a quiet restaurant and made awkward small talk about David's thesis project. Then, halfway through the meal, Robert had set down his fork with unusual deliberation.

"Your mother asked me to tell you something. Before she died. She made me write it down so I'd get it right."

Robert had pulled out a folded piece of paper from his wallet.

Unfolded it with hands that trembled.

Read in a voice that was trying hard to remain steady:

"'Tell David that his father loves him though he's terrible at showing it. Tell him that some people love through planning and providing rather than presence and emotion. Tell him that's love too, even when it doesn't feel like what he needed. Tell him I understand his father's limitations and I hope David will learn to understand them too.'"

Robert had refolded the paper. Returned it to his wallet.

"She was right. I am terrible at showing it. I do love you. In my own limited way. And I'm trying to be present better than I was when she needed me."

David had sat across from his father, seeing him differently. Not as the parent he'd wished for, but as the person Robert was—someone doing his best with the emotional tools he'd been given.

"I know, Dad," David had said. And found he meant it. "I know you do."

Now, standing at the Thursday gathering with his father beside him, David understood more fully what his mother had been teaching him. How to see people for who they were and love them anyway. How to accept what they could give rather than resenting what they couldn't.

Robert's expression did something complicated—understanding mixed with old pain. "She was good at that. Better than I deserved."

They stood together watching the gathering, father and son finding it easier to be present together than to articulate what their relationship was becoming.

Progress didn't always look like dramatic reconciliation. Sometimes it looked like arriving consistently, trusting that the presence mattered when words failed.

Jeremy appeared with his guitar, having apparently decided the gathering needed music. He settled on the porch steps and began playing soft background melodies—nothing dramatic or attention-seeking, just gentle accompaniment to conversation and laughter.

Maya joined him after a moment, harmonizing with a voice David hadn't known she had. Soon others were singing along to familiar songs.

Eileen found David in the garden where he'd retreated to water newly planted herbs, seeking a moment of quiet in the midst of gathering. She slipped her hand into his without speaking.

They stood together watching fireflies begin their evening dance while music and laughter drifted from the house.

"This is what she meant," Eileen said quietly. "About gardens at rest. Not empty. Full of life in the quiet moments."

"I think you're right."

They returned to the gathering as dusk deepened into evening, the porch lights creating warm circles of illumination. And somewhere in the midst of it all, David sensed his mother's presence—not as grief or absence, but as ongoing influence working through multiple people's hands.

The next morning, David woke early and found one final note from Marie.

This one tucked into her Bible at Ecclesiastes 3—the passage about seasons and times for every purpose. The note was longer than most, written in the careful handwriting she'd used when matters were deeply important.

His hands trembled as he unfolded it.

His vision blurred before he started reading.

Because he knew.

Somehow he knew this was the last one. The final message she'd left him.

He sat down at the kitchen table. Took a breath. Started to read.

David,

If you're reading this, it means you made it through the hardest seasons and you're starting to believe that life can continue after terrible loss. I'm proud of you. Not for being strong (though you are) or for not falling apart (though I hope you didn't), but for learning to tend what matters when the work is difficult.

The garden will teach you everything you need to know about faith, if you let it. How growth requires patience. How abundance comes from careful attention rather than desperate control. How the best work can't be rushed. How dormancy isn't death but preparation. How love planted well continues producing long after the original gardener is gone.

I won't see what you build with this house and garden, but I trust it will be good because I know your gift for caring. Not plants alone—people, relationships, broken places that need gentle attention. Trust that gift. Don't try to be me or Dad or anyone else. Be yourself, paying attention to what needs care and offering what you can without trying to control outcomes.

The garden at rest isn't about producing constantly. It's about being at peace with seasons of rest, trusting that rest serves growth even when nothing visible is happening. Learn to love the dormant seasons of your heart. They're not empty—they're full of quiet preparation for whatever comes next.

One more thing, honey: I need you to tell your father something for me. Tell him I understood. That loving through planning was loving too, even when I needed different care during my dying. Tell him I don't regret asking him to stay away—it was the kindest action I could take for both of us. But I do hope he'll be present for you in the ways he can. He's better at practical love than emotional presence, and that's okay. Not everyone has to tend the same way.

And David? I'm sorry I didn't tell you about the separation. I wanted to protect you during your final semester, and then everything happened so fast. You're allowed to be angry at me for that. Anger at the dead is complicated, but it's honest, and I always valued honesty over comfort.

I love you. I'm proud of you. Thank you for holding my hand at the end and for being brave enough to keep living after I was gone. That's the gift children give parents—the promise that love continues working through them when we can't be there to see it.

Plant good seeds. Nurture them patiently. Share the abundance. Trust the dormant seasons. Remember that the most beautiful gardens are the ones that learn to be at rest while remaining peacefully expectant of whatever will grow when conditions align with possibility.

All my love, always, Mom

David sat at the kitchen table reading the note three times.

Tears streaming down his face.

Not from grief alone. From the complex emotion of being known so completely by someone who'd prepared him for this moment though she couldn't be present for it.

His throat closed. His eyes burned. These tears were different—not the drowning grief of March, not the violent breaking of the storm, but simple, honest tears. The kind that came when you realized someone had loved you enough to keep teaching you after they were gone.

"She knew," he said to Samantha, his voice rough. "She knew I'd need this now. She knew I'd find out about the separation and... she wanted me to understand."

"She knew *you*," Samantha corrected gently. "And knowing someone means being able to leave what they'll need when you're gone. That's what love does—it plants the kind of seeds that don't sprout until the right season, then feed more than the planter ever saw."

David folded the note and placed it in Marie's Bible, marking the passage about seasons and times and purposes.

His mother's direct address of the separation, her explanation, her lack of regret, her hope that Robert would be present for David—all of it landed with weight. She'd known David would discover the truth. Had prepared for that discovery. Had wanted him to understand that releasing his father wasn't weakness but grace.

"She forgave him," David said. "At the end. She understood his limitations and loved him anyway."

"She understood that people show up in different ways," Samantha said. "That loving through planning and provision was loving too. She released him from what he couldn't give so he could give what he could."

The scholarship would start in January. Eileen would begin her commute in three weeks. Jeremy would return to Portland. The garden would produce through September and then begin its dormant season.

Life would continue forward with all its uncertainty and possibility.

David was ready for it now. Not confident in specific outcomes. Trusting the process that had brought him from March's raw grief to August's peaceful expectancy.

He'd learned to tend what mattered. To pay attention. To be present consistently. To trust growth that happened underground before becoming visible. To believe that love planted well continued working long after the original gardener had gone.

That evening, David and Eileen walked through the garden together in the golden light that made everything look both real and magical. They moved slowly, companionably—two people who'd learned to work well together and were learning to be together in ways that extended beyond collaboration.

"What are you thinking about?" Eileen asked, noting his contemplative expression.

"My mom's final note," David said, pulling the letter from his pocket. "About gardens at rest and peaceful expectancy. And about the separation. She addressed it directly. Wanted me to understand why she asked Dad to stay away. Wanted me to tell him she understood."

Eileen read the letter, her eyes moving over Marie's handwriting with attention. "This is beautiful," she said when she finished. "And true. She was giving you permission to rest when rest is needed. And she was giving you, and your father, permission to be human. To have limitations and be loved anyway."

"She was teaching me about faith. Not the type that requires certainty or perfect understanding. The type that appears daily and does the work even when outcomes are uncertain."

They reached the end of the garden where Marie's apple tree stood, its branches heavy with developing fruit that wouldn't be ready for harvest until September. The tree his grandfather had planted when she was ten, before he taught her how to prune and graft and coax fruit from reluctant wood.

David thought about timing, about how forcing growth or rushing harvest created inferior results, about how the best work took its own time regardless of human impatience.

"I love you," he said to Eileen, the words both new and inevitable. "And I'm grateful we're building this together. Not the community programming alone. A life that makes room for both our callings while supporting what matters to each of us."

"I love you too," Eileen replied, kissing him with easy affection. "And I'm grateful you're patient with process. That you understand building sustainably requires time and attention."

They stood together in Marie's garden as evening settled and fireflies began their ancient dance. Two people learning to trust that love could grow in the midst of loss. That new work could be built while honoring what came before. That faith was mostly a matter of being present consistently and paying careful attention to what needed care.

The garden rested around them—not empty or abandoned, but peacefully expectant of whatever would grow when conditions aligned with possibility.

Tomatoes ripened on their vines. Beans climbed toward light. Herbs spread with enthusiastic determination. And underground, invisible but essential, roots continued their patient work of preparing for what would come next.

"Garden at rest," Eileen said quietly.

"Peacefully expectant," David agreed.

They walked back to the house hand in hand as stars began appearing overhead and the night's first cool breeze rustled through corn stalks and tomato plants and the apple tree that would give its fruit when fruit was ready, regardless of human impatience or need for immediate results.

Inside, Samantha waited in her seafoam-colored pot, her leaves catching lamplight. "Good walk?" she asked.

"Good walk," David said. "Good day. Good summer. A decent start on a life."

"That's all anyone gets," Samantha said. "One day, one season at a time. Tend what's in front of you. Notice what needs care. Trust that showing up matters more than having a perfect plan. Your mother knew that. You're catching up."

David made tea and settled into Marie's chair by the window, Eileen beside him on the small sofa where they'd spent so many evenings planning and dreaming and learning to build together.

Outside, the garden rested in darkness. Inside, lamplight created circles of warmth where people gathered to work through daily life and plan for tomorrow.

This was what Marie had been building toward. Not a museum of perfect preservation. A living space where love continued working through multiple hands. Where abundance was shared. Where community formed around the patient work of caring for what mattered.

The house had become home. The garden had become classroom. The inheritance had become invitation to build new work while honoring what came before.

"Thank you, Mom," David whispered into the quiet evening. "For the garden. For the house. For Samantha. For all the notes and journals and careful planning. For teaching me that the most beautiful gardens are the ones that learn to be at rest while remaining peacefully expectant. For showing me how to love people through their limitations."

He closed his eyes.

Peace that had been earned through months of honest work and patient learning settled in his chest.

Tomorrow there would be more harvest. More planning. The ongoing labor of building sustainable life that served purposes larger than individual comfort.

Tonight there was stillness. Not empty. Full of quiet preparation for whatever would grow next.

The garden at rest in his heart had learned to hold all seasons now—grief and gratitude, memory and hope, loss and love intertwined, limitation and grace.

He was ready for whatever came next, trusting that the work of caring would continue, that community would sustain what individual effort couldn't, that faith was mostly a matter of being present consistently and believing that attention itself created conditions for growth.

His mother's love was still working. He could see it in the garden, in the people who kept arriving, in what she'd taught him about accepting people as they were.

Always trusting that spring would come when the time was right.

Always believing that the most beautiful gardens were indeed those that learned to be at rest while remaining peacefully expectant of whatever would grow when conditions aligned with possibility.

Epilogue

Six Months Later

WINTER HAD SETTLED OVER the garden with the quiet authority of a
season doing its essential work.

David stood at the kitchen window on a Saturday morning in mid-January,
watching snow fall over beds where tomatoes and beans had grown so abundantly
months ago. The garden slept deeply now, but it was not empty. Beneath the
frozen surface, roots continued their patient work of preparing for spring.

Classes had started two weeks ago. David was learning to balance academic
requirements with community programming that had grown beyond what he'd
imagined in August. The guest room had hosted three families so far, providing
respite for parents whose children were receiving treatment at the hospital.
Weekly workshops continued through winter, focused now on indoor gardening
and season planning rather than active harvest.

David was seven, standing at this same kitchen window on a January morning
watching snow fall over the garden. His grandfather Marvin stood beside him,
coffee in hand, looking out with the same contemplative expression David now
recognized in himself.

"Is the garden dead?" David had asked. The bare beds looked so empty
compared to summer's abundance.

"No, honey," Marvin had said, his voice carrying the patience of someone
who'd watched fifty winters come and go. "It's resting. Sleeping. All the plants
are storing energy underground, getting ready for spring. You can't see the work
happening, but it's happening."

He'd knelt down to David's level, pointing through the window. "See those
raspberry canes? Look dead, don't they? But come May, they'll leaf out and by

June you'll have more berries than you can eat. The roots are alive down there, waiting for the right conditions."

Young David had pressed his nose to the cold glass, trying to imagine all that hidden life beneath the snow.

"That's what faith is sometimes."

Marvin's voice had been gentle.

"Trusting that good work is happening when you can't see it. Believing that spring will come when everything looks dead. Your mom's learning that now too—she's better at remembering it than I am."

Now, sixteen years later, David stood at the same window understanding what his grandfather had been teaching. That winter wasn't failure. That dormancy served growth. That the work continued when nothing was visible.

Marie had learned it from Marvin. David had learned it from both of them. And now he'd pass it forward to whoever needed to hear it.

Eileen's car pulled into the driveway for her weekend visit, the rhythm they'd established over the fall. She emerged carrying coffee and the excited expression of someone who had news to share.

"The hospital wants to expand the program," she announced as she came through the door, stamping snow from her boots. "They're getting requests from other facilities about replicating the model. They want you to present at a regional conference in March."

David experienced the familiar mixture of excitement and nervousness that came with possibility expanding beyond comfortable boundaries. "That's... that's good?"

"That's very good," Eileen confirmed, kissing him in greeting. "It means what we're building matters to more than our immediate community."

They settled at the kitchen table with coffee and the stack of seed catalogs that had been arriving all month—Marie's careful planning continuing through subscriptions she'd maintained, her influence shaping what would be planted when spring arrived.

"Your mother would be proud," Samantha observed from her spot by the window. "Of what you've built. Of how you've let her vision grow into work that serves others. She'd also tell you that you're allowed to be nervous about expanding—that growth always comes with uncertainty. Like how plants get stressed during transplanting though the new location is better. The stress doesn't mean the move is wrong. Adjustment takes time. Root shock is normal."

Eileen's eyes found Samantha's leaves, the way they'd been doing more often since autumn. She didn't hear every word the way David did—more like catching the melody without all the lyrics. She heard enough now to nod at the observation, understanding what David had been experiencing all summer.

"I am nervous," David admitted. "What if I can't sustain this? What if school gets overwhelming, or the programming exceeds my capacity, or I fail people who are depending on this space?"

"Then you'll adjust," Eileen said with the practical wisdom he'd come to depend on. "You'll ask for help. You'll scale back where necessary. You'll trust that doing what you can is enough."

Through the window, David could see the garden under snow—barely visible except where bird feeders marked Marie's oak tree and raspberry canes poked through white drifts. The garden his grandfather Marvin had started fifty years ago, that his mother had tended for thirty, that David was learning to steward for whatever came next.

Three generations of patient work, all leading to this moment.

David was nineteen, home for winter break during his sophomore year. He'd found his mother in the kitchen on a snowy January morning, looking out at the garden while making her morning coffee.

"I always loved winter in the garden," Marie had said when she noticed him, making space for him beside her. "Everyone thinks spring is the most hopeful season. I think it's winter."

"Winter?" David had been skeptical. "When everything's dead?"

"Not dead. Dormant. There's a difference." She'd gestured toward the window with her coffee mug. "In winter, the garden gets to rest. No pressure to perform or produce. Quiet preparation for what comes next. The plants aren't stressed about bloom time or fruit production. They're just being. Storing energy. Getting their roots deeper."

She'd turned to look at him then, with that expression that meant she was teaching an important lesson.

"That's what I want for you, honey. Permission to have dormant seasons. Times when you're not producing or achieving or impressing anyone. Times when you're just being. Getting your roots deeper. Preparing for whatever comes next."

"You mean like having a bad semester?" David had joked, uncomfortable with the intensity of her attention.

"I mean like being human," Marie had corrected. "Like letting yourself rest without guilt. Like trusting that the quiet seasons are doing essential work even when nothing looks impressive from the outside."

Now, standing at that same window six years later, David understood.

She'd been teaching him this lesson long before he knew he'd need it.

Outside, the snow continued falling, adding to the blanket that protected dormant plants and enriched soil with moisture that would support spring's growth. Inside, David and Eileen made plans for the coming season—what to plant, who to serve, how to expand programming without losing the intimate quality that made it effective.

The work would continue. Community would keep gathering. Love would keep working through multiple hands.

Marie's final note remained tucked in her Bible at Ecclesiastes, marking the passage about seasons and times and purposes. David read it often, finding in her words permission to rest when rest was needed, encouragement to trust the process, assurance that love planted well continued producing long after the original gardener had gone.

The most beautiful gardens, Marie had written, *are the ones that learn to be at rest while remaining peacefully expectant.*

David understood now.

Understood that stillness and productivity weren't opposites. That rest served growth. That faith was mostly a matter of showing up consistently and trusting the process when outcomes remained uncertain.

Tomorrow there would be more work. More planning. More patient tending of what mattered.

Tonight there was peace—earned through honest labor, sustained by community, grounded in faith that had been practiced daily until it became not belief alone but lived experience.

The garden at rest lay in winter darkness, full of quiet preparation for spring that would surely come when the time was right.

THE END

Interlude: Renewal

The stillness is not empty. It is alive with memory, with unseen roots, with hope waiting quietly. The garden does not ask us to forget what has been lost. It asks us to tend what remains, to carry love forward into the next season.

"Beauty for ashes, the oil of joy for mourning, the garment of praise for the spirit of heaviness." — Isaiah 61:3
God does not erase sorrow; He transforms it. What feels like ashes becomes soil. What feels like ending becomes seed. The garden does not demand perfection, only tending.

From Ellen's last journal entry:
"If love has taken root in you, then I am never far away."

AUTHOR'S NOTE

Dear Reader,

This story began with a question that haunted me through my own seasons of loss: What if healing doesn't mean fixing everything that's broken, but learning to tend what remains with such care that new life can grow from the wounded places?

I wrote *Still Garden* because I've witnessed something profound in kitchens and around dinner tables where authentic community happens: the people who create the safest spaces for others are rarely those who've avoided suffering, but those who've learned that sharing their broken places creates permission for others to be honest about theirs.

David's journey from isolated grief to chosen family reflects a pattern I've observed again and again, that our greatest capacity to love others emerges not from our perfection, but from our willingness to let our scars become visible. His mother Marie's faithful preparation for death becomes the foundation for his ability to build a table where others can bring their losses without shame. Jeremy's guilt about abandoning friendship during illness teaches him how to show up for difficult moments instead of fleeing them. Eileen's experience carrying the grief of dying children prepares her to understand that some losses we carry, not cure, and that healing work is rarely solitary. Her partnership with David emerges not from romantic rescue but from shared purpose, two people learning to tend both gardens and grief alongside each other. Even David's father Robert, whose absence during Marie's illness created wounds that don't heal quickly, learns that showing up imperfectly but consistently matters more than waiting until you know the right thing to say.

This isn't a story about overcoming grief or finding closure. It's about discovering that healing happens in community, around shared tables, through the slow work of tending hope together. The deepest satisfaction often comes not from having all the answers, but from learning to sit with hard questions alongside people who understand that some wounds become wisdom when they're shared.

David discovers his mother's greatest gift wasn't the garden itself, but teaching him that tending, whether plants, people, or grief, is fundamentally the same practice: patient attention, consistent presence, trust in processes we can't control. Maya's journey from trying to replicate her brother's art to discovering her own voice teaches him the difference between preservation and transformation, that the best way to honor those we've lost is to let their influence grow through us into something they never could have imagined but would recognize as rooted in their love.

I invite you to consider your own story through this lens:

What losses have taught you how to be present for others who are struggling?

Where has your experience with imperfect relationships prepared you to love people as they are?

How might your private healing be longing to become shared hospitality?

The talking plant in this story is, admittedly, fantastical. But the wisdom Samantha offers, that growth happens slowly, through patient tending, in seasons we can't control, is as practical as soil and sunlight. Every day, people discover that their willingness to set an extra place at the table creates space for unexpected family. Every day, communities form around the understanding that we heal best when we learn to share our stories without trying to fix each other.

Your pain has prepared you for purposes you can't yet see, but only if you're willing to let your wounds become the wisdom you offer freely. The question isn't whether your pain has meaning for someone else, but whether you can trust that your raw honesty might be the thread another person needs to see that even unfinished mending is still healing.

In a world that often encourages us to grieve privately and present polished versions of our lives, *Still Garden* suggests a different path: that our broken places, tended in community, become our most generous gifts. That the strongest relationships are those rooted in shared honesty about how hard life can be. That love doesn't end when bodies fail, it learns to work through those who carry it forward in ordinary acts of hospitality and care.

May you find the courage to tend your own still garden, and may you discover the joy that comes from creating space around your table where others can learn they're not alone in their questions.

With gratitude for the tables you set and the stories you share,
Cisco Mills

P.S. If you're reading this while carrying your own difficult questions about loss, friendship, family, or faith, I invite you to consider that your struggles might not be obstacles to overcome but preparation for the kind of presence others need. Your experience with betrayal might be preparing you to forgive imperfectly but genuinely. Your season of depression might be equipping you to sit with others in darkness without trying to fix them. Your complicated family relationships might be teaching you how to love people who can't love you back the way you need.

Look for the "still gardens" already growing in your community, not metaphorical ones, but actual gardens, actual kitchens, actual tables where the work of presence happens. Sometimes healing begins as literally as putting your hands in soil or sharing produce you've grown with neighbors whose names you're learning. Places where people gather not to solve each other's problems but to share meals and stories and the understanding that we're all on the way to being mended. And if you can't find one, perhaps you're being called to set the first table. After all, every chosen family begins with someone willing to say, "You're welcome here, as you are, for as long as you need."